STOLEN

DANTE'S VOW

NATASHA KNIGHT

Copyright © 2021 by Natasha Knight

All rights reserved.

No part of this book may be reproduced in any form or by any electronic or mechanical means, including information storage and retrieval systems, without written permission from the author, except for the use of brief quotations in a book review.

Cover by CoverLuv

Photo by Rafa Catalana

Click here to sign up for my newsletter to receive new release news and updates!

NOTE FROM NATASHA

Dear Reader,

Stolen: Dante's Vow is a spin-off of the *To Have and To Hold Duet*. Although it does stand alone, I recommend you first read With This Ring and I Thee Take as many of the characters and some backstory have already been established.

You can find With This Ring here and I Thee Take here.

Thank you and enjoy!

Natasha

PROLOGUE 1
DANTE

Five years.

Five fucking years. That's how long it has taken me to find her. And the only reason I did was word circulating about Petrov having been duped.

Felix Pérez going into hiding.

Bastard.

I climb out of the car at the entrance of The Hudson Hotel. An icy drizzle pelts me as I adjust the collar of my coat before looking up at the penthouse windows more than twenty floors up.

She's here.

It's her.

It has to be.

The second SUV comes to a stop behind ours and as Matthaeus flanks me, three more men fall in line behind him. I push my hands into my pockets and walk toward the entrance. A bellman opens the door. I don't miss the widening of his eyes when the light from a passing car dances across my face. Maybe it's not my appearance that's got him freaked. Maybe it's my entourage. Because we look like trouble.

And we are.

I make my way to the concierge desk and give the attendant my name. Well, not my real name. The name of the asshole who paid extra to get his turn early in the night. Before she's used up. He's dead now.

The attendant can't quite keep eye contact. I blink, watching him as his eyes move over the eyepatch, the deep, still angry X-shaped scar across my cheek. I let him look. Let him clear his throat in embarrassment as he makes a point of rearranging his desk while asking for identification.

I pat my pockets. "Guess I forgot it."

He finally forces himself to meet my gaze, his neck and face flushed.

"Envelope," I say, holding out my hand. I don't have time for this buffoon.

"Yes, sir." His hand trembles as he hands the envelope over. He wants me gone and I can't blame him.

I check my watch. We have to time this exactly right. I walk toward the elevators followed by my men. As if to oblige us, the doors slide open just as we get to them, and we step inside. I rip the envelope open, press the key into the slot marked Penthouse and let the doors slide closed. Matthaeus sets the black duffel bag on the floor, unzips it and hands each of the men an automatic rifle. They have suppressors in place, although there's really no way to muffle that sound. But if all goes to plan, it won't matter.

An upbeat tune plays in the background as I stare at my own face in the mirrored doors. I make myself look. Make myself see. I wonder if she'll be scared when she sees me.

My phone buzzes. I reach into my pocket, take it out, scan the text. Cristiano telling me the soldiers are in place, both inside and outside the property. Chopper is on its way, and they've secured our exit.

If I can get out.

If.

Because he thinks this is a shit idea.

But no, it's not *if* I get out. I have no intention of dying tonight. Not until I've killed that fat fuck Petrov. Not until I've buried my knife in Felix Pérez's gut. Not until I have their blood and the blood of anyone else who touched her on my hands.

Then, I can die.

Only then.

He reminds me again of Petrov's soldiers nearby, the distraction we arranged only giving us minutes inside the suite. He asks one more time if I know what the fuck I'm doing.

I text him a pirate emoji, along with the middle finger, then silence my phone. He'll be pissed but this is mine. What happened to her happened because of me. What happened to all of them happened because of me. All while I simply walked away.

So, as the elevator approaches the penthouse, I crack my neck and pull my pistol out of its shoulder holster. Then twist the silencer into place and hold the weapon at my side.

Because tonight is the beginning of their end.

Tonight, I take back what they stole.

PROLOGUE 2
MARA

"Nothing personal, my dear."

I jerk out of his grasp. *Nothing personal.* Should that mean something to me? Does he really think it can?

He grips my jaw, forcing me to look at him. His calloused fingers are rough. Bruising.

I grit my teeth, fist my hands. I want to fight him, but I don't. I'm still scared. Even when that little voice in my head tells me maybe it would be better if I fought.

If he lost his temper.

If he just killed me.

Because what's coming will be worse.

My eyes burn with tears and the moment he sees them, his expression changes. His head tilting to the side, one knuckle of his free hand wiping away the drop making its way down my cheek.

"Sweet girl." His thumb presses against my lower lip. "Pretty girl. It's too bad it had to be this way."

He releases me and I step backward.

"Just let me go," I try even though I know it's no use. *It's not my fault*, I want to tell him. But that doesn't matter, not to him. And besides, in a way, it is my fault. I told. I was warned not to. Hell, it was beaten into me not to tell. To forget. But I didn't. I never could, no matter how much I tried.

He moves his mouth into a smile that if I was naïve, I'd think may be meant to comfort. But I'm not naïve. Any innocence I had, he stole. Or maybe it was Felix before him who stole it.

"If I do that, then there's no lesson for that snake, is there? No, Mara," he tries out my name. It sounds strange on his tongue, his accent too thick, the disgust he feels too palpable. "But Leonard will stay with you," he says, gesturing over his shoulder to the soldier. "He'll make sure you're not hurt. Not too badly at least," he adds as if an afterthought. As if I'm a fucking afterthought.

I catch Leonard's eye. One corner of his mouth curves upward into a sneer. What I'd give to dig my nails into his eye sockets and scratch his eyes out of his head. What I'd give to hurt him just once. Because I have no doubt he's going to enjoy the next few hours.

Petrov turns, walks toward the soldier and gives him instructions in Russian. I try to understand what he's saying but in the last five years he's only ever spoken English with me and instructed anyone who encountered me to do the same, so the few words I've managed to pick up don't help. Not that I need to understand what they're saying to know what's coming. He explained that part in great detail. Relished it, I think.

I put my hand to my hip. I swear I still feel the burn of his punishment. But it was my own fault. I should have kept my mouth shut.

And then what?

How much longer did I really expect him to keep me alive when he was already growing tired of me. I'm not as young as I used to be, and he likes young.

My stomach turns at the thought, and I channel all my hate into his back, his thick shoulders, wide middle. Into the roll of fat around his neck and his small head with its military style close-cropped hair. His hair is receding and the bald spot at the crown is widening. He sprays something on his scalp that he thinks hides it, but everyone laughs behind his back. The problem is no one dares do it to his face.

I walk to the window and draw the heavy, burgundy drapes back. He spared no expense renting the presidential suite for the event. My farewell.

It's raining. I look out at the street below, the people like ants twenty floors down. I'd jump if I could open it, but the windows don't open. I guess the hotel isn't taking any chances. And besides, I know myself. I'm too much of a coward to do that.

Dropping the curtain, I go into the bathroom again desperate to get away from them even if it's just for a moment. It's beautiful. The lap of luxury with its claw-footed antique bath, the marble floors. The fresco of fields and fields of wild red poppies blowing in tall green grass on all four walls, the bluest sky I've ever seen on the ceiling. I wish I could run into those fields. Feel the delicate petals against my legs, the grass soft under my bare feet.

But then he calls my name.

It's time.

I wish I could be sick, but I haven't eaten all day. He hasn't fed me. It wouldn't do for me to puke all over his friends.

I walk back into the bedroom and see the third man who has just entered. The doctor. Seeing him here makes me shudder.

"Take off your clothes," Petrov tells me.

I drag my gaze from the doctor to Petrov, feeling the blood drain from my face as my knees begin to wobble. "Please just let me go," I try one final time.

"Do you need an injection?"

I glance to the doctor who takes the ready syringe out of his pocket. I know those injections. They make my arms and legs useless, my body no longer under my control. But they leave my mind untouched and alert. I'll know everything, feel everything, but I won't be able to fight. Won't be able to do anything but lie there and take it and know every second what is happening to me.

I shake my head. I don't want an injection. Not yet. I'll try to get one hit in so at least I'll know I did something. I didn't just roll over and play victim.

I begin to undo the buttons of my dress.

Petrov nods, watches as I disrobe. I'm naked underneath so it doesn't take long. He walks around me, and I know he's looking at his mark. He chose the spot so anyone who touched me would know I'd been his. His discarded property. Used goods. Felix will be pissed when he sees it. He won't be able to sell me. Not for a good price anyway. That's a blessing, right? In a way?

At least he won't touch me tonight. Hasn't since he found out the truth.

Petrov stands facing me again. He lifts my hair off my shoulder.

"After the good doctor has his turn, he will be in the next room. If you cause any trouble, he will administer the injection. No questions asked. Understood?"

"You're going to let him—" I try to instill steel into my words but my voice breaks.

He mutters a curse in Russian then asks again if I understand.

I nod. Because it's not just my voice that's breaking. It's me. And I'm still scared.

"Sir." A soldier peers his head through the door. "Service elevator is here."

"What's wrong with the normal elevator?"

"Out of order," the soldier says.

"Fine," Petrov answers, irritated. He appreciates appearances and taking the service elevator is beneath him. He looks back at me for what I guess is the last time. "So pretty still. It really is too bad," he says. He turns and walks out the door and for one brief, stupid moment, I entertain the idea that he means it. That he's sorry I'm not who he thought I was. That he's sorry to have to do what he's about to do. Because that's the strange thing when you're kidnapped. When there is a single person in your life who controls every aspect of it. Who decides whether you eat or go hungry. Whether you live or die. In a way, you want to please them. You feel safer with them. It's utterly idiotic, I know this. Stockholm Syndrome. Maybe it's because this monster you at least know.

I shake my head, snap myself out of it. Because he's gone and the lights are dimmed, and I watch in disgust as the doctor steps toward me.

1

DANTE

Energy crackles around me. I'm ready. We all are. Ready for the kill.

The elevator doors slide open, and I look up at the camera, smiling wide. I flip my middle finger up. I want to be sure Petrov knows it was me who took her. I want him to have no doubt. And I want him to know I'll be coming for him next.

Classical music comes from inside the penthouse. I wonder if that's to make what's going on inside seem civilized. Elegant even. I'm sure what's happening to her is anything but. I hear laughter, glasses clinking together. Sounds like a fucking party. But I guess for them, it is.

It takes the two men standing just inside the suite a moment to stop staring at me and realize we're not invited guests. It takes them another to register the weapons we're carrying as my men fan out and the sound of silenced automatic rifles disrupts the classical music. Guns are drawn, bullets flying.

I shift my gaze to two of the guests standing by the window, drinks in hand just waiting their turn at her. Something about them, in particular, pisses me off. Maybe it's their casual stance, their relaxed manner. Maybe it's their pleased, smiling faces. Whatever it is, I veer off plan. I'm supposed to go straight to the bedroom. Grab her. Get out.

But I can't.

Maybe it's that I want their blood on my hands. Maybe it's just that I like the kill.

Either way, tonight, they die.

For a moment I wonder if the sick fucks are father and son. They share that same weak chin. When the younger one sees me coming, his smile morphs into an expression of terror. Dad's faster. His gun is in his hand, but not before I've taken aim between his eyes and pulled the trigger. His body jerks, the tumbler of whiskey slipping from his hand. Shattering against the polished hardwood floor.

The younger one looks in shock from me, to him, and back. He takes a step backward. I take one forward. Lowering my gun, I reach for the dagger at my hip. He opens his mouth to scream like a little girl when I push it into his gut and draw up with one swift tug of my hand.

The scream turns into a grunt or gurgle or some combination of both. His hands close around mine, body hunching forward as I give one more tug before shoving him backward and pulling my knife from his stomach. He's down, bleeding out next to dear ole dad. I wipe the blade on his pant leg before replacing it in its holster. I should wash my hands.

But then I hear it. The muffled scream. Her scream.

And something pulls at me like I'm tuned into it. Into the girl who has become my obsession.

I turn toward the sound coming from behind a closed door, and for one moment, I can't move. Just for a moment. Then I'm stalking toward what must be a bedroom.

She screams again, louder this time as I kick the door down surprising the soldier with the hard on. He's watching the man looming over the slight woman on the bed. That man has got his pants down around his knees. I don't waste time on the soldier. I just put a bullet between his eyes, and he drops instantly.

The man stumbles off the bed in a panic and I see her. For the first time in fifteen years, I see her.

It's dark in here. Lights dimmed. Heavy curtains drawn shut.

But it's her.

And again, for one moment, I'm transfixed.

She's naked on the bed trying to hide herself. Of course, she's naked. What did I think they'd be doing in here, playing cards? Her face is framed by long, white-blonde hair, her eyes shiny, bright and wide with terror.

"I fucking paid," the man starts, forcing my attention away from her. Drawing it back to him. He'll regret that in about one second because the rage inside me has become a living, breathing thing. The pulse a fire in my veins.

He's finally got his flaccid dick back in his pants and is zipping them up.

"Petrov agreed I get to go first."

"Is that right?" I ask, stepping toward the man who must be sixty. Fucking pervert. "Petrov's not here, is he? But I'll tell you what." I cock my gun, step close enough the toes of my boots are touching the tips of his shoes. "You can go first. Straight to hell." I raise the pistol just a little, just so it's at the level of his dick, and pull the trigger.

He screams and so does she. She's squirming away. She should.

"We gotta move," Matthaeus says, touching his earpiece. "Soldiers are on their way."

I drag my gaze from the pervert cupping the place his dick used to be and glance at her. Again, it's like I'm struck. Paralyzed.

"Dante!" It's Matthaeus.

I shake away the strange sensation and I see how his blood has splattered her face and hair like a stain. Like something foul on a clean thing. A pure thing. She's wide-eyed, mouth open in a stunned O, holding a pillow up against herself to hide her nakedness.

I step closer to the man on the floor and set the bottom of my shoe over his bloody hands. I press. "How old are you?"

"What? Fuck. Fuck! It fucking hurts!" He sobs.

I crouch down, fist a handful of hair and tug to make him look at me. "How fucking old are you?"

"Sixty-two."

"You're old enough to be her fucking grandfather, bastard."

"Petrov...he said..."

"Did you put your dick inside her?"

"What?"

"Did you put your wrinkled old dick inside her?"

He tries to shake his head. "No. No. I wanted to look... I... Petrov..."

I bring my gun to his gut and pull the trigger. I don't want to hear another word from him.

A heavy hand falls on my shoulder. "Dante."

I turn to look at Matthaeus, seeing her in my periphery when I do, feeling things I shouldn't be fucking feeling, not here, not now.

"We have to move," Matthaeus says urgently.

I step toward the girl but when she gets a glimpse of my face, she recoils. I stop, draw back into shadow. I should know better.

"Where are your clothes?" I ask, trying to soften my voice. It's impossible. She's terrified. I see it.

She points a trembling hand at a light green dress draped over the back of a chair. I grab it, hand it to her.

"Put it on. Hurry."

She nods but is shaking too badly to actually get the dress on. From outside I hear the chopper.

"Sixty seconds before we have a dozen soldiers on us," Matthaeus warns. "We're cornered in here."

I holster my weapon, take the dress from her, and pull it over her head. It's baggy and long, a summer dress for a winter's day. Without hesitating, I wrap an arm around her and hoist her over my shoulder. She lets out a yelp but we're moving, Matthaeus and my men on my heels, out of the bedroom. We're running to the door that will lead to the roof where the chopper is waiting.

Petrov's soldiers are close. I hear their boots echo through the penthouse as I open the door and hand her to Matthaeus. He'll get her on the chopper.

The door below opens, slamming against the wall as the last of my men get out. I see the first of Petrov's soldiers and ignore Matthaeus's shouts for me to get on the helicopter. I want to be sure my message gets to Petrov tonight. So, I shoot, taking out the first three before a bullet hits my arm. Searing pain slices through me. Memory takes me to a different place, a different time. I drop the door and just barely haul myself into the chopper as it lifts off, veering just out of range of their bullets.

2

MARA

He's hurt. Blood is seeping through his fingers where he's holding the wound on his arm.

One of the other men, the one who carried me into the chopper, tugs my seatbelt tight and clicks it into place, drawing my attention from the one with the scar like an X on his face. The one with the patch over his eye. He places a headset over my ears and reaches under the seat to take out a small box. A first aid kit. He hands the hurt one something to put over his bleeding arm.

There are six of us inside the chopper plus the one flying it. The soldiers are anxious, charged, there's an energy about them, adrenaline high. I hear them talk about what happened through the headset. They laugh about this one's face or how that one screamed. They smell of sweat and exhilaration. It's almost palpable, the scent coming off of them. Intense. They clean off their rifles and put them into a black duffel bag. Even now, after so many years in captivity, it's terrifying to see those killing machines.

I watch them but what I want to do is look at *him*. Because I feel him looking at me.

And I know him.

I sneak a glance. He's leaning back so his face is mostly in shadow, but I see the shine of the eye without the patch. Bright green. I wonder what happened to the other one. I think how the color doesn't fit him. He's a hard man. A killer. But that color is like spring. Like promise.

"Don't be scared," he says, and my heart does exactly the opposite. Its already frantic pace picks up making it pound against my ribs. But I think it's his voice that's doing it. Not his words. Like a deep rumble vibrating inside me.

The chopper veers at an impossible angle and I gasp, gripping the edge of the seat as rain pelts the glass door. It's picked up, coming down harder than it was. Below us is the black water of the Hudson River. And we're flying too close to it.

"You're safe," the man with the patch says.

I shift my gaze up to his. Force myself to look at him as we near a low but wide building and prepare to touch down in the large, mostly empty parking lot.

I know him. Not his man's face. His man's body. But his eyes.

Eye.

And I feel it. The tug of something buried deep inside me. So deep it's almost dead but not quite. Not yet.

The landing is bumpy. The men pile out, one of them hoisting the duffel bag over his shoulder like it weighs nothing. Soon it's just him and me left inside the helicopter. I remain where I am, unsure of what to do. He's still studying me like he can't believe it's me. He's already undone his seatbelt and is taking off his headset. I take mine off too.

"Here," he says, coming to sit beside me. When he reaches to undo my belt, his hand brushes my bare arm and I gasp. He draws it back. It's like an electric shock. Something sparking and alive, a charge of pure electricity. He feels it too. I see it on his face.

It's then I start to shiver, realizing how cold it is outside. How cold I am. I'm barefoot and wearing a summer dress in wintertime. I'm naked underneath.

I wrap my arms around myself. Petrov used to take care with me, in the beginning. He grew less and less careful as time wore on. When he found out the truth, found out Felix had betrayed him and made a fool of him, he stopped altogether. My clothes were taken away and I was moved out of my comfortable room to a different one. A small, dirty one.

Not that it bothered me so much. A prison is a prison whether you sleep on a feather bed or a dusty old mattress in a corner. But my new room was cold. Freezing. I can't remember what warm feels like anymore.

I wonder where Petrov is now. If he knows what's happened. I wonder if he'll punish me for it when I'm returned to him. If I return on my own, maybe it will be less bad. If he doesn't have to come after me. The time I ran before, he had to get me, and I still remember his punishment. Still remember how I couldn't get out of bed for days after.

That brings me to another possibility. This could be a game. A trick of his. It wouldn't be the first time.

"Hey," the man says to get my attention.

I blink, his voice drawing me back to the present.

He touches my chin to lift my face to his and my breath catches when I fully look at him. It's like his eye, it belongs in a different body. A young boy's body. Not this man with the deep X at the center of his right cheek. This man whose face has been sewn together. This close I can almost make out each stitch across the angry-looking scars.

He turns his head so I can see the other side. The beautiful one. And he is beautiful. The eye without the patch darkens and he doesn't quite look at me for a moment.

"You're cold," he says, voice different. Like he's trying hard to soften it. He frees me of the seatbelt. "We'll get inside. You can warm up." He pulls his jacket off and drapes it over my shoulders.

It's heavy and warm and I smell him on it. Something about the gesture makes me want to cry.

"I'm not going to hurt you." When I don't reply he tries again, voice louder. "Do you understand what I'm saying?"

I draw back at his tone. He sounds angry.

He mutters a curse under his breath and shakes his head. "Okay, let's go," he says. He steps out of the chopper then turns to me. When I don't move right away, he just reaches in and lifts me out like I weigh nothing. I grip his shoulders for balance. He's big. Strong and solid. And for one instant, we remain like that, him staring up at me, me down at him, the blades of the chopper whipping my hair around.

He shifts my position so he's cradling me against his chest. He ducks his head and carries me to a door that one of his men is holding open. He feels different than Petrov. Holds me differently.

The sound of the chopper's blades fade as the door closes behind us and we're moving up a staircase. It's dark inside, the lamps barely lighting our way. The boots of the men ahead of us are loud against the metal stairs. But a few minutes later, once we've climbed another shorter set of stairs, we're inside what looks like a large warehouse. The walls are unpainted brick, the exposed beams supporting the roof.

He sets me down. The cement floor is cold against my bare feet, although it's not as cold as it is outside.

I back away a few steps and take it all in. Eye-patch man talks to one of the others but keeps watching me. There's a kitchen against one wall. It's all stainless steel, wood and brick. The table has six chairs around it and behind me is a living space with a few leather couches, a coffee table. Sitting on top is a bottle of whiskey and a half-full glass. A large television is mounted on the wall.

Someone starts some music. It's loud, heavy metal. Not the classical Petrov always listened to. I like it.

Most of the walls don't have windows, but the ones that do are made up of small panes framed inside steel that span from floor to ceiling. A hallway leads to half a dozen closed doors. I wonder what this place was. Not a home, or not meant to be.

I hear my name then and turn to find eye-patch man watching me but talking to someone on his phone. His eyebrows are furrowed, gaze intent on me. He nods at whatever the other person is saying.

One of the men laughs from the kitchen area and I look over to find them standing around the counter, drinking beers. They're quick to adjust their expressions when they see me watching them.

A moment later, eye-patch man disconnects the call, tucks the phone in his pocket and comes toward me.

I take a step back. Instinct. I'm always backing away from men.

He stops, puts his hands up, palms toward me. "I'm not going to hurt you, Mara."

My heart thuds. He knows I'm Mara. Not Elizabeth.

"I knew you before," he continues. "A long time ago. I used to bandage your knees when you cut them. Tie your shoelaces."

I feel my forehead wrinkle as I listen to him.

"I'm Dante. Lizzie's big brother."

Dante? No. Dante is dead. They're all dead. I know because I watched them die.

Is this a trick? A game of Petrov's? His latest, cruelest punishment?

"Do you remember me?" he asks.

I don't reply.

"Do you remember Lizzie?" He takes another step toward me, and I realize I'm shaking my head as I back up.

"You're safe. I'm not going to hurt you, Mara."

I shake it more frantically. "I'm not Mara," I say, my voice no more than a hoarse whisper.

He stops when he hears me, smiles. "You understand me."

Why wouldn't I understand him?

I clear my throat so he can hear me. "I'm not Mara. I'm Elizabeth."

There's a shift in the energy of the room. "No, you're not." His voice grows hard like he's angry. He must see my panic at this change because he takes a deep breath in and sounds calmer when he speaks. "Lizzie had green eyes like mine. And she didn't have a star-shaped birthmark on the back of her shoulder." He gestures to my right shoulder.

How does he know about my birthmark?

"It's small. Probably smaller now. You've grown up," he says, peering around as if to see it. "But if you know where to look, you can see it." He sounds sad as he faces me once more. "And then there's the fact that my sister died fifteen years ago."

I shake my head hard as he blurs through the tears that fill my eyes. I know. I know she died. I watched her die. But this isn't safe. I'm not safe if they know the truth.

"I'm not Mara," I say again, looking at the door we came in through. It's just beyond him. There's even a red exit sign over it.

He walks toward me, and I scoot sideways. The men have stopped laughing, stopped talking. Someone turns the music off. The silence is abrupt and jarring. They're watching us. I feel their eyes. And I'm not sure I'll make it to the door. I hear the sound of a beer bottle being set on the table. It's that quiet. But I don't turn. I keep my eyes on the one in front of me. The one with the broken face.

"Let me take you to one of the bedrooms. You can rest."

No. No way. I am not going into a bedroom. I'm not going where they can hurt me. Not without putting up a fight. Never again.

"You can have a hot bath. Lie down. I'll get you some warmer clothes." All the while as he speaks, I realize he's coming closer, herding me farther and farther from the exit.

"Just let me go." I try. I don't know why. It hasn't ever worked before.

He stops moving. "Sweetheart," he says, looks at me like he feels sorry for me, and I hate that look. I hate their pity. Anyway, it's not real. "Where would you go?" he asks.

My back is at the wall. I close my eyes, take a deep breath in, and press my fingernails into my palms. It hurts but it helps. Helps to make me strong. I remember Helga. She was a bitch. A horrible, sadistic bitch who got what she deserved. I remember Scarlett. Remember what she did. How she hit Helga with the lamp over and over again. How she killed her. Scarlett thought she could save us.

I need to be strong like her. I need to remember to be strong because they like it when you're scared. Like it when you cry.

I straighten, open my eyes to look at him again. "Where would I go?" I ask.

He cocks his head to the side.

"Away from you," I tell him, my voice sounding more determined than I feel.

He smiles again, nods like he's proud of me and wipes the corner of his lip with his thumb. "I'm glad to hear you have some fight in you."

I eye the knife he has in a holster on his belt. He's still talking but I tune him out. I need to concentrate. I'll get one chance. And when he takes a step closer, I lunge at him, surprising him, my fingers closing around the hilt as he catches my waist. He laughs a little as he takes one step backward, so I don't slam into his chest, his arms wrapping around me as if he wants to be sure I don't fall.

That's good. Because he doesn't feel it when I slip the blade from its holster and bring it to his dick. If there's one thing I know, its men become babies when their dicks are threatened and it's the one sure way to get their attention.

From the kitchen comes the cocking of four pistols, but I don't look away. I can't risk it.

"Relax," eye-patch man says but he's not talking to me. He's telling them. I can tell from the tone of his voice.

"Get away from me," I hiss, keeping my voice low like they do when they really want to scare you.

He laughs as if that was funny. I think he's crazy.

He must be. His reaction is all wrong and for a moment, it confuses me. And that's all he needs. One single moment.

He's fast. Faster than Petrov. Faster than Felix. Faster than any of their soldiers. And before I know it, he has his big hand wrapped around my wrist and is pulling it away from his dick. I feel the pressure of his grip but he's not hurting me. Or at least he's trying not to.

"That's sharp," he says, expression hard but not angry. He squeezes my wrist enough to force my fingers to uncurl so he can take the dagger. He doesn't look away once as he tucks it back into its holster and I feel myself deflate, feel my shoulders slump.

I'm too weak. I've always been too weak.

"Please let me go," I say, feeling my lip quiver. "Please just let me go. I'll go back. I won't tell him where you are. I promise."

His eyebrows furrow. "You think I'd let you go back to that bastard? Petrov and those others will never lay a hand on you again. I will tear them limb from limb before I let them near you," he says, the disgust in his voice like sandpaper against my skin.

I try to pull my wrist free, but he won't let go. I look at it, see how big he is. My wrist looks like a doll's in his giant hand. It's scarred too. But a line of red sliding down his arm catches my attention. He's bleeding again.

When I look up, he's studying me and there's that feeling again. Something familiar and warm. Like I'm safe.

"I knew you before. A long time ago. I used to bandage your knees when you cut them. Tie your shoelaces."

He said he's Dante.

I remember Dante. Remembering the feeling that belongs to that memory. But he's lying. He's not Dante. He can't be. Dante is dead. They're all dead. I saw their bodies. Saw the blood. I don't think I'll ever get the sight of it out of my head. Ever forget the terror in Lizzie's eyes when her killer advanced on her. She was just a little girl. We both were. She didn't even have a chance to scream.

"Mara. I need you to relax, okay?"

I blink, remember where I am. I'm hyperventilating.

He lets me go. I move away from him. But I don't run to the exit. There's no point. He's right. Where would I go? Besides I'm outnumbered. Not to mention they have guns.

"Matthaeus," the one claiming to be Dante says as I sink onto the floor and hug my legs. I close my eyes, hide my face in my knees and think about the song Flora taught me. It helps a little at least. If I can see the words and hear her sing the song. I just have to see the words and listen for her voice.

"Mara." Dante's voice sounds urgent. He's close

but I don't open my eyes. Not even when I feel his big hand cup the back of my head. He's gentle. But some pretend to be gentle and those are the ones you really have to watch out for. They're the ones who hurt you the most.

"Here." Another man says. I still don't open my eyes.

"Just a pinch, Mara. It'll help relax you and when you wake up, I'll be there with you," he says as the hand that was cupping my head pushes it slightly to the side.

I register his words then. They creep in along the edges of the song, and I realize what he means. What he's going to do.

The pinch. An injection.

The one that makes sure I don't fight.

My eyelids fly open, but when I try to push my head back and get away, his grip tightens and a moment later, I feel the prick of the needle and I know it's over. I'm done for.

3

DANTE

Her body relaxes, arms falling away. I wrap her in my arms as she slouches. I stand. She weighs nothing. Like a little bird. A broken little bird.

Dried blood smears her face. Her lips are parted just slightly, hair hanging over my arm. It's long and needs to be washed. Golden strands are crusted with the blood of the asshole I killed in that bedroom. One of her arms rests on her stomach and the other hangs limp.

"Shit," I mutter.

"You had no choice. It's better if she sleeps anyway, given what we need to do. When she wakes up, she'll see she's safe," Matthaeus says. He's been with me for the last five years. Cristiano hired him as a bodyguard when I couldn't defend myself and he's become a friend. Someone I trust.

"I don't think it's going to be as simple as that," I tell him.

"When is anything simple?" he asks. Never when it comes to me, I think. "But you have her back. Get her settled then I need to look at your arm."

"It's nothing. The bullet grazed me. Idiots have bad aim."

"Still."

"Fine. After." Matthaeus has some medical training which, given what we do, is a good thing.

The men start the music again, but it's not as loud. I carry her into the back bedroom. My room. It's the quietest and the most comfortable. Matthaeus lives here too, and the men have rooms when they need them. It's our base in the northeast. My uncle used to own the building. I should burn it down, except that I like this one.

But wait. No. He's not my *uncle*. I have to get used to calling him dad.

A feeling of disgust turns my stomach at the memory of *Uncle* David. The only image I can ever conjure up anymore is that of him sitting at the desk in that hotel room. His hands pinned to it with a steak knife and a letter opener, head blown half off.

I did that.

Patricide.

Although does it count as that if you hadn't really processed that the man you killed was your father, not your uncle? That he'd been lying to you all your life.

That he'd raped your mother.

Which explains some shit at least. Not that I can blame mom. She tried to love me. Maybe she even did.

Fuck.

My steps slow as I grit my teeth, steel my spine. I shove those thoughts aside. Now isn't the time to wallow. I need to take care of her. She needs me. And I haven't been there for the last fifteen years when she really needed me. I need to get my head out of my ass and be here for her.

I open the bedroom door and step in, closing it behind me. Inside is a large mattress set on crates with a heavy comforter. The makeshift bed is unmade. Instead of a nightstand I have a crate turned upside down but most of my shit is on the floor. A charger for my phone. A laptop. Another gun. Candles too. Sometimes the power goes out here.

The walls are bare brick, the beams exposed, and there's a decent size bathroom attached. Instead of a dresser I have my clothes stacked on a table set against the far wall. Shoes underneath it. Two chairs, shoved against another wall beneath the huge windows, hold my books.

The furniture David had in here was very different. Top-quality custom-made shit. Just like in all the rest of his houses we had no idea he owned. Ever since the reading of his will, where he left me everything, I've celebrated my inheritances with a bonfire. I have one at each property I claim. First the furniture. Then, after I've looked through every possible place he could have hidden more information from my brother and I, the houses themselves. The two penthouses will be harder to set fire to, but I'll figure it out.

I lay her down. She really does weigh nothing. Her head lolls to the side a little, but otherwise, she doesn't move. God. I haven't seen her in fifteen years, but I swear, out there, when her lip began to tremble and the dimple on her chin deepened, I glimpsed the girl she was. The little girl with the crush on her best friend's big brother.

Cristiano used to laugh when she'd come to me for the slightest thing. When she and Lizzie fought over a toy or when she fell and hurt herself. She rarely went to her grandmother. Always came to me instead as if I were her hero.

But that was a long time ago. She doesn't remember me. Not to mention the sight of me probably scares her half to death now. And I can't blame her for forgetting. Some days I wish I could forget. Or at least I used to. Now, I make myself see it all again. Make myself remember. Because what happened, happened because of me and I owe it to them to remember.

I take my gun out of its holster and set it on the makeshift nightstand then think better of it and put it on the stack of books across the room. I put my dagger next to it.

I look her over, her small, bare feet pale against the dark bedding. She's too thin, I can see it even with the dress on, her face gaunt. Even so, she's beautiful. There's no hiding that. And I remember how bright and blue her eyes were just moments ago. Full of life. Full of fire.

But I also remember how she crumpled after her attempt at an attack. How quickly she gave up.

With a shake of my head, I walk into the bathroom, switch on the lights, and run the tap. I scrub my hands and splash water on my face, studying myself in the mirror but only momentarily. I never look at myself longer than I need to. I pick up a washcloth and soak it with soapy water, then return to her.

I clean her face first. I can't wash her hair until she's awake but at least I can clean the dried blood off her cheek and lips. I take in her features, see how she's developed. I notice her high cheekbones, wide forehead, eyebrows shades darker than her hair, lashes thick and black and impossibly long. Her lips are parted slightly, the top lip fuller than the bottom. She looks like a doll. An angel. Fucking beautiful. A sleeping angel who has woken up to a nightmare every fucking day for the last fifteen years of her life.

My mind returns to what they did to her. How they took the innocent girl and dirtied her. I swallow hard, almost choking on the lump in my throat. The green dress is stained with blood and dirt. At least the blood isn't hers.

Suddenly I can't stand the thought of their blood on her.

I look at her again and consider for one moment not doing it. Not cleaning her. Because when she wakes up wearing my clothes what will she think I did? Given what I saw today and what I know must have happened to her over the course of most of her life, I can't blame her.

But I won't allow any part of them to stain her, so I undo the few buttons on the dress. Then, not having any way to pull it off her without moving her, I grip the two sides and rip them apart with one tug. I tear away the thin straps, set the pieces of it on either side of her, and look at her.

She's naked underneath. I knew she was. But seeing her like this, in my bed, this woman with breasts fuller than her frame would suggest, her stomach flat, skin stretched tight over protruding bones, pale, flawless skin right down to the V between her legs, it's fucking with me.

Fuck. What is wrong with me? This is Mara.

But she is not a little girl anymore.

I already knew this, so what the fuck is my problem?

I force myself to focus on the damage. Because it's not quite flawless skin, is it? Not really. I see the healed scars. Not too bad, but still, the fact they are there at all pisses me off.

I swallow, my eyes falling to the slit of her sex. My breathing is shallow, uneven and I make myself look away but only after noting the hair is gone. She's been shaved bare for them.

For those bastards.

That's the part I concentrate on. Not this woman's body she's grown into. Not the beautiful face made gaunt from malnourishment and constant stress. I focus my energy and my rage. Rage at those men in that penthouse. Rage at Petrov. And Felix Pérez. At all the men like them including my uncle-father. And I clean her, reciting their names over and over in my head.

I lift one arm, wipe it down. Do the same with the other. There's a small gold bracelet on this one. I don't take it off. As I move to her body, I try not to see her curves, not to feel the softness of her skin beneath the washcloth. Try not to watch her nipples tighten as I wipe away the filth of the men who've touched her.

I clean her legs, her feet, scrub the dirt from the bottoms. I keep my thoughts on those bastards as I part her legs and clean between them. This part is harder. But it's when I'm finished with the front and roll her onto her side that I freeze. That my blood comes to a boil, and I fist my hands so tight the washcloth drips water onto the mattress.

"Fucking. Bastard."

Because here, too, are more scars. Some deeper across her shoulders, her upper back. Her ass. But the thing that is getting this visceral reaction out of me, that has me gritting my teeth hard and vowing vengeance for the thousandth time is the mark on her hip. Fresh. Not yet healed. Probably infected.

A letter *P* branded into her skin.

Branded.

Fucking burnt into her skin.

4

MARA

Consciousness comes slowly. It's like I'm in a thick fog at first. This is always the case when I wake from a drugged sleep. I think it's my mind's way of protecting me. Making me feel like I'm safe for just a little while longer.

I hear a sound, water running, and people talking in the distance. Or maybe a TV. I'm lying on a bed. A different bed than mine. And I'm warm, the blanket over me comforting for its weight. I don't recognize the scent around me. Petrov always smelled faintly of food masked by too much cologne. This isn't that smell. This is the smell of a man. Of leather and sandalwood and something almost tangibly dangerous. But this scent doesn't turn my stomach. It makes me want to inhale deeply.

I blink, my eyelids heavy, and slowly open my

eyes just as the sound around me changes and a door opens.

With a gasp I bolt upright and stare at the man entering the room. Because I remember where I am. That warehouse-like building. I remember the soldiers who stormed the penthouse and killed everyone in it. Remember this man, the one with the leather eye patch—the one claiming to be Dante—who rescued me from that hell.

Who then drugged me and put me in this bed.

"Good morning," he says with what I can hear is false cheer.

Morning? I glance to the windows, see the gray sky, the heavy clouds. It doesn't look like morning.

"Well, evening, really," he corrects as if reading my mind.

I turn back to find him watching me. Steam bellows out of the bathroom behind him. He must have been showering. That's what the water was. The other sound is a TV. A sitcom maybe. I hear the audience laugh on cue.

"There's a bottle of water for you. You're probably thirsty." I glance at the bottle of water on a makeshift nightstand beside the bed but don't touch it. "And hungry. Just let me get dressed and I'll make us something to eat."

I turn back to him. I am both thirsty and hungry. But I'm not sure if the water is drugged.

"It's not drugged," he says, and I wonder if he can read my mind. "I don't want to drug you again."

Then why did you? I want to ask but don't.

He looks at me for a moment longer and I wonder about his eye under that patch, wonder how he got the deep gashes across his face.

He buckles the belt on his jeans as he heads toward the table where a pile of clothes is stacked. I take the bottle, twist off the cap and drink as I watch him because I'm too thirsty not to. I take in his powerful, naked back. Watch how his muscles work as he moves. So different than anyone I've seen. I also see the scars. See the bandage wrapped around his arm with the faint pink of blood.

He got shot getting me out of that penthouse. That has to mean something, doesn't it?

He chooses a shirt then turns and heads toward me. He slips his arms into the charcoal button down. He hasn't wiped the droplets of water off his shoulders, and they leave dark spots on the shirt. He tucks the shirt into his jeans never once taking his eyes off me. I feel my face go hot.

"You slept all night and most of the day. Do you feel better?"

I look down at myself then, notice it's not the dress I'm wearing but an oversized hoodie. I lift the blanket a little to peek underneath. Okay, that's it. Just the hoodie.

"Mara?"

My gaze snaps back to his and I'm about to tell him I'm not Mara when I remember we've had this conversation. Remember what he'd said about Lizzie's eyes being green. Mine are blue. And the birthmark. I remember that too. Lizzie used to say I must be special to have a star on the back of my shoulder. It was more pronounced when I was younger but it's still there. We used to pretend that maybe my father was a king from a far-off land of magical beings.

Dante sits down on the bed. I draw my legs up and after buttoning his shirt, he rolls up the sleeves wincing when he pushes the one over the bandage.

"Did you touch me?" I ask, trying to keep my eyes level on his. Trying to focus on the good eye and not keep looking at either the patch or the scar. Not wanting to care that he's hurt. I notice he tries to turn the good side of his face toward me. Like he's trying to hide the damaged half.

"I cleaned you up as much as I could while you were sleeping then put you in one of my hoodies so you wouldn't be cold. I have some clothes for you though. I thought you'd want to put them on yourself after a shower."

"What does it mean exactly that you cleaned me up?"

"I cleaned the blood off you. Cleaned the dirt off you. I did not touch you in any inappropriate way. I would not." His voice hardens at the last part as if I were accusing him of just that. Maybe I was.

But again, like with the water, I believe him. I don't know why but I guess he doesn't have a reason to lie. I'm here. I'm his. I can't get away from him. We proved that last night. And he can do whatever he likes to me.

"Why did you drug me then?"

"Because you were getting upset. I didn't want you upset."

I try to make out if that's all. I feel like he's leaving something out. I study his good eye. It's familiar, like Lizzie's.

But the Dante I knew was a boy. This is a man.

The Dante I knew was killed before he had a chance to become a man. This man is a cold-blooded killer.

"Would you like to eat something before you have a shower?"

I'm hungry but I want to be alone for a few minutes. I want to be sure he didn't touch me or do anything else to me. I shake my head.

"All right," he stands. "Bathroom's in there. You'll find everything you need but if I forgot anything, I'll be inside, okay?"

"Is there a lock on the door?"

"Yes, there is."

"Can I use it?"

He's momentarily confused by the question but

recovers quickly. It's not so strange a question. Petrov would test me. See if I'd use the locks he'd put on and take off the doors. He said I was his. That I would always be available to him. And he'd punish me when I locked any door, even the bathroom. He always knew, too, even if it was for an instant. Just for one little second so I could feel a little in control. A little safe.

"Yes, Mara," he says, smiling that sad smile. "You can lock the door. You can take your time and I'll wait for you inside. You're safe here. Safe with me."

"No, I'm not."

He opens his mouth to say something but changes his mind. He moves to pick up his phone from on top of a stack of books. He slides his finger over the screen and then types something quickly using both thumbs before turning back to me.

"Holler if you need anything," he says, and walks to the door. He opens it and the sound of the TV grows louder.

"Dante's dead," I call out when he has one foot out of the bedroom.

He stops at that and turns, his hand on the doorknob.

"I saw them. They all died," I tell him.

"That's not true. I wasn't on the island. And Cristiano survived. You met his wife, Scarlett."

"Scarlett?" I feel my forehead furrow.

He nods. "They started a family. They have a

little boy. Well, more of a little hellion," he says proudly. "And another one on the way."

"She's alive?"

He nods. "Because of you. You made that deal with Petrov and saved her life."

No, I didn't. I hadn't been smart in how I'd said it, but I only realized it later. And I don't like that he is trying to flatter me. I'm about to tell him so when his phone buzzes and he turns his attention to it.

"That'll be Cristiano. They're anxious to hear from you. Your grandmother especially."

My grandmother is dead. They killed her too. Felix told me. Showed me the pictures. I'd been five at the time, but I still remember the mess they made. The ruin they left in their wake.

Why is he doing this? Why is he lying to me like this? Playing with me. Is this one of Petrov's tricks? Did he stage it all only to punish me again? He's done it before. He likes playing with me. Making me fall into his traps for his sadistic pleasure.

"Is this a test? A trick?"

"What?"

I push my fingers into my hair trying to think.

"Have a shower, Mara. Get cleaned up. Put on fresh clothes. Then we'll talk. I'll tell you all about them. We can even call them."

I stare up at him.

"Lock the door if you want. I won't hurt you or punish you."

I study him and as much as I want to believe him, I can't afford to. I look down at my lap, thinking what to do. How to get back to the penthouse.

"All right?" he asks, taking a step back into the room, back toward me.

He dips his head to see my face, eyebrows high and I want to believe him.

"What happened to your eye?" I ask before I can stop myself. I don't want to care.

He straightens again, expression hardening a little. "There was an explosion. I lost my sight in that eye soon after."

"Explosion?"

"Five years ago. The night Petrov took you. The night Scarlett killed Helga."

He knows all of that? He was there, in that house? If he was there, then why did he let Petrov take me? If he cared so much, why would he let Petrov have me? It doesn't add up.

"Go get cleaned up. We'll talk after."

I nod so he'll leave and watch him finally walk out of the room. When the door closes, I take a moment to really look around. It's a big room, bigger than even Petrov's bedroom was. But his was tacky. This is minimal. Industrial. I like it. Even the mattress is set on piles of crates. No bed frame.

One wall has large windows without any curtains. I climb out of the bed, the cement floor cold. No carpet. The first thing I do is go to the door and lock it. I have the feeling if he wanted to, he could kick it in pretty easily, but I do it anyway.

I walk to the window, put a hand against the glass. It's cold and a light snow has begun to fall. On the pavement below I see the remnants of the last storm from a few days ago. It's black slush now. It had been cold the last time I was in the city too.

I see why he doesn't have curtains here. There isn't another building nearby, not a high one at least. We must not be in the city proper. Assuming we're still in New York although the helicopter ride wasn't very long so I think we are. Maybe New Jersey.

The urge to pee has me turning to go into the bathroom. I check out his things as I go, a few sweaters, some shirts, jeans. His wallet is sticking out of the pocket of the jeans, and I glance to the door before slipping it out. He must have forgotten it was here.

I bite my lip as I touch the soft black leather. It could be a test, so I just decide to have a look. See if he really is who he says he is. I open it but inside only find cash. No ID. Not even a credit card. Convenient. I count the money. Eight hundred-dollar bills.

I close the wallet and slip it back into his pocket. I won't take it. What would I do with it anyway? I go into the bathroom, switch on the light, close and lock the door. This is spacious too and everything looks new and nice. I run my fingers over the stone countertop as I head to the toilet. I really need to pee. I pull the hoodie up—it's big enough that it falls to mid-thigh—and pee. That's when I notice the bandage on my hip over the *P*.

When I'm finished, I wash my hands and twist a little to inspect the dressing in the mirror. I peel it back and see the remnants of a white ointment. Did he do that? It hurts less than it did, so I gently press it back on and look at my face, my hair. I look gaunt, shadows under my eyes, my cheeks hollowed out. My stomach growls as if reminding me why that is.

I don't need a reminder. I'm hungry. Always hungry. I've been starving for years.

On a stool across the room is a pile of folded clothes with tags still on them. I guess they're for me. Jeans, a sweater. Underthings. A pair of boots. All new.

I should shower before I put them on, but I just splash water on my face in the sink and return to the bedroom. Because I'd seen something at the window.

I go to it and look out, watch the train that runs along the elevated track not too far away and I realize I don't hear it. He must have the place soundproofed. A fence circles the parking lot around the building but it's old and not maintained. Not as secure as I'm used to.

And when I press my forehead to the window, I see the ladder I'd just glimpsed against the wall of the building. I can't tell if it's broken. If it reaches all the way down to the parking lot. I glance at the closed bedroom door then back to the window. I unlock it. It's easy. Too easy. But the window itself is jammed and harder to open. It takes a few minutes but soon enough there's a creak and I push it up. It only goes half-way then gets stuck again but that's all I need.

Bending I stick my head out into the cold evening and see the remnants of the fire escape. The ladder is intact, and it goes almost to the parking lot. That last part I'd have to jump but it looks like it's only a few feet. I can do that.

I hurry back to the bathroom and switch on the shower, leaving the bathroom door open as I pull off the hoodie. That's when I notice the band aid stuck to the crease of my forearm. I take a minute to look at it, peel it back to see the miniscule puncture. Another injection.

He doesn't want to drug me. Yeah, right.

I yank the band-aid away and let it drop to the floor. Quickly, I put on the folded clothes, fresh underthings, a warm, soft sweater. No coat, though. I'll need a coat.

After slipping my feet into the boots I put his hoodie back on over top of my clothes, catching that faint scent of him. The feeling it gives me goes against what I'm thinking, against the warning in my head that this is all a lie. A trick.

I shove the feeling away and leave the shower

running when I return to the bedroom, pausing when I see the wallet again, knowing there's eight-hundred-dollars inside. I slip one of the bills out. I may need it when I get out of this room. I don't know how far I am from the hotel. The Hudson, I remember the name. Like the river.

I head to the window and pause when I hear men's voices inside speaking quietly. I wonder if they're all still here, but I can't think about that right now. Fear paralyzes. I know that well.

I can't be afraid.

So, before I get to that point, I bend down and climb out of the window. The landing is not quite stable, the metal of the ladder rusty and cold. I hold on tight as I toe the first rung, just barely managing to touch it. My heart races and my breath mists in the morning air. The hoody catches on something, tearing, and I feel a sting as I swing the other leg out, but I don't care. I'm out. And I climb as fast as I can manage, which isn't very fast because it's so cold my fingers are freezing. I'm also scared of falling. But soon I'm at the end of it and I look five or six feet down to the ground. It seems higher now that I'm here.

But I have no choice.

So, I turn carefully and when my back is to the wall, I take a deep breath and jump.

5

DANTE

"This wasn't what we fucking agreed!" Cristiano bellows.

I bite into a piece of crispy bacon, enjoying the saltiness, the texture. I eat the rest of the strip. "Any word on that fuck's location?"

"Dante," my brother starts. I can almost hear him forcing himself to breathe, to calm down. "You were going in to get her. To bring her home safely. That was the plan."

That was *his* plan. I want Petrov. He's at the top of my list of assholes to kill and I'm not leaving the city until he's dead. After what I did last night, I know he'll crawl out of whatever hole he disappeared into. He won't be able to resist.

"Charlie?" I ask, again, ignoring my brother. He and Charlie are in his office back at the house in

Italy. Charlie's been monitoring for Petrov's location but nothing as of last night.

"Come home," Cristiano says. "Bring her home. Get her safe. We'll go back together. I want him as much as you do."

"She is safe. And I'm not leaving the city until I take care of him."

"He'll be on high alert."

"That's the point."

"You're reckless, Dante. You're going to get yourself killed. Please, for fuck's sake, wait until I can do this with you."

After giving birth to Alessandro, Scarlett and Cristiano's little boy, Scarlett miscarried twice and now that she's five months pregnant, he's taking extra precautions to keep her and the baby safe. I'm pretty sure my brother hasn't told her about last night yet. She'll lose her shit when she hears.

"You have a family to look after, Cris," I remind him.

"You're my fucking family too."

"This one's for me and I'll take care of it," I finish. I check my watch, look at the closed bedroom door. "I gotta go. Charlie, you still there?"

"I'm here, Dante."

"Call me as soon as you hear anything."

He's silent.

"I mean it. Cristiano means well but I'm not going to let him get himself killed."

"I'll call," Charlie says reluctantly, but he agrees with me. Now that Cristiano has his family, there's more at stake for him. I'm a one-man show. No one will miss me when I'm gone.

Not that I plan to be gone just yet.

"Good." I disconnect the call and tuck the phone into my pocket. I put another strip of bacon into my mouth and chew. There's a low rumble in the warehouse. An unusual sound now that it's otherwise quiet. I sent the men away so as not to scare her. She's skittish. Understandably so.

After a few minutes, I check my watch again. That rumble repeats and it bothers me. I hear the shower, but something doesn't feel right. Setting my coffee mug down I walk down the hall to the bedroom and knock first, but there's no answer which isn't surprising considering the shower is going.

I try the door, but it's locked as I expected, so I pull the ring of keys out of my pocket, unlock the door, and open it thinking I should make some noise so as not to startle her even though some sixth sense is telling me I fucked up. That I'm going to find the room empty. And it takes all of a moment for me to see my mistake. The open window.

"Fuck!"

I make my way to the bathroom, confirm the shower's empty. Water left running. Clever. I reach in and switch it off, my sleeve getting wet. The clothes are gone. My bad again. I shouldn't have left her alone. Shouldn't have left her with an out. She didn't have a coat. That's in the other room. She probably wore my hoodie on top.

I return to the bedroom, go to the open window, see the strip of cloth caught on a rusty nail. I recognize the material of my hoodie. I should have pulled the rusted old fire escape out.

A train rattles by. That's the rumbling I'd heard inside through the open window. The place is soundproofed otherwise. We're about a fifteen-minute drive outside the city and it's noisy as hell out there. I look at the train, at the myriad of tunnels created by the elevated tracks. At the bums gathered around fires they've made in barrels. At the snow that's begun to fall.

I send a text to Matthaeus telling him to send the men out to look for her. He confirms before I've even grabbed my wallet from on top of my jeans. I shove it into my pocket as I hurry through the warehouse, putting my shoulder holster in place, tucking the pistol into it. I throw on my coat and head out into the icy night to find her and bring her back.

6

MARA

It's bitterly cold. I'm shivering as I make my way beneath the train tracks, not really sure where I am or if I'm even going in the right direction. But at least under here I'm partly shielded from the snow that is now coming down hard.

It's getting darker too. I've only been walking for about twenty minutes, maybe half an hour. I have to ask where I am. How to get back to the hotel or I could be going in circles.

Cars speed past me and there are so many people. My hood is up, and I've got my hands shoved deep into the pockets, that hundred-dollar bill crumpled in my palm.

The trains that go by overhead are frighteningly loud. I hear another one coming and look up at the rumbling tracks, to see them vibrate with the weight of it. I back up a few steps to get out from under it, scared the whole thing will collapse on me. Suddenly, I'm stepping into a pile of sludge as the back of my boot hits the pavement and I go down on my butt on the curb. At least I didn't land in the sludge.

Wet snow has gotten inside my boot and it's cold. I dig some of it out. This close to the ground I swear I smell urine and other things I don't want to think about. Someone laughs and I look up from my seated position to find three men huddled around a fire at the next corner. They're watching me.

"Come here, sweetheart."

Sweetheart. The man claiming to be Dante called me that, too. But it didn't sound like this.

"Warm up," one of them says. The other grins, showing a black hole where his teeth used to be.

I straighten, shake my head, turning fast, but crash right into another man.

"I'm sorry!" I start, bouncing back. The only reason I don't fall is because someone else catches me from behind.

I look up at the first man, then turn around to the second. I pull out of his grasp. They're heavily bearded, hair outgrown and dirty, smelly.

"Nothing to be sorry about, pretty girl." He smiles. The teeth he still has are stained. He reaches out a dirty hand in worn gloves and fingers strands of my hair.

I back away a step, tug my hood back up.

The three in the far corner start to walk toward us and instinct takes over. I turn and run, only to hear the scream of horns when I do, the screech of brakes. I scream too, a car stopping inches from me.

One of the men behind me laughs and after a quick glance I charge across the street as the car window opens and the driver screams at me. I run for as long as I can without looking back, until I'm out of breath and have a cramp in my side. As I slow, I look over my shoulder sure the men are behind me. But the coast is clear. Just cars on the road and people rushing down the stairs from one of those platforms. A train must have just pulled in.

I stand there for a minute catching my breath, hand on my side. I look at the people in coats, some carrying briefcases, some talking into wireless earbuds in their ears. I follow a group of four women who walk down the street and enter a diner. I stop outside, my stomach rumbling at the smell wafting out, as the door swings closed. I'm so hungry. God, my stomach hurts.

The place is busy with people having food at the counter and sitting in the fifty's style booths. Some have fancy drink glasses. The women are led to one of the few empty booths.

I take a deep breath in and walk toward the door, too. It chimes and I look up at the source of the sound. A little bell. I think everyone will turn to look at me, knowing I don't belong here, but no one does.

I step up to the counter and look at the meals the others are already eating. Plates of pasta or hamburgers and fries. My mouth waters but I don't have time to eat. I need to hurry. This could all be a test. And I need to get to the hotel as fast as I can, or the punishment will be worse. Petrov is a sadist. He probably has someone watching me now and is gleefully counting the minutes. A stroke for each that he'll make me count out. That's one of his favorite punishments.

I look at the people around me, trying to work out which one works for him.

"What can I get you, hon?" a woman asks, and I turn to find a plump, middle-aged woman with graying blonde hair cleaning the counter before me. I feel that hundred-dollar bill in my pocket.

My stomach growls and I look behind her at the rows of candy and bags of chips.

"Um..." I point. "Chips please. And a candy bar." I want warm food, but this will have to do.

She looks at me curiously for a moment and I wonder if it's her. If she's the one working for Petrov.

"Sure thing," she says.

I take the now-crumpled bill out and set it on the counter. I push it toward her, and her eyebrows go up.

"That's only a couple dollars. You don't have anything smaller?"

I shake my head as I shove the candy bar into the

pocket of my jeans and take the bag of chips. I hurry toward the door.

"Hold on there, honey."

I stop, turn and it feels like everyone in the place is staring at me. I feel my face flush with embarrassment.

"Your change," she says.

"Oh." I walk back to the counter and shove the money she hands me into my pocket. "Do you know where The Hudson Hotel is?"

"The Hudson?" Her drawn-in eyebrows disappear into her hairline. "The swanky place in the city?"

I nod.

She looks me over. I look down at myself too and I'm sure she's thinking someone like me doesn't belong in a hotel like that. She's right.

"You can take the train to Washington Street and it's a couple of blocks walk from there."

"Washington Street?"

She walks to the end of the counter toward the window and points up. "That one. East-bound. It's about six stops."

I look up, nod. "Thank you," I say, and walk out into the cold as I open the bag of chips and cram a handful into my mouth. I hurry up the stairs to the platform where I just miss the train. I mutter a curse and duck under the shelter to try and keep dry.

7

DANTE

I stand on the decrepit street trying to catch a glimpse of her. She only had maybe a ten or fifteen-minute head start on us, but she's vanished. I look into alleyways and eye the bums huddling around their fires. I climb up and down the stairs of the trains wondering if she's up there. She'll be freezing in what she's wearing, and I don't even want to think about what would happen if she got herself cornered in one of these alleys. This is not the best neighborhood.

"Anything?" I ask Matthaeus as he crosses the street toward me.

"Nothing."

"Fuck." I walk to the bums at the far corner, smell the stench of liquor and body odor from here. Three turn toward me, one of them with a grin that shows his lack of teeth. "You guys seen a girl out here? About this tall." I gesture to the middle of my chest. "Wearing a gray hoodie. Blonde hair."

They look at each other then over my shoulder.

I follow their gaze to another man who is bending to pick up what looks to be a discarded still-smoking cigarette butt. He puts it to his lips and takes a drag. I turn back to the others and take out my wallet. "Well?"

They glance down at it and the one without the teeth talks. "Pretty little thing." He pauses, eyes on my wallet.

My fingers tighten around the leather, and I grit my teeth. I take out a hundred-dollar bill. "She was here?"

He holds out his hand and all their eyes follow that bill as I hand it over. "Talked to Bart over there for a minute then ran off."

"Bart." I turn to find the one with the cigarette staring at us. When he sees my expression, he tosses the butt away and takes off down the street.

Matthaeus and I both go after him and it takes about half a block before I've got him by the collar, his back against the wall.

"Where is the girl?"

"I didn't touch her."

I give him a shake. "Where is she?"

"Ran away. That way." He points.

I toss him aside and Matthaeus and I take off in that direction, running several blocks before we slow down as a throng of people rush down the stairs of the platform above.

"Fuck! Get the fuck out of the way!"

But this is New York so no one does. That's when I see it. My hoodie. A strand of long white-blonde hair escaped from beneath blowing in the cold wind as she rushes to board the train.

"There," Matthaeus says, seeing her at the same time.

We shove our way through the mass of people but we're too late. The train doors close and it's already leaving the station before we're even on the platform. I catch a final glimpse of her and look up at the train line.

"I know where she's going," I say, realizing something. Remembering what she said.

"Where?" Matthaeus asks, looking at me like I'm crazy.

"The hotel." This line will take her near it.

"She's going back there? Why the fuck would she do that?" he asks.

I look at him briefly before flying down the stairs to wave down the next cab, practically throwing myself in front of it.

"She asked if it was a test. A trick," I say as the driver hits the gas when I toss a hundred-dollar bill into the seat beside him with the promise of another hundred if he gets us there at the speed of light. I watch out the windshield, the snow slowing down traffic. When we're about two blocks out I turn to Matthaeus. "Keep going in the cab. Watch the subway exits. I'm going on foot to the hotel."

"Petrov's men will be looking for you."

"Better they find me than her, don't you think?" I push the door open, slamming it closed behind me, before he can say more. I hurry down the sidewalk, keeping my head down against the heavy fall of snow. At least there's less people out.

I'm about a block away when I see Petrov's soldiers. Matthaeus was right but like I said, better they find me than her. They're standing at the front entrance of the hotel looking like a couple of goons. I pull my baseball cap down at the front. I always wear a hat these days. Helps to have something to cast a shadow over my face so people don't fucking stare at the half-monster coming at them.

I scan the intersection, glad it's a busy one, and cross to the other side, giving the finger to the asshole who almost runs me over. It's when I'm turning to watch the stairs coming out of the tunnel that I see her. She must have gotten off at the earlier stop. She has the hoodie up. Most of her hair is tucked inside it and she's hunching against the cold. She stops when she's in the middle of the block and looks up at The Hudson straight ahead of her. She doesn't see me watching her but I'm half a block away between the hotel and her. The snow has become a white wall between us.

She moves quickly heading straight to me in her haste to get back to the hotel.

I start to move toward her, hoping to block her from the soldiers' view. Her steps have slowed. She has her head down against the snow. Someone walks out of the liquor store just as she's passing the door and collides right into her, knocking her backward. She stumbles and I'm only a few steps away then. I don't look behind me, hoping we're too far for Petrov's soldiers to see us.

The man apologizes, moves past her.

And that's the moment she sees me.

She freezes in place, mouth falling open in surprise. And it takes her a split second to make the decision to run. She spins and takes off, but she doesn't go back down the sidewalk. She takes off into the street, looking back at me as she does, she doesn't notice the SUV that's coming down the road straight at her.

The driver hits the break, but the road is slippery, and the SUV goes into a spin, blaring his horn. She stops, turns to the sound and over every other noise, I hear her scream. I charge toward her, not knowing whether it's adrenaline giving me the speed I need or maybe fate fucking giving me a break for once, but I wrap an arm around her middle and pull her out of the SUVs path just before it would slam into her. I don't stop running and I don't let go of her until we're around the corner and out of sight of the hotel. She's squirming but I don't care. A few moments later, I hear the horn of the taxi and Matthaeus pushes the back door open. I get her inside, forcing her head down as we pass the hotel and Petrov's men back to the warehouse.

8

MARA

"What the fuck were you thinking?" Dante barks when we're back inside the warehouse. I back away from him as soon as he lets me go.

Matthaeus is here too. He rode with us to a place about an hour from where we got into the taxi. We changed cars, then drove back to the warehouse in case Petrov's men followed us.

"Take it easy," Matthaeus tells Dante.

"Just take care of the fucking locks," Dante orders.

Matthaeus looks like he wants to say something but changes his mind, glances at me then disappears down the hall. I watch him go and some part of me wants to ask him to stay. To be a buffer between Dante and me.

"I asked you a fucking question!"

I startle, Dante's tone commanding my attention. He pulls his baseball cap off and hurls it across the room, pushing a hand through his hair. Some of it flops over the right side of his face, partially obscuring the patch.

"What the hell were you thinking?" he asks.

He's angry? I'm angrier. I breathe a sharp breath in and step toward him. "I was almost back! I almost made it!"

"For fuck's sake." He looks at me like he can't believe what he's hearing. With a shake of his head, he moves to where the bottle of whiskey sits on the coffee table. He lifts it and one of the empty glasses, pouring, then straightens and watches me as he drinks it in one swallow before pouring a second.

I'm so angry I charge at him, wrestle the bottle from him and smash it against the far wall. The sound is strangely satisfying. Making me feel in control, powerful. At least for a split second.

"You fucking jerk!" I slam my hands hard enough into his chest to almost budge him. "I was almost back! It's not fair!"

He captures my wrists and holds my arms at my sides. "Fair? What the fuck are you talking about? Don't you get it? You're not going back. I'm taking you home. Don't you want to go home?"

"Home?" Now it's me who can't believe the words coming out of his mouth. "What home do you think you're taking me to exactly? I have no home. Don't *you* get it?" He loosens his grip and I slip my wrists free. Tears burn my eyes. "You're just making it worse." My voice breaks but I scrub my eyes and steel my spine. "I'm leaving!" I spin on my heel and walk toward the door.

"Leaving?" he snorts. "Like hell you are!" His steps are heavy behind me.

I close my hand over the doorknob, turn it, open it. In the same instant his big hand is flat against the door over my head, pushing it closed before I get it all the way open. He turns the key in the lock then pockets it before leaning down close to me. So close, I can feel the heat coming off him, smell his aftershave. It makes me shudder, makes the hair on the back of my neck stand on end. And it puts my body on high alert.

Because when he's this close, something happens to my insides.

"You're not going anywhere without my say so," he says and my breath catches. His voice is low, a vibration against my skin sending a chill down my spine. "Understand that."

When I can breathe again, I slowly turn to face him. He's so close that all I see is him. All I breathe is him, his big body in front of me, arms caging me in. My heart is racing, my stomach in knots as I force myself to look up at him. But I can't keep eye contact. Can't take how his gaze is drilling into me.

I turn away. Force myself to think. To not feel

what it is I'm feeling. I need to steel myself against him.

"I'm going," I say to his chest, my tone somehow firm in spite of my quaking insides. It's not fear exactly, though. Fear has a different texture. A different smell.

He gives me a one-sided grin like he's humoring me. I set my palms against his wall of a chest, trying to shove him away but it's impossible to budge him.

I need to get out.

I slide my hands up to his shoulders feeling the contour of powerful muscle beneath and strangely, I find myself lingering, curious. I shift my gaze to his broad chest, to my hands small on the wide expanse of his shoulders. My heart pounds against my chest and I lick my lips before shifting my gaze back to his and I wonder if he can hear my heart beating.

But when his expression changes, the way he looks at me different, I catch myself.

What am I doing? I need to get out.

He clears his throat and nods and I swear he looks like he's about to call me a good girl but that's not what this is. I'm not his good girl. I'm not anyone's good girl. I never was, not for any of them.

Instead, I grip his shoulders and jerk my knee up between his legs, ramming it into his groin.

He grunts, hunching forward. It hurts, I see it on his face. Feel it in the tight barely controlled grip of his hands when they close over my shoulders, pinning me to the door as he manages the pain.

"Christ. Fuck," he mutters, breathing hard. He draws one hand into a fist, and I think this is it. He's going to hit me.

I let out a pathetic whimper, all my bravado gone. I curl into myself, tuck my chin, cover my ears with my hands and keep my arms tight to my torso to protect my stomach. But the hit doesn't come. No slap. No punch to my temple or my belly. Just that fist slamming into the door above my head, rattling it in its hinges.

"I'm not going to hit you," he says through clenched teeth, voice like sandpaper.

It's a trick. He's waiting until he can see my face. Watch me when he hurts me.

"Look at me," he commands.

I hope it's a slap. Fists hurt more than flat hands. But I can't bring myself to look up. To just get it over with.

"I said look at me."

I shake my head.

"I'm not going to hit you. I wouldn't. Ever. Just look at me."

I still don't.

"Please, Mara."

His tone twists something inside me and before I can stop myself, I shift my gaze. I look up at him, confused, off balance. Unsure what to do. I shouldn't have hurt him, but I'm confused by my reaction to him. That feeling in my stomach when he's close like this. When he's looking at me like this. Confused that he won't hit me. Won't make me fight him. It's what I know. It's what I can do. I'll lose. That's a fact. I always lose. But fighting helps. Like I'm not just giving it to them. Like I'm not complicit in my captivity.

"Don't fucking do that again, understand?" he says.

That's it? Just that? I need him to fight me. Doesn't he get it? This other thing, this other way he is, I can't make sense of it. So, I curl my hands into claws and scratch down both sides of his face. I scream like some wild animal as I do, forcing him to hurt me back. Needing him to.

He curses under his breath and grips my hands, pulling them away. My fingernails are bloody and his grip is tighter than it's been. Red lines form on his cheeks and I know they sting. Still, all he does is look at me like he pities me. Like I'm some pathetic thing to be pitied and I can't stand it.

"Fight me!" I scream. "Fight me like a man!"

"I know the kind of men you've been around, but let me tell you something," he starts, pulling my wrists behind my back. "Men don't fight women. They don't hit women." He releases me and looks me over. "Go inside and get out of those wet things."

That's it? I turn around to try the door again, but

it's locked. He has the key which is why he's not bothering to stop me.

"Let me out of here!"

"So you can go back to Petrov?"

"Yes!"

"That's not happening. That's never happening. He will never get his hands on you again. I'm taking you home."

Home. God. There it is again.

"Don't you remember your home?" he asks.

"I told you. I don't have a home."

"Yes, you do. With a grandmother who loves you. Who wants you back. With people who care about you."

I shake my head, cover my ears to try to tune out his words. I can't hear this. I don't want to remember this. I can handle anything else. Beatings. Their hands on me. But this is too hard. Because this reminds me of everything and everyone I lost. The life that was stolen before I had a chance to live it.

"That was the last of my whiskey," he says then, gesturing to the smashed remnants of the bottle.

"Punish me then." I try because I need him to. I need him to hurt me because if he hurts me then I know where we stand. I understand that. In a way, I understand pain.

His forehead wrinkles and he studies me. I wonder what he sees. If he's reading my mind.

"Do it," I push.

"No."

"Yes!" I grab hold of his patch and am about to yank it off in my rage when he catches my wrists. The next thing I know, he knocks my legs out from under me and hauls me over his shoulder. My wrists in one hand, the other arm wrapped around my thighs. He stalks down the hallway with me across his shoulders. I can hear a drill going but before I can see where it's coming from, he opens another door and dumps me on a bed. Then he's on top of me, his weight crushing my lungs making it impossible to breathe.

"Don't do that. Don't ever fucking do that. Am I fucking clear?"

"Why? Are you afraid I'll see you for what you are?"

A moment passes between us, strange and fraught with an edge of danger and something else. Something dark. After the pause he releases my wrists to stretch my arms out to the sides.

"Am I fucking clear?" he asks, voice low. When I don't answer right away, he continues. "I'm being patient with you, Mara."

"Don't do me any favors."

We're so close, I'm not sure what's going to happen. I'm panting. Worn out. And he's breathing heavy, gaze searching my face, falling on my mouth.

I lick my lips because for a moment, I think the strangest thing.

I think he's going to kiss me.

The room goes dead silent, even the drilling has stopped. But after an eternity, he leans away.

I blink, remember myself as my face flushes with heat. Does he know what I was thinking? Did he read my mind again?

"Fuck," he mutters, looking away, shaking his head as he releases my arms, starts to lift his weight from me.

But then everything changes.

Because that's when I feel it. Feel him.

He must know the instant I do because he shifts his gaze away and clears his throat, climbing off the bed. He stands, scrubs his face and I sit up. Before he can turn away, I see it. The erection he wants to hide.

"I don't want to hurt you," he says almost hoarsely. "Christ. It's the last fucking thing I want."

I get to my feet. Watching as he adjusts himself before turning back to me. He knows I know. He must.

"You're like him. Just like him."

He's quiet for a very long moment, studying me intently before he answers. "I'm not like him."

"I felt you."

His jaw clenches.

"You may say you don't want to fight me, but you got hard doing it. So how are you different?" I ask, not looking away.

"Mara—"

I step toward him close enough that we're almost touching. "Tell me how you're different," I hiss.

His jaw tightens, gaze hardens. "Tell me something first. What would he do now? Petrov."

I press my lips together.

"Comfort you?"

I don't bother to answer. He knows anyway.

"Tell me. Is that what he'd do? Because I don't think so. I think he'd hurt you."

"Stop."

"And I don't think he'd just use his hands. I've seen the marks, Mara."

Shame washes through me. "I said stop."

"And he wouldn't stop there, would he? Wouldn't stop at hitting you."

"Shut up!" I scream, taking a step away only to have him take a matching one toward me.

"He'd touch you."

I feel my face crumple and cover it with my hands, trying to rub away emotions I haven't let myself feel in so long.

"Hurt you in every way."

I turn to run away but he catches my arm and spins me to face him, backing me into the wall. He sets one big hand against my belly to keep me there.

"Understand one thing," he starts, leaning his face down to mine. When I try to look away, he leans in closer. "I am not him. I am nothing like him. Don't ever accuse me of being like him."

I swallow the lump in my throat and wrap my arms around myself when I begin to tremble with a cold that's so deep inside me I'm afraid I'll never get warm again.

"Just let me go," I try, my voice coming out weak.

"No," he says and there's that look again. The same one from yesterday. But I was wrong. It's not pity. It's more. And it's harder to look at. "I won't let you go, Mara. That's the point."

I search his face, shake my head.

He looks at me straight on and I can see the broken side of his face, the two deep crisscrossing gashes. I think he's letting me look.

"Dante didn't look like you," I say. My words wound him. I see it. He turns his head a little, so I only see the good side again. "Why are you lying to me? Telling me you're him?" A tear slides down my cheek.

He watches it fall as if transfixed, then wipes it away with the pad of his thumb.

"Why?" I ask again.

"I'm not lying to you, and you know it." His voice is quieter. Darker. "They told you you were Elizabeth because they thought they'd taken Elizabeth. They were supposed to have taken her."

More tears flow from my eyes.

"Then when they realized their mistake, they told you that you had to *be* Elizabeth."

I bring my hands to my face to wipe away the

tears that won't stop falling. I shake my head. "It's not true." But it is true. I remember them arguing in the very beginning. When I wouldn't stop crying. When they realized what I was saying was that I wasn't Lizzie.

I don't want to remember this. I can't.

He reaches out, brushes my hair back and when I meet his gaze something strange passes between us. His fingers make contact with my face as he wipes away more tears and there are those sensations like before. Strangely, I find myself wanting his touch. His hands on me. Something I've never wanted before. Something I never thought I could want. And when he pulls me to his chest, I don't fight him. I just let him hold me for a long, long time, feel him kiss the top of my head, strong arms keeping me to him.

"I won't hurt you, Mara. And I won't let anyone else hurt you again."

I want to wrap my arms around him. Let him carry me, give in to him. Give myself over because he is so much stronger than me. Maybe he can take the weight, the mess of the last fifteen years.

But he pulls away too quickly and I'm left feeling cold again. I wrap my arms around myself once more.

Alone.

Always alone.

And besides you can't just give away fifteen years. Hand it over like it's a coat you take off.

"I was off the island that night," he says, drawing me out of myself. It sounds like a confession. Like something heavy inside him. "I'd snuck out for a girl. But that was all planned. So that bastard could murder my family. We thought you'd died. We just assumed they'd gotten rid of your body. It took Cristiano years to get better. And he was different after. Until Scarlett, at least." I watch as he tells his story. "It was Noah who recognized you from a picture in Lizzie's room. He remembered you."

"Noah?"

He nods.

In the rags of my memory is a little boy named Noah. But that was a very, very long time ago. I remember that he was kind to me.

"That's not possible," I say.

He cups my face with both hands, uses his thumbs to wipe my tears. He's gentle, so gentle, this giant of a man, this killer. But I can't believe him. Doesn't he know that?

"I never even looked for you. God. I never even looked."

His pain is palpable.

I pull out of his grasp, turn my gaze away. I don't want to see it and I don't want to feel what I'm feeling. I can't do this.

"Stop," I tell him.

"And then you were so close, in the same fucking house." He's angry at that last part, his emotions shifting so erratically, so violently.

"I said stop. I don't want to hear any more."

"But that bastard had already taken you and after the explosion," he stops, looks away from me, shakes his head. "It took me five more years to find you, but I never stopped looking once I knew. I swear." That last part is like a confession and a plea in one. I look up at him, at the agony on his face.

"I said I don't want to hear it," I say because I have to.

"You're not going back to him, Mara. You don't have to be afraid of him anymore."

I close my eyes. "You have no idea what you're saying. You don't know how powerful he is."

And I can't do this. I can't listen to this. I can't start feeling again. It's easier if I just don't feel. I can manage it then. And the pain, sometimes the punishments help. It's stupid, I know.

He's still talking but I try to tune him out. I sing Flora's song in my head. I close my eyes and sing. His thumb comes to my lips. I must be mouthing the words.

"Your grandmother—"

My eyelids fly open, and I slam both hands flat into his chest. "Stop it! My grandmother is dead! They're all dead. And I don't want to hear about how *they* died, and *I* lived all because somebody made a stupid mistake! I don't want to hear any of it!"

I swing one arm up to his face, almost get my hand around the eyepatch but he catches me. He drags both arms over my head, holding them against the wall, leaning in so close I smell the scent that was on his pillow.

"I said not to do that," he says, tone low, voice like gravel.

"Why not? Are you afraid I'll see what I already know? You forget that I watched you kill that man at the penthouse. You liked it. I saw that, too."

"He deserved to die. They all did."

"Only monsters enjoy the feel of blood on their hands."

He snorts, one side of his mouth curves momentarily upward. "I never said I wasn't one. But I'm not *your* monster."

That makes me pause. I need to think. "Why are you doing this? What do you want with me?"

"I want you safe. I want you home."

"I already told you I have no home and I will never be safe."

"You're safe with me."

I twist, tug at my arms but it's useless. He just stands there like it's costing him no effort at all to keep me in place.

"Just let me go."

"I'll let you go when I'm ready. When you've heard me."

"What if I don't want to hear you?"

"Well, that's too bad, sweetheart."

There it is again. *Sweetheart*. I blink, open my mouth to say something but I can't remember what.

"You used to make me little hearts cut out of pink paper and leave them on my pillow. Always pink with you. My brothers would laugh so fucking hard."

"I hate pink," I lie. I don't feel either way about pink. I shake my head. I need to stop this. For fifteen years I have been learning to store the few memories I had away. And I do remember. I remember the boy, Dante. I've always remembered him even when all the other faces faded, his somehow remained. Even over my own grandmother's. But I learned to keep those memories locked up in a box until they were all but forgotten. Until there was no lost life to cry over. Until there was no one to miss so much it made it impossible to breathe.

"Why are you doing this to me?" I ask again, eyes warm with quiet, never-ending tears.

"Why am I making you remember?"

I don't answer.

"It hurts. I know. It's why you want me to stop but you have to face it now."

"No, that's not why. Let go." I twist and turn but he doesn't give, not an inch.

"You suffered the most out of everyone."

"You don't know me." I realize then there's only one way to make him stop. I have to wound him like I did moments ago but harder.

"You're strong, Mara. A survivor."

"I'm not that." I know what I am. Weak. A coward. I don't know what he reads in my expression or my body language, but he lets me slip my wrists from his grasp, keeping his hands on the wall. He leans into them to keep me caged as he looks down at me.

"But you need to stop and face the past. It's the only way to have a future."

"A future?" Doesn't he understand that for someone like me, there is no future? No hope?

"And I'll be with you. It hurts. I know. Fuck, do I know. That's why you want me to stop, but—"

"No, you're wrong. That's not why I want you to stop," I say, cutting him off, my voice clear, not choked. Because I need to end this now. I need to make him stop now before it gets too far, and I can't stop it anymore. Before I can't put the lid back on Pandora's box. So, I change tactic. "You want me to tell you I believe that you're Dante? What if I did? What would it matter?"

His eyes narrow as he takes in this change.

"You need me to tell you it's okay? Is that it?" I force myself to keep going. To not give in to the weakness that has me hugging my arms to myself.

"You want me to say that I'm okay now that you've rescued me? That you're my hero?"

"I'm not a hero. I know that," he says through gritted teeth. I've hit a nerve. I see it. Guilt. That's his Achilles' heel.

"Tell me, is that what you want? Why you came for me now? *Fifteen. Years. Later. Fifteen years too late?*" I don't have to work at pretending the anger I feel. The rage. I just have to direct it at him. No matter how much I know it's wrong.

"Mara," he sounds calm, but that calm is fading. He has anger inside him too. A rage as violent as mine.

"Do you know what my life was?" It's hard to speak around the lump in my throat, but I keep going. Pushing him, poking at that rage, nudging it to the surface. "Do you have a single fucking clue?"

He exhales, blinks away momentarily like he can't quite look at me. The breath he draws in is tight.

"Do you think I can ever go back after all that happened? Go home? What would I go back to? A life I don't remember? One I never got a chance to live? One where I watched my best friend murdered because they thought she was me?" My voice breaks.

He steps away, runs a hand through his hair. "Fuck, Mara. That wasn't your fault. You know that, don't you? Please tell me you fucking know that."

I step toward him, steel my spine, and stand up

straighter. "You want to know how I know you can't be him? Can't be the boy with the bright green eyes who was a hero to me back when there weren't any monsters to slay?"

His lips draw into a tight line, and I know if I say what I'm about to say, I will cut him deeply.

But I can't not say it.

I can't stop.

"Because Dante would never have let what happened to me happen."

9

DANTE

Fuck.

You can hear a pin drop.

She's right.

She is absolutely right.

Those last words cut into me like the shards that tore me apart in that house. She could have slapped my face and it would have been less violent. Less painful.

I look down at her not quite believing it, the words themselves echoing as if bouncing off the walls. Repeating. Repeating.

"Because Dante would never have let what happened to me happen."

She stares up with her wide blue eyes, accusing and innocent and terrified at once. Her face is pale, the skin around her nose and eyes pink from crying. She's waiting for my reaction. Ready for an attack like earlier when she curled into herself thinking I'd hit her. Assuming I would.

Fuck. This has gone off the rails. Everything so very different than I could have anticipated.

I knew she'd be confused. I thought she'd remember me though. It was arrogant, to think it. To assume I'd swoop in and rescue her, and we'd all live happily ever after.

Newsflash, asshole. Kidnapped girls who have lived their lives in captivity don't get happily-ever-afters. And neither do monsters. I am one, inside and out. I let her see that with her own eyes. Couldn't shield her from my true nature.

"Matthaeus." I don't take my eyes off her as I say his name, sounding much calmer than I feel. I wonder if she hears the current just beneath that false calm.

Neither she nor I look away when Matthaeus comes into the room. He probably heard every fucking word.

"Watch her. She tries anything, give her something to help her sleep."

Her eyes narrow and her mouth tightens but she remains silent. She doesn't look away from me, those vivid blue eyes familiar, twisting something inside me.

He nods tightly.

I walk away, unlock the door, and get out of the apartment, letting the door slam shut behind me. I hadn't taken off my coat, so I button it against the icy wind when I get through the downstairs door. I walk blind through the empty lot, out the broken gate. I don't look back at the warehouse. It's one of David's. Harder to dig up than the others. He had wanted to make sure no one would know about this one, at least when he was alive. I can't imagine him having spent much time inside it. Not his style. He had it stocked with weapons though and I know he's had men stay there. I saw the trash they left behind. I wonder what kind of operations he ran out of the place.

But that's not what I'm thinking about now.

I'm hearing her words repeat in my head. *"Dante would never have let what happened to me happen."* I let them take me under as I walk for half an hour before finally getting too fucking cold to be outside any longer. I turn the corner and walk into the first bar I see, a run-down, smelly hole in the wall.

But it's dark and there's liquor, so it'll do.

I walk up to the bar and the two men sitting nearest the empty stool are quick to vacate their seats. I open my coat, shake off the snow. I don't bother taking it off before I drop onto the stool. I push my wet hair back and it stays back, putting my face on full display for the barman who to his credit, doesn't flinch. He just stands there eyeing me while drying a glass. He's a big guy. Bald. Bearded and tattooed. He nods in greeting.

"Whiskey," I say.

He sets a glass down in front of me, uncorks a new bottle and pours.

"Leave the bottle." I take a hundred-dollar bill out of my wallet and set it on the bar. Not that this whiskey's worth that.

He eyes the bill but doesn't take it just yet. "Sure thing." He walks to the other end of the bar, and I pick up the glass, swallow the contents. I catch my reflection between the bottles of liquor in the tarnished mirror behind the bar. I see why the men who scurried away did. I look wrecked. And scary as fuck.

I pick up the bottle and the glass, then pour. I have to do that since I lost my eye. Can't just pour something out into a cup that I'm not holding. Depth perception is still a challenge, but I work around it. Shrapnel hit my eye the night of the explosion, but the doctors thought they could save it. I knew when I opened them there was a problem, but I figured that was the bandages obscuring my vision. In time it became evident I was losing my sight in my right eye. Then it got infected, and well, here I am. A patch like a pirate.

Alessandro likes it. Thinks it's cool.

I smile at the thought of my nephew. Miniature Cristiano. He had Scarlett buy him an eyepatch as soon as he understood why I wore it so I wouldn't feel like I stuck out. He was irritated his wasn't leather like mine though.

I swallow the rest of the contents of the glass and pour again. Christ. This hasn't gone like I expected, but she's right. What did I think? That I'd fucking swoop in like some knight in shining armor and slay the beast and then what? She'd forget everything those bastards did to her and go back to living the life she was meant to live? A life she's never known?

Fuck. I don't want to think about it all, but I need to. I need to do this with her. Like I said. I owe it to her.

This all happened because of me. Because David raped my mother. Got her pregnant when she only wanted to be free of him. So, to punish her, he had that bastard Rinaldi violate her, then made her watch as her husband and children were massacred.

Not me, though. I didn't die.

And I have a feeling if she'd had a choice, if she could have sacrificed me to save them, she might have. I wouldn't blame her. I was the living, breathing reminder of the violence done to her. A secret she had to keep from her husband, the man I knew as my father but wasn't. I still wonder what he'd have done if he knew. If he'd have been able to love me. To stand the sight of me.

Pouring another glass, I take a sip, leaning back in my chair. The liquor is starting to do its work.

She was never cruel or even unkind to me. She

loved me. I know she did. But sometimes I'd find her watching me and it always felt off. I understand now why that was.

But that's all past. She's dead. Gone fifteen years now. The men involved are all dead. And I killed the one who orchestrated it all.

Not that it gave me any satisfaction. It couldn't. Not when I learned the truth about him. About how I was conceived. Not when I learned that Mara was alive. Kidnapped and sold. A slave to the highest bidder.

She was unlucky from birth. Her mother died in a traffic accident soon after she was born. No one, not even Lenore, ever found out who her father was. Mara got stuck with us for an adoptive family.

Christ. What a family we are to get tangled up with.

I am sorry that I never looked for her. I will forever hate myself for that. I assumed she'd been killed. Believed David when he told me they probably dropped her body in the ocean. Why not kill her when they killed everyone else? It didn't even occur to me that they'd have mistaken her for Elizabeth and had plans for her that, in some ways, were worse than death.

No. Nothing is worse than death. It's what Cristiano says. Alive is better. Always.

Alive is possibility. Hope.

But that's just it. She has none.

I forgo the glass and bring the bottle to my lips, seeing the eyes of the barman and a few other patrons as I drink about a third of it. The only reason I stop is my phone buzzing in my pocket.

I set the bottle on the counter, wipe my mouth with the back of my sleeve and pull the phone out. It's Charlie. I swipe the green bar and put the phone to my ear.

"Charlie."

There's a pause. "Are you drunk?"

"My, what big ears you have."

"Where's Matthaeus?"

I pick up the bottle, pour, splashing some onto the counter. That could be the amount I've already drunk and not necessarily my one-eyed status.

"Not here," I tell him.

"You're not at the warehouse."

"Check my location?"

"You're out alone?"

"What did you find?"

"For fuck's sake, Dante. Do you think it's wise to be out on your own drunk or well on your way to being drunk when Ivan Petrov has his men scouring the city for you?"

"Does he?" I smile, drink more whiskey. "Then he got my message."

"Yeah. Not very bright to leave a fucking calling card." He means my big smile and the fuck-you to the camera before we went into the penthouse.

"It's what will get him out of his hole," I pause when I see the barmen's eyes on me, but my glance is all it takes for him to look away. Mind his own fucking business. "Where is he? I assume that's why you're calling? And I assume you haven't told my brother since he's not on the line with you."

He sighs. "No, I haven't told Cristiano. He'll get on a plane the instant I do, and I agree with what you said. His family needs him here right now."

"Smart. So, where the fuck is that bastard?"

"I'll tell you what. You get yourself home. Sleep it off. Then call me when you're sober and Matthaeus is at your side. We both know you need someone with a little sense to keep you from getting your head blown off."

"I'm not planning on getting my head blown off just yet."

"Yeah, well, it's that last part that scares me. I dealt with this with your brother. I don't intend on doing it again with you."

I grit my teeth. I know what he means. I know Cristiano planned to kill Rinaldi and that was it. It was as far as his plans went. He thinks I didn't know.

"Where is he? Where's Petrov?" I ask, no note of sarcasm in my voice, trying to make myself sound as sober as possible.

"Like I said, get home. Sleep it off. Then call me. And try to remember there's more at stake than just your life, Dante. You just got her back. Not to mention Matthaeus and the rest of your men." He disconnects the call before I even open my mouth to reply.

I tuck the phone into my pocket, pick up the bottle and look straight ahead as I process, my mind circling back to Mara. To that moment when I was on top of her. Fuck. What was I thinking? I hadn't meant for it to go like it did. I hadn't meant to be fucking turned on but she's right. I was.

Christ.

There's something strange between us. Something I hadn't even considered. An electrical charge.

I just have to remember electricity kills.

And yeah, her accusation, she was right on that too. To some extent, I am like that bastard, Petrov. I like the kill. But I won't hurt her. Ever. And whether she likes it or not, I'm hers now.

Her protector.

Her monster.

The one who will slay all the other monsters in her world.

10

MARA

I stare at the door for a long time after he leaves. After I've heard the downstairs door slam shut so hard it rattled the glasses on the counter.

He's gone. Walked out.

It's what I wanted. At least for him to stop. But now that he's gone, I feel alone. Cold. Feel the empty space where he was.

Matthaeus comes toward me, stopping a few feet from me.

"You should get out of those wet things. Have a warm shower. I'll make something to eat. Come on."

We walk into the hall, and he gestures to Dante's open bedroom door. I wonder if he's not afraid that I'll try to run again.

"I changed the lock on the window. There's no way out. I also took the locks off both the bedroom and bathroom doors."

I shift my gaze back to Matthaeus, disliking him for this. He's loyal to Dante. That's clear. I study him, his eyes a warm brown, hair almost the same shade as his eyes. Square jawed like all of them. Big, like all of them. Soldiers. Killers.

"The brand on your hip is infected."

I feel my face flush. He saw it, too?

"I left a fresh bandage and ointment you'll need to put on it in the bathroom. Do that after your shower and if it hurts, let me know. You'll need to clean it and put that ointment on twice a day."

I don't reply.

He gestures to the bedroom. "Go. Ten minutes or I'll come in there and get you."

He means it. I know it from his expression. He's the first to turn away. He walks into the kitchen. He's not afraid to give me his back. Not afraid of me. I get it. I have no doubt he can overpower me and, more importantly, he won't hesitate to. He's been given the green light by Dante. Besides, I'm pretty sure he doesn't think I'm worth the trouble they went through.

So, I walk down the hall, guilt gnawing at me for what I said. For that look on Dante's face.

Inside the bedroom I notice Matthaeus hasn't just taken the lock off the door but removed the doorknob altogether. Same with the bathroom. I can't even close either door. And there is a brand-new lock on the window. He's been busy.

I head to the bathroom, stripping off my boots and wet things, hanging them on the drying rack because I'm not sure I have other clothes. The bandage on my hip is already peeling so I pull it the rest of the way off and try not to see the angry red *P* there. I touch my hand to the skin around it. It feels hot.

I switch on the shower and step under the flow. It feels good. So good. The water is steaming hot and for a long minute I just close my eyes and let it wash over me. I don't even care that the brand stings. I try to forget what just happened. The things I said. The look on his face.

He is Dante. I know that. Part of me knew it from the first moment I saw him. I'd never forget those eyes.

I open mine then.

He lost one of his eyes. I'm sad about that fact. And as I pick up the shampoo, his shampoo, I think about how awful I was to him. How I hurt him when he's the one person who wants to help me. Wants to save me.

But he can't save me. And it'll be better for him, and for me, the sooner he understands that.

I scrub my hair, smelling him all around me. That scent familiar from the bed. I shampoo twice then a third time. He doesn't have conditioner, but I don't care. I want to cut it off anyway. Get rid of it.

I use his bodywash too and am aware of the time

so, for as much as I want to stay under that hot flow, I switch off the shower and reach for a towel. I make a turban out of it for my hair then take a second one, wrapping it around myself. At the counter I look at my reflection, feeling as tired as I look. I pick up the toothbrush that's still in its package and brush my teeth, dry my hip gingerly then put some of the ointment on and bandage it again.

Apart from the underwear, my clothes are too wet to wear so I go to the pile of his things. They're folded neatly. I pick a warm, oversized sweater that smells like him, pull the towel off my head and put it on. It comes to the middle of my thighs.

I go back into the bathroom then and open the drawers to look for a brush and a pair of scissors. I find neither, only a small comb with teeth too close, some shaving cream, a couple of razors. A box of condoms.

I pick those up, think about him, how he felt when he got hard.

The fact that he got hard wrestling me.

I should feel disgusted. Angry. But I don't because I lied. He's not like them. He's nothing like them. And my mind naturally imagines his hands on me, his body on top of mine. His weight pressing me into the bed.

I close my eyes, setting one hand to my stomach to quiet the fluttering. I put the condoms back in the drawer and wonder what's wrong with me. How can I even think about that? About any man in that way ever again? But everything feels different with him.

Inside another drawer I find his aftershave. Glancing quickly at the door I twist off the lid and inhale deeply. Then, before I can think better of it, I tilt the bottle, dab some onto my fingertips and press them to the pulse at my neck.

It's weird. I have no idea why I do it. As soon as I do, I close the bottle and immediately try to wash it off when I hear footsteps.

I grab a towel and dry my hands, my heartbeat picking up.

"Mara?" It's Matthaeus.

I set the towel back on the rack and walk out of the bedroom.

He looks me over with concern. "Give me your wet things. I'll put them in the dryer."

I go back into the bathroom, grab the pile of clothes on the drying rack and hand them to him. I then follow him out of the bedroom and into the living area. He opens a door off the kitchen and disappears. A moment later I hear the tumbling of a dryer.

"Did you put the ointment on?" he asks when he's back.

"Yes."

"I'd like to have a look at it—"

"It's fine." I turn to the stove where soup is

bubbling in a pot. It smells wonderful and my stomach growls loudly.

"Sit down," he says, hearing it too.

I sit at the table. A moment later, he sets a deep bowl of tomato soup with meatballs in front of me, along with a basket of bread, a dish of butter, and a glass of water.

He takes the seat across from mine with his own bowl and an already open beer. He sets the bowl down and leans back, eyeing me as he drinks from the bottle. It's hard to hold his gaze so I focus on my soup, blowing on each spoonful and trying not to tip the bowl straight down my throat. I am so hungry.

It's awkwardly quiet as we eat and every time I glance out the window I see how heavy the snow has gotten. I can't help but think about Dante out there. Wonder if he's okay.

"He risked his life to get you out," Matthaeus says.

"He shouldn't have." The words are out before I can stop them but what I want to say is I'm sorry. That I know he did. But it's not that I don't mean what I said. Dante shouldn't have risked his life for me because Petrov will hunt him down and kill him for taking me. "I don't mean—"

"More?" Matthaeus gets to his feet, cutting me off.

I nod.

He takes my bowl and ladles more soup into it. I

am quick to spoon up a meatball. "What I mean is Petrov will come after him," I tell Matthaeus once he sits down again with his second bowl.

"That's the point."

I put my spoon down and study him. "What?"

"That's the point," he repeats as if I've just not heard.

"Then he'll get himself killed. You know that. Petrov will kill him and you and all the others, too. You don't know him like I do. You shouldn't have taken me from him."

Matthaeus sets his elbows on the table and leans toward me. Any kindness is gone as his eyes bore into mine. "I'd love to see that mother fucker try."

I lean away, feel goosebumps rise along my arms, the hair on the back of my neck standing on end.

He grins, relaxing back in his seat. After a long minute he checks his watch. "You should go to bed."

Guilt gnaws at me. "Do you think he's okay?"

"Now you're worried about him?"

I lower my lashes.

He sighs. "He'll be fine. Just needs to blow off steam."

"He's all alone out there," I say, my gaze out the window.

"I sent men to keep an eye on him. I can track him."

"Track him?"

"I've known Dante a while. Know not to let him go out there alone."

I smile a little. Well, I try to move my lips into a smile. I don't know the last time I really smiled. Can't remember what my own laughter sounds like.

"Thank you," I say quickly, pushing my chair back and standing. I'm about to go into the bedroom when I see a pair of scissors hanging on a magnetic strip on the wall along with a few sharper knives.

"Don't," he says as if anticipating I'll grab one of those knives.

I turn to him. "The scissors."

"No."

"I want to cut my hair."

He looks confused.

"Please. I just want to cut if off."

He studies me for a long moment, then stands, gets the scissors, and hands them to me. He follows me down the hall and into Dante's bedroom. I guess he's afraid I'll hurt myself.

In the bathroom I stand in front of the mirror looking at the mess of too-long hair. It's so knotted I just grab a handful, and, without a moment's hesitation, I snip.

Matthaeus stands in the doorway watching, expression fixed, not giving anything away. I hack more hair off, so the end result is a not-quite even cut to my shoulders.

I set the scissors down and peer closer at my

face, touch my hair. I can almost get my fingers through it now. I have never cut my own hair. Never been allowed to say what I want to do with it.

I turn to him, hold the scissors out to him. "Thank you."

He nods, takes them from me. "Are you okay?"

It's a strange question to ask and I'm not sure if he means about how I just hacked off my hair, or about when I was out on the street, or the last fifteen years. I don't know how to respond so I nod.

"I'm inside if you need anything."

"Okay," I say, and then he's gone. I bend to pick up the hair I cut off and drop it into the trashcan. Then I walk back into the bedroom toward the window. I turn the chair around to face out, grab the blanket off the bed and wrap myself in it, then take a seat.

Tonight, I'll keep vigil. I'll watch for Dante like he watched for me.

11

DANTE

Matthaeus has the TV on but the volume off and he's cleaning a pistol. He's got it all taken apart, parts lined up in military precision on the coffee table. He looks up at me when I walk in, expression unchanging.

I've known Matthaeus for five years. At first, he pissed me off. Fucking standing in the way of anything I wanted to do that wasn't okayed by my many doctors during my recovery. He was the one who'd draw the short straw every time and sit with me when Cristiano thought I needed to be on fucking suicide watch. I never intended on suicide. That would have been the most selfish thing I could have done. I needed to get her back. That was why I'd survived that night. That was the only reason. The fact that my brother thought I could have some normal sort of life while she was out there was typical, actually. Like he's the only one of our family who should suffer. Like he should carry my pain along with his.

This responsibility, though, this guilt, it belongs to me. Whether he can accept it or not.

He became the head of our family the day his father and our older brother, Michael, were killed. I was young and while he lay in a coma, I waited for him. I didn't suspect for a minute it was my uncle making sure he remained as he was. I just trusted him blindly. He was all I'd had then.

Fuck. Bastard.

But I won't wallow. David's dead now. He paid. Not enough, but he paid.

I'm convinced the only reason David kept him alive was because of me. At least at first. He adapted his plans then. Always knew how to make the best of any situation. Once Cristiano finally woke from the coma, he turned him into his own personal killing machine.

I shake my head, take off my coat and hang it on the hook. It takes three times before I manage it as I sway on my feet.

"Don't fucking send men after me," I tell Matthaeus. I'm sure he knows me well enough to know that I'd see our guys in the car outside the bar. "I don't need fucking babysitting."

"Not smart to be out there getting drunk when Petrov's got his soldiers searching the city for you," Matthaeus says, shifting his attention back to the gun.

"I got the lecture from Charlie already. Where is she?"

"Asleep."

"Did you sedate her?"

"No."

"Good." We both knew I didn't want him to.

I walk into the kitchen and get a beer out of the fridge. Cracking it open I drink a long swallow. My gaze is down the hall. I want to be there. In the bedroom. With her.

"Tests came back clean. No STD's. She's not pregnant and hormone levels indicate birth control."

"Good." This is something, at least. Matthaeus swabbed her and took blood that first night while she was passed out.

I set the beer down without finishing it and, without another word to Matthaeus, head toward my bedroom. I see her before I step inside. She's passed out on the chair in front of the window, wrapped up in the thick duvet, her head at what's got to be an uncomfortable angle. I look at her for a long minute in the light coming in from the window, streetlamps reflected off snow.

Something's different. I move toward her, peer closer. She's cut her hair. It's just at her shoulders now. I reach out to touch it, feel the soft waves fall through my fingers.

She moves, mutters something, but stays asleep. The blanket shifts a little. She's wearing one of my sweaters. It's big on her and her shoulder is exposed. I touch the star-shaped birthmark. It's smaller than it used to be. She's grown into it.

I push the hair back from her face.

She's a woman now. I don't know what I thought when I started this quest. She was fifteen when we learned she was still alive. Still a girl. Now, although I sometimes see glimpses of that girl, looking at her like this, eyes closed, face soft, her lips full and slightly parted, what I see is the woman she's become. This beautiful, broken creature. A stranger but not.

And I find myself remembering how she felt beneath me.

No, not a girl anymore.

Her body, the softness, the curves, those of a woman. But still too young for the things she's seen. For the things she's experienced.

I move closer and slip one arm around her shoulders, the other behind her knees. She smells like me. My shampoo. My soap. My aftershave.

She startles, her eyes fluttering open, her back going stiff. One hand comes to my chest, and she pushes readying to fight, eyes suddenly wide with panic.

"Waiting up for me?" I ask, and she realizes where she is.

Her body relaxes. She blinks, shifts her gaze away. She's stubborn. Good. It's probably one of the things that's kept her alive so long. Kept the fight from going out of her.

I hold her tighter, carry her to my bed. The blanket drops to the floor. My sweater has ridden up, so I catch a glimpse of her panties. Just white cotton. Plain. But not. Not at all. Not on her.

And why the fuck am I thinking this? Am I looking at her like this?

When I meet her eyes, I find them on me. She saw me looking. I clear my throat and tug the blanket up to cover her.

She takes it, adjusts it.

"You smell like a bar," she says.

"Perceptive," I tell her as I walk toward the bathroom. I need to piss. I see the hole on the door where the doorknob used to be. Fucking Matthaeus. He's nothing if not thorough. "So, were you?" I call into the room.

"Was I what?"

"Waiting up for me."

"No," she calls back, her tone defensive.

"Little liar." I chuckle.

I lift the toilet seat and piss, flush, then wash my hands, unable to avoid looking at my face in the mirror as I do.

Dante didn't look like you.

The shadow of my smile vanishes. No, he did not. But Dante, the boy is gone. Long gone. He was gone before Cristiano ever woke up. He died the day I walked into my house and found my family massacred. The only thing that saved me at all was finding Cristiano still breathing, still fighting for his life.

I bend to splash water on my face not wanting to see this man's face. A monster's face. I'm not sure how she can stand to look at me. I switch off the bathroom light and stalk back across the room to find her sitting up watching me.

"What?" I ask, moving toward the bed.

"Are you drunk?"

I slip the holster off my shoulder, keep the gun inside and set it on the makeshift nightstand.

"Not drunk enough." I am about to take off the patch. I do when I sleep. But I think better of it. I reach back to pull my shirt over my head and drop it on the floor. It stinks of this too-long day. I then undo my jeans.

"What are you doing?" she asks, pulling the duvet closer.

I pause, look at her. "Not playing twenty questions." I push my jeans off. She gasps but I catch her looking before she makes a show of turning away.

"Don't worry, I won't take the briefs off, and I won't touch you."

She turns back to me as I pull the blanket up and get into the bed. "You're sleeping here?"

"It's my bed."

She pushes the blanket away and swings one leg out, but I catch her wrist.

"You'll stay."

"I'll sleep somewhere else, thank you."

"It wasn't a question and I'm fucking tired so lie down and go to sleep and don't make me fucking chase you around the apartment."

"Why?"

I lie down on my back but keep her wrist in my hand. It's tiny. I stare up at the ceiling "Because I didn't child-proof it."

"What does that mean?"

I turn my head to look at her. "You cut your hair."

She reaches up with her free hand and touches it. I see her hesitate.

"I like it," I say. "Now lie down and go to sleep. You're safe from me."

"What do you mean you didn't child-proof it? I'm not a child."

I let my gaze drop to her chest where the too big sweater exposes skin, the soft swell of one breast. "No, you're not. But after today's escapades and until I can trust you, you'll be supervised by myself or Matthaeus."

She seems to accept this and lies down. I still don't let go of her wrist.

"Why did you come for me?" she asks after so long I wonder if she hasn't fallen asleep.

"I told you that. You just don't want to believe it."

"He's going to kill you when he finds you."

I look over to find her staring up at the ceiling, her profile outlined by the cool light reflecting off the fallen snow.

"Is that what you're scared of?" I ask her. "Or just plain scared?"

She doesn't shift her gaze and doesn't answer right away. I watch a tear slide down over her temple. "Both."

I already knew the answer, knew there could only be one answer, it does something to me. Twists something inside me.

Over the last five years, I've felt hate mostly. Apart from those closest to me, I trust no one. I've come to expect the worst from people. But this, that nod, her lying beside me so small and scared, it fucking does something to me that somehow hurts more than any of the rest of it.

I get up on one elbow and turn to her. "Hey."

Nothing. She still doesn't look at me, but I can see she's crying quiet tears.

"I can tell you that you don't have to be scared anymore but I don't think that will make a difference."

She wipes the back of her hand over the tip of her nose.

"I'm here now, Mara. And I may not be the boy you remember, but I am the man you'll come to know. The man who will destroy your demons."

She turns her face a little, eyes wide and I see her wanting to believe.

"I'm never going to let anyone hurt you again. Ever. I swear it on my life."

12

DANTE

The night is short. She doesn't sleep peacefully. Not for more than an hour at a time. I wonder if this is normal for her. If nightmares always plague her. Make her nights so restless.

I woke her twice when it got bad. This last time she seemed to wake herself up. She went back to sleep easily enough only to be haunted by more demons. It's only when the first light of the sun shines through the window that she finally falls quiet and by then, I can't sleep. So, I make coffee and sit on the couch with Matthaeus, who is an insomniac worse than me, to video call Charlie. It'll be early afternoon in Italy.

He answers on the second ring, and I see he's at his home office.

"Glad to see you in one piece," is his greeting.

"You look like you've slept about as much as I did," I reply.

He turns to Matthaeus. "Matthaeus. Thanks for keeping an eye on him."

Matthaeus just nods once.

"Petrov," I say, taking a sip of my coffee.

"Petrov," Charlie says and the screen switches to a different view. The interior of one of David's—now mine—penthouse properties in the city, the rooms torn apart, furniture shredded, art broken to pieces, antique furniture destroyed.

"The Wallingford property," Charlie says.

I smirk. "I guess I should send him a thank-you card. Saved me the trouble."

Charlie's face is back on the screen. He is unamused. "I know you don't care about the properties you inherited, and I understand why, but you could donate the furniture, give it to a charity. Make something good out of something bad."

"I don't want to stain anyone else's life with anything David touched. Is that what you're so upset about? The broken crap? It's just stuff."

"No, Dante. What I'm upset about is if he can find the penthouse, it's only a matter of time until he finds the warehouse location."

"It's buried deeper. You know that. And besides, I already told you. I'm not hiding. What aren't you telling me?"

He glances at Matthaeus for a moment, then the

screen flips again, and I realize why he looks like he hasn't slept. He hasn't. I read the handwritten message on a torn off sheet of letterhead that once belonged to David.

You sent a message. I'm sending one back.
Return.
My.
Property.
Red's. Midnight. I'll reserve the cellar for you.
If you're late, she gets hurt. You show up on time and only you'll get hurt.
You don't come at all, and I have my friend pick up your nephew and take him out for an ice cream cone. I hear he has a sweet tooth.

THERE'S A PHOTO NEXT TO THE NOTE OF ALESSANDRO and Scarlett in a café somewhere. They'd have been guarded. There's no way Cristiano would let them go anywhere without protection so the fact that he has this photo at all is alarming.

"Does Cristiano know about this?"

"Yes. He's doubled the guard."

"Good." I re-read the note.

Red's. A private club in downtown Manhattan owned by one of Petrov's sons.

Matthaeus opens his laptop and starts typing.

"Do you have a contact inside?" I ask Charlie.

He looks hesitant.

"Neither Mara nor Scarlett not to mention Alessandro or anyone else is safe until he's dead and you know it," I add.

"You can't take her near that place. I'm sure he'll pick you up before you get close to the club."

"I don't plan on taking her. But I won't be able to take a weapon in."

"No, you won't." The screen switches again to show a couple of shots of a large mostly empty room with a counter taking up one wall. There's a large deep, dirty sink, tile floors, a drain in the center of the floor. Makes clean up easier. The wall behind the counter is tiled too and on the counter are various items which at quick glance may appear to be for use in a kitchen.

But this isn't the kitchen at Red's.

"The cellar," Charlie says.

I take in the single round table. It's small. Two chairs set across from each other. Several more chairs along the wall. A set of handcuffs dangles off the rung of one of the chairs at the wall. Deep red stains the grain of the wooden back and seat.

"If you walk in there, you may not walk out."

"You have a contact inside?" I ask again, still looking at the shot of the cellar. Memorizing my limited options.

"Yes. But this is more than risky. They own the damn building."

"We got Scarlett out of that house and that was riskier. My men will be nearby."

"The cellar exit is sealed," Matthaeus says, turning the laptop around to point out a photo of the exterior of the building. "Closest exit is the front door."

"You can't be thinking to do this," Charlie says.

"What's the alternative?" I ask him and he's quiet. He knows there isn't one. Petrov needs to die. Period.

"What do you need inside?" he asks.

"You can't go to the cellar," Mara says before I can answer. She's standing barefoot on the edge of the living room, her hair like a white cloud around her, hands at her sides, eyes locked on me. "You won't come out if you do."

13

MARA

Dante and Matthaeus both look up at me at the same time. I pull the sleeves of Dante's sweater down and tuck my hands inside.

"You should go back to bed," Dante says, getting to his feet.

"I mean it. I know what happens in the cellar."

"How do you know?"

"I've been there. Once. Only for a few minutes." That was enough.

"Why were you there?"

I shift my gaze to my bare feet. It's why I'm cold. The floors are so cold here.

"Mara?"

I look back up at him. "There was a soldier once. Samuel. He was...nicer to me than he should have been, I guess."

Dante and Matthaeus are both watching, and I am aware of the man on the phone or computer that I can't see.

"He was my friend. Someone saw us holding hands once. It wasn't anything, he was just..." I shake my head, force the tears back and swallow the lump in my throat. It's a memory, that lump, with too much emotion balled up inside it. It's one of the ones that makes it hard to breathe. "He was going to leave. He was going back home. But they didn't let him go. Petrov had me tell him which hand he held mine with then made me watch when they sawed it off." I will never forget that night. I look away. "Sometimes, I swear I can still hear that saw work through the bone over his screams."

"Jesus Christ," Matthaeus mutters and I give a small shake of my head to clear it.

"They took me out of there after that. I think they killed him then. I never saw him again. This was his," I say, pulling the sleeve up and showing them a delicate gold bracelet. "He gave it to me and when Petrov found out, he decided to let me keep it. He wasn't going to at first but then changed his mind. He said it was so I could remember our friendship. But really, it was so I remember what happens to my friends."

Dante's jaw is locked so tight I wonder if his teeth will crack. He walks toward me, takes my hand, and pushes the sleeve farther. He touches the thin gold chain.

"Take it off," he says.

I shake my head.

He looks at me and I remember what he said last night. About the boy Dante being gone. This man now in his place. This man who would destroy my demons.

"The bracelet makes me remember him. Not what they did to him. And I want to remember him."

He studies me for a long minute then finally nods. I wonder if he's aware he's still holding my hand.

"Do you remember Charlie?"

Matthaeus turns the phone around and I look at the face on the screen. The man is older than them, middle-aged, I guess. And he has a patch of gray in his hair. He's smiling.

"Hello, Mara. It's good to see you."

I blink once, twice. Study the man, then shift my gaze up to Dante. I shake my head.

"It's okay," he says, and Matthaeus gets up, taking the laptop and the phone into another room.

"I'm hungry," I tell Dante.

He nods, leads me to the table where I sit down in the same chair as last night. I wince when I do and touch my hip.

Dante doesn't miss it. "Let me see it."

"It's fine. I just have to be more careful."

"It's not fine. It's infected. If the ointment isn't enough, we'll need to get you something stronger."

"You really can't go to the cellar," I say, changing topic.

"We'll discuss the cellar after I get a look at the brand."

"There's nothing to see."

"I'll judge for myself."

"You'll listen to me if I let you look?"

"I'll hear what you have to say."

I study him, not sure, but it's something. So, I stand and lift the sweater enough to expose the side of my hip. I look away when he bends closer, holding my breath so as not to gasp when he draws my panties down a little, enough to be able to peel the bandage away. I know it's not meant in any way but to look at the damage, but I can't help that flutter in my stomach.

"Does this hurt?" he asks, pressing the skin around it.

"A little."

"We'll get you something stronger today." He puts the bandage back on and adjusts my panties over it.

I sit down more carefully and watch as he takes eggs out of the refrigerator and scrambles them along with several strips of bacon. My mouth waters at the smell and I watch him standing at the stove barefoot in jeans and a T-shirt, doing this very domestic thing. I remember him last night when he stripped off his clothes. When he lay down beside me and it took all I had not to curl into him. To let him hold me. I have to be careful with him. Losing people hurts and I can't let myself get to a place where it will hurt when I lose him. Because I will lose him. I know it.

He plates the food and sets it in front of me, then opens a drawer to hand me a fork and knife.

I start to eat as he pours coffee into a mug and sets it in front of me before refilling his own. I pour cream and three heaping teaspoons of sugar into it. Dante watches. I stir, then pick it up and drink a steaming sip, savoring the sweetness, this simple thing of eating breakfast. Of feeling hungry and wanting to eat.

"It's sound proofed, the cellar," I tell him as he watches me. "Elegant people upstairs drinking fancy drinks while downstairs men have their hands sawn off before they're killed." I eat a strip of bacon wondering if he finds it strange that I can talk about this while casually eating. Because it is strange. It says something about me. Something a little terrifying.

"Is that what the dreams are about?"

I stop chewing, look up at him. I remember him waking me once or twice. I always wonder how loud I am. If I scream in real life when I scream in my nightmares.

"No, not really," I say. I don't want to talk about that. "He took me to Red's a few times. I met one of his sons. I don't even think he found it strange that his father brought me there. That I was his property. I don't think anyone did."

He doesn't say anything, just watches and listens. I eat every bite, drink all of my coffee then sit back in my chair and put one hand over my belly.

"Would you like more?"

I shake my head, push my plate away and look up at him. "If you go, you'll die."

"You don't know me very well."

"You will."

"Mara—"

"And if you die, then I'll die."

"It won't come to that but if it does, Matthaeus will get you out. Get you home."

"You said you'd listen if I let you look."

"I am listening."

"But you're not hearing me. You're gambling with your life and my life. Everyone who is involved is in danger."

"Mara—"

"I want a gun."

He furrows his eyebrows, chuckles. "You're not getting a gun, sweetheart."

"Stop calling me sweetheart!"

His mouth moves into an entertained grin. He opens it to speak but must think better of what he was going to say because he shakes his head and pauses. "Have you ever handled a gun?"

I fold my arms across my chest. "No."

"Well, you're not going to start now." He's humoring me. I see it.

"I need one to protect myself."

"I'll protect you."

"Not when you're dead, you won't. And you're going to be dead if you go to that meeting. It's what he wants. For you to walk into his trap. He's the master of setting traps." I grip the edge of the table and lean toward him. "You don't know him. I do." I push my chair back and stand. "And I'm wasting my breath because you're a liar. You were never going to listen to me." I stalk toward the bedroom.

"Hey." He comes after me, but I don't stop. I'm almost to the bedroom when he catches my arm and spins me to face him. I crash into his chest then bounce backward. He steadies me, walking me until I'm up against the wall.

I look up at him, heart racing. I take my lower lip between my teeth and his gaze shifts to my mouth. For a moment, he just looks at me and it's not with pity. It's different. And there's that flutter in my belly again.

It's the way a man looks at a woman.

He clears his throat and shifts his gaze to my eyes. "I'm not a liar, Mara. I did listen."

"But you never planned on taking what I'm

saying seriously." I try to tug free, slip away, but he tightens his grip, his jaw tensing. "Let go."

"Stop fighting me."

"Let me go and I'll stop fighting."

He chuckles at that, and for a moment, his expression is lighter. But when I wriggle again, he fixes his face, leaning closer. "I'm not going to let you go. Hear that and hear it well." He dips his head down so his face is inches from mine. "Do you remember what I told you last night?" he asks more quietly so only I'll hear him.

I stare up at him, feeling him shift his grip from my wrist to my hand. His thumb rubs the inside of my palm as his fingers weave together with mine. No one's ever held my hand like this. Ever.

"Do you?" he asks.

I bite my lip, nod.

His gaze falls to my mouth again and he has to clear his throat before he continues. "I mean it. I'm going to kill Ivan Petrov for what he did to you."

"What if you're wrong?"

"I won't be—"

"What if you don't come back?" I feel my eyes mist.

He shifts one hand to my face, cupping it, his touch gentle. "I will. I promise."

I find myself leaning into that touch. I want to believe him. I want so much to believe him. But I know the man he's up against. "You can't kill him. He's unkillable."

He comes closer and with his chest touching mine, he presses my back to the wall. I breathe in his aftershave. Feel his heart beat against his chest. Feel my nipples tighten in response to having him so close. It's so strange. My body's reactions are so different than they have ever been with any man ever.

I lick my lips and look up at him. The green of his eye has darkened, and his breathing is tight.

"I'm going to kill him," he says, voice low and gravelly. He takes my hands in his interlacing his fingers with mine again. He leans his cheek close to mine so the scruff on his jaw scratches my face. His mouth is at my neck and when I turn my head a little, his lips graze me. He doesn't pull back, not right away.

I suck in a breath and hold still when he brings his mouth to my ear, lips brushing the shell of it.

"I'm coming back to you. I promise you that," he whispers, and his breath sends a shiver down my spine. I feel myself curl into him. It's like a magnet, like we're two magnets drawn to each other by forces outside of our control.

I lick my lips. Can he hear how hard my heart is beating?

He takes another deep breath in, and I wonder if he can smell his aftershave on me. If he knows I put it on. If he understands why I did it. He draws back then, and I look up at him.

"Do you trust me?" he asks after a long minute.

I nod. Because for some reason, I do. For some reason, I know if anyone can kill Ivan Petrov, it will be Dante Grigori.

14

DANTE

I swear I can still smell her scent if I concentrate. My aftershave on the throbbing pulse at her neck. And I know I need to stop this. Because this isn't how this is supposed to go. But somewhere in the years as I planned to rescue Mara, the girl, she has become Mara, the woman. And it's the woman I can't get out of my head.

I'm three blocks from Red's. My head not quite in the game because it takes me a minute to register the two men approaching me as Petrov's soldiers.

"Gentlemen." I look them over. "I use that term loosely."

Neither of them even meets my gaze. An SUV screeches to a halt near us. The front tires bump up onto the sidewalk. I'm thrown against it. After searching me and relieving me of my pistol—I didn't bother bringing anything else—they shove me into the backseat, and one climbs in beside me. There's another one already in the vehicle so I'm sandwiched between them.

"This is cozy," I say as we head toward Red's. At least I hope that's where we're headed because I don't have a backup plan. Matthaeus will be tracking me though. The benefit of having this patch. A phone they'll take from you. But the tracker is embedded into the patch itself.

Cristiano doesn't know I'm doing this. Charlie is buying me time but taking a chance. If things go wrong, he'll be the one answering to my brother.

A few minutes later, we drive past the entrance of the high-end private club. The vehicle comes to a stop at the mouth of an alley. I'm ushered out, met by two new men, one of whom zip-ties my hands. I'm grateful the idiot does it in front of me and not at my back. They each take an arm and walk me toward the alley entrance. From here I can see the sealed exit of the cellar at the far end.

The steel door is held open by a soldier who tosses the butt of his cigarette onto the ground. I walk in through this dingy back entrance. No one's here and I guess this isn't even the staff entrance.

I pick up the smells of food and hear the bustle of a busy kitchen. At the far end of the room, I see the small, round window in a door that leads to where those smells are coming from. I wonder if any kitchen staff know what happens just below their feet.

Another man stands at a second door. He opens it and I'm hustled inside. This doorway leads to a staircase too narrow for both my guards, so one goes ahead and the other behind me. I'm tempted to kick the legs out from the one in front of me but hold back.

I look around the large but dingy space, recognize it from the pictures. They didn't do it justice. Or maybe it's been used since those photos were taken. And photos can't capture the smells of a place. Bleach and basement with an undercurrent of blood and fear.

I think about Mara being brought here. Mara made to witness what they did. That's good. That makes my blood boil.

Two men lean against the counter talking. Along that counter I see several butcher knives and various other tools they'll use to torture me. Or so they think. They straighten when we enter, and I note the hazmat like suits they're wearing. I'm going to guess that's to intimidate. It's overkill if you ask me.

I'm planted unceremoniously into one of the two chairs at the table my back to the staircase. I would have preferred the other seat.

The soldiers who accompanied me down walk back up the stairs. The door slams shut loudly behind them.

"You know it's polite to offer your guest a drink," I say to the two idiots tasked with keeping me company. They're to my left for which I'm grateful. My peripheral vision to the right is nonexistent.

They don't reply. But I don't have to wait long before I hear the door open, hear the low grumble of voices speaking Russian.

I think of Mara then. Of how she must have felt every time the door to her room opened and he entered. And I think about how she is. Quiet. Intense. Dark. What would she have been like if they hadn't taken her? If she hadn't been on the island the day of the massacre? If she'd had a chance to lead a normal life.

"You're not very intelligent, are you Mr. Grigori?" Petrov says from behind me.

I crane my neck to watch the hulking man remove his coat and hand it to another, shorter man in a suit and hat. No hazmat on this guy. I guess he thinks he's leaving before things get messy.

I move to rise to my feet but a hand clamps down over my shoulder and shoves me back down. "And you're even fatter than your pictures show." I smile wide as I take in one of the men who turned Mara into the lost girl she's become. "I thought they said it was the camera that added ten pounds."

His smile disappears and his lips settle into what I guess is his usual scowl. He unbuttons his jacket and pushes it back to show me the shoulder holster containing his pistol. He lowers himself into the seat across from mine.

"Where is she?"

"Not here."

"You think I'm playing a game?"

"Why would I think that?"

"My men are destroying the second penthouse as we speak."

"I thank you for that. It saves me the trouble."

He sits back, beady eyes narrowed, assessing me coldly. "You've destroyed each property your father left you."

My jaw ticks. He knows David is my father. How the fuck does he know?

He grins. He must see my reaction. Well, good for him. I'll give him a fucking sticker.

"What's the matter, didn't like daddy's gifts?"

"Fuck you, Petrov."

"No, I believe you are the one who's fucked at the moment. Where is my property?"

"She's a human being."

He cocks his head. "No. Property," he says, studying me. I school my features. "Something pretty to own and discard when it's used up."

I want to kill him. "Why do you want her back? She's not who you thought. In fact, didn't she make a fool of you?"

It's him with the tick in his jaw this time. At least

I think that's a tick. I can't quite make out muscle movement beneath the layers of fat.

"She and Felix, that is. That tiny little nobody Felix Pérez, along with a fifteen-year-old-girl, made a fool of the great Ivan Petrov. Tell me, are your friends still having a good laugh at your expense? Oh wait, you don't have any friends."

He's quiet, still assessing. He's not a stupid man. I know that. And I need to be careful. Push him just enough. But not too far. Not yet. It would have been better if he'd put his pistol on the table between us. Given me a second option. But as it stands, I only have one.

"How did it feel walking into your home only to find the blood of your family staining the floors? Is it strange to live there now?"

Fuck.

"But you don't live there," he continues when I don't react. "I'm sure your brother and his family are relieved at that. The son of their family's killer sharing their roof, their table, it would be too much for anyone to bear."

"Tell me something, does your wife know you like to fuck fifteen-year-old girls? I hear your boy doesn't seem to mind. Like father like son?"

He's not upset by this. I didn't expect him to be. "You know you really should be thanking me."

"And why is that?"

"If it weren't for me just think of all the men who would have used her all those years."

I force myself to breathe. To not react.

"I paid for her virginity. And oh my, was it worth it." He grins. Self-satisfied prick.

"Fuck you. How's that for a thanks?"

His grin vanishes. "You're wasting my time. Where is she?" His tone is sharp, eyes dead.

"Somewhere you won't find her."

"I have eyes and ears everywhere."

"You're not getting her back, Petrov. Ever."

"I'm sure she misses me. Misses my hands on her. And I miss her, too. Miss the way she called my name when she came."

My hands fist in my lap.

He grins, leans toward me. "She tastes wonderful. Have you had a taste yet? Something about eating a young, virgin pussy."

I grit my teeth, force myself to regulate my breath.

"Tell me have you felt her tight cunt squeeze your dick yet? Or hear her screams when you take her ass?"

I lean toward him too because this is what I want. What I need for this to work. I slide my bound hands along the underside of the table. Feel the edge of the tape. The tip of the blade pointing toward Petrov's gut. Charlie's contact knew which seat he'd be in.

"She has a set of lungs on her, that girl," he

continues, smiling now, showing teeth that are too small for his fat head spaced too far apart from each other. "I wonder if you'll scream as loud when we cut you into a hundred little pieces before I put you out of your misery."

I close my hand around the hilt, peel it from the table slowly so the duct tape doesn't make a sound. I'll have one shot at this. And I may still die. It depends on how fast he dies. How quick his soldiers are. One of them has his back turned. He's rearranging the tools of my eventual torture.

"Now my son, he had a special preference for her mouth. I told him it was risky. I never did manage to break her spirit completely."

"Tell me, do you think she even felt your dick? Rumor has it it's, well, smaller than expected for a man your size," I say, not that I have a clue. I lean forward some more, gripping the knife hard. It's shorter than I'd like but it'll have to do.

He puts his hands on the table, neck and face growing red with anger.

Hell. I've hit a nerve. Maybe it's the truth after all.

"That's about the size," I gesture to his hands. He looks down at them. "The pinkie." I grin, extending my arms as far as they'll go beneath the table, grateful for his gut being the size it is. "Length and width I hear." This last part I say in a lowered voice, so he leans toward me to hear. It's just enough.

He doesn't even have a chance to answer as the

knife slides into his gut like it's cutting through butter. The blade is short, but very sharp.

There's a momentary pause, a grunt that only I hear. He blinks, shifts his gaze back to mine, a look of surprise on his face.

"Is that right?" I ask, drawing the knife up a little, watching his eyes widen. "Size of your pinkie would you say?"

A line of blood forms on the corner of his mouth and I pull the knife out, letting it fall to the floor as I shoot to my feet, turning the table over so it lands on its side between me and the two at the counter. In one step I'm behind Petrov wrapping bound arms around his neck and drawing his pistol from its shoulder holster.

Over the crashing of the table comes the cocking of guns and I duck behind Petrov, his bulk shielding me as I shoot one of the guards. He goes down as his gun goes off, missing both me and Petrov. I have the advantage of surprise. They didn't expect this.

The second one is next, the butcher's knife in his hand will do him no good now as his eyes widen in surprise and I pull the trigger, sending the bullet into his stomach before I turn to the one holding Petrov's coat.

The least assuming one.

He's faster than the others. I underestimated him.

His weapon is aimed at my heart but before he

pulls the trigger, I shift right. It's not far enough but it's not my heart. I stagger backward, my arms linked around Petrov's head, zip-tied wrists stopping me from falling back.

Pain shoots through me. I glance down at the bloody circle, the bullet lodged in my shoulder. It's not my shooting arm and I get a shot off before he can. My aim is a hundred times better. The bullet puts him on his knees, eyes still open before a second one between the eyes drops him face first onto the dirty tile floor.

The sound of a gun being cocked comes from the one I got in the stomach, and I turn. We pull our triggers at the same moment. My bullet takes him out but not before his is lodged next to the first in my shoulder.

Pain shoots through me, the room spinning. Petrov moves and I lean closer, stretch the arm of my injured shoulder around his neck getting under the layer of fat that is his chin. I squeeze my eyes shut momentarily to manage the pain in my shoulder, forcing in air. I need to finish this. If I pass out now, I'm dead.

I open my eyes and look down. He's still somehow sitting in his chair, hands on his stomach, blood seeping through his fingers. He's close to death but not close enough. I force his head up, forearm tight under his throat. Sweat drips from my head onto his face and nausea leaves a bitter taste in my mouth.

The knife I used to stab him with is lying at his feet. It's a steak knife. I don't miss the irony. I used a steak knife to pin David to that desk.

But now's not the time to revisit that night. I shift my gaze to Petrov.

"Which of your boys fucked her?"

He groans, and I squeeze my forearm.

"Which. One?"

Nothing.

"Tell me or I'll kill them both."

No answer. But to be fair, I'm not sure he can speak judging by the blood seeping from the corner of his mouth.

I don't give a fuck about that though.

"Both it is then." I set my hand on the side of his head and give one hard jerk, the snapping of bone satisfying even if his death is too swift. "That was for Mara, you sick fuck, you sick son of a fucking bitch."

15

DANTE

Petrov's body hunches to the side, his bulk pulling me along, making me stagger. I draw my arms from around his broken neck. For a moment, his head hangs at an odd angle just before he goes crashing down, the chair tumbling after him.

I breathe, look around. I'm left with four dead bodies in this hole. My shoulder is pouring blood down my arm, seeping through my shirt and coat. I raise my bound hands to touch the area and wince.

Feeling dizzy and too hot, I take an unsteady step toward the counter, pain making my vision go black for moments in time. When I get to the counter, I set the gun down and grip the edge, looking for what I need. I find a small sharp knife and pick it up, turning it to slice through the zip-ties. It takes a full minute to do it but when it's done, I turn on the tap and splash cold water on my face.

"She tasted wonderful. Have you had a taste yet? Something about eating a nice, young, virgin pussy."

I look over at the dead man as I pull a couple of paper towels from the dispenser and wipe my face then check his pistol for bullets. Two left.

"Tell me have you felt her tight cunt squeeze your dick yet? Or hear her scream when you take her ass?"

I walk toward him, look at his still open but empty eyes. I spit on the side of his face before walking toward the smaller man. I pick up his gun, check the chamber and tuck it, too, into the waistband of my jeans. I take off my bloody coat and switch it out for the one he was wearing. It's a tight fit but it'll have to do. I also take his hat and put it on my head. I'm recognizable enough with the patch so I'm hoping this will give me some cover.

Because I'm not finished here yet.

If his sons are upstairs, I'll have to kill them too.

So, I make my way back up the stairs, gripping Petrov's gun at my side when I open the door. There's no one here. I smell cigarette smoke, though, and glance at the door that leads to the alley. It's cracked open and the smell is coming from that direction. I guess Petrov didn't let them smoke inside. How conscientious of him.

I walk toward the kitchen, and I can almost hear

Matthaeus shouting at me as I push the swinging door open. This isn't the plan.

"Now my son, he had a special preference for her mouth."

My blood boils.

It's noisy in here, lots of staff. I put my hand into my jacket pocket to keep the gun out of sight. The lady at the counter closest to me turns when I enter. She gasps when she sees me grip the edge of her workspace, gaze catching on the bloody print my hand leaves there.

I should get out. Come back with my men. That would be the smart thing to do. But Petrov managed to evade me for five years. I'm not taking a chance on that happening with his offspring. I put a hand to my shoulder, suck a deep breath in and focus on what he said about his son. About what he did to Mara. I look around the kitchen, locate the door a waiter carrying a tray exits from and follow him into the restaurant part of the club. I pause there, grateful it's dimmer in here.

I've never been inside Red's before, although I've seen pictures. It's huge and lavishly decorated, catering to a high-end crowd. Dress is formal, the wine expensive, the food elegant. I scan the restaurant for either of Petrov's sons. Viktor and Sacha Petrov. Viktor is first-born. Red's belongs to him. He looks like a younger version of his father. Sacha, the slightly smarter of the two—or at least the more sober—looks like his mother. And they couldn't be more different.

If I had to guess which son Petrov was referring to, my money would be on Viktor. But just in case, I'll take them both out.

Neither are in the dining room though. The tables reserved for the family are set apart from the rest on raised dais. Pretentious pricks.

I cross the dining room toward the club room aware I'm getting looks. Aware I need to hurry this up and get the fuck out of here before Petrov's soldiers or sons realize I walked out of that cellar.

The music at the club room is the same as that in the restaurant but a little louder. The place darker, more shadowy, the highlights being the various stages upon which beautiful women in various states of dress dance.

The majority of the guests in this room are men but there are women too. I don't care about any of them, though. Not when I see the room set apart on a mezzanine level. It's glassed in and two men and one woman are seated at an elegant table as a waiter pours the woman a glass of wine.

It's Viktor I recognize first. He's built like his father. He stands from the table, throwing his napkin to the floor as he takes a call. He walks to the window and surveys his club.

I back into the shadows of a sculpture of some Greek goddess, her tits at eye level. I watch Viktor, then see the door to their private room open and several soldiers walk in. He tucks his phone back into his pocket and turns to them.

I take a step toward the stairs that will lead me up to that room, stumbling once as I do, the room spinning. Just then there's a loud pop. I jerk my head toward the sound, tugging to get the gun out of my pocket. But it's not a bullet I heard. I see the group of people laughing around the freshly opened bottle of champagne. I push the gun back out of sight.

Breathe. Process the dizziness. Get a fucking handle on my vision fading in and out of black.

I reach my other hand out to steady myself, not sure what I'm reaching for but hear the crashing of crystal as I knock a tray out of the waitress's hand.

Fuck.

I glance at the stairs I'm heading toward. See the half-dozen men dressed in suits that fit too tightly across their chests rush down. See the effort it takes for them to slow their steps and smile tightly at the guests as they scan the room. I notice one zeroing in on where the sound came from. I crouch down along with the waitress to pretend to help her clean but keep my gaze on them.

I'm so close. I just need to get into their glass cage. I can see them. Both brothers still there. The woman gone now. I don't know where she went. They're standing at the glass wall searching the place. I'd shoot now but I know that glass is bullet-proof. Petrov is—was—meticulous in protecting himself and his family. He wouldn't miss that detail.

I get to my feet when the soldier heading toward us is interrupted by another waiter. I turn, weave through a group toward the stairs, my hand still in my pocket, Petrov's gun cool in my grip when another hand falls heavy on my shoulder.

The injured shoulder.

I wince, grit my teeth to keep from crying out.

"I think you should leave," a man I don't know says. "You're outnumbered. By a lot." He squeezes my shoulder. "And not exactly up to the task."

"Who the fuck are you?" I ask, turning to look at the man as I shove his hand from my shoulder. He's got his head down too, as if he is also trying to stay out of sight.

"There are about a million cameras in here. This was stupid," he adds as if I give a fuck what he thinks.

"Who the fuck are you?" I ask louder this time.

Another man approaches on my other side and they each take an arm. "This way," he says as they lead me away from the stairs that would take me to the brothers' perch.

I turn back in time to see another maybe ten soldiers descend those same stairs, several rushing toward the kitchen. We get to a set of double doors where the first man discreetly hands a folded bill to the one standing sentry. He glances around, pockets the bill, and pushes the door open.

Once we're outside, an SUV pulls up, the back door opens, and I'm escorted into yet another vehicle. I take my pistol out of my pocket as the car pulls too fast away from Red's, just as soldiers hurry from the door in the alley they took me in from.

"Again," I ask, shifting my gaze to the first man, very aware how everything seems to be spinning. How sweat is dripping down my forehead and into my good eye. I meet the stranger's eyes. "Who. The. Fuck. Are. You?" I cock the pistol and aim to his stomach.

He grins. "I'm the man saving your fucking life. Although I'm not quite sure it's worth my time."

The one on the other side of me grips my gun hand, which is already unsteady, and twists it back, relieving me of Petrov's pistol. We're driving fast, too fast, and cars honk their horns as we speed through a red light, sending two vehicles crashing into each other while we slip past. It's like a fucking movie.

The driver laughs, drives a few more blocks before slowing at the command of the first stranger. A moment later, I'm tossed out onto the curb on my ass, the vehicle barely slowing, the pavement unforgiving as I crash down and watch the fuckers drive away.

16

MARA

"He's alive?"

I hear them through the radio, Matthaeus shouting orders, a car's tires screeching. The soldier they left behind to babysit me looks up at me, nods once.

Alive!

Goosebumps cover my arms as my heart races.

He's alive!

I can't believe it.

But an hour later, I hear them. Hear their boots on the metal stairs outside. I rush to the door when it opens. Matthaeus and another soldier walk in, Dante almost passed out between them, face bruised, one arm soaked in blood, wearing a coat too small and too tight on his shoulders.

"Dante!" I rush toward him, shocked and relieved he's here. Really alive.

One of the guards intercepts me as Dante manages to lift his head momentarily before they take him to his bedroom and disappear inside. The soldier won't let me enter so I stand in the hallway and listen. Smiling every time I hear the low rumble of his voice. Happier than I thought I could be to know he survived. Know he didn't die in that terrible cellar.

"Do you ever stick to the fucking plan?" It's Matthaeus.

"I'm alive, aren't I? It's fine."

"It's not fucking fine. And this is going to hurt."

I think I hear Dante's groan and I push against the guard to let me in. He doesn't budge so, after pacing for ten minutes, I drop to a seat on the cold cement floor, my back against the wall to wait.

It's more than an hour before Matthaeus finally comes out. He looks tired. Exhausted. He's talking into his phone in Italian. I know it's Italian and I know I spoke it once, but I don't speak anymore. I understand what he's saying though.

I get up to see Dante but again, the soldier stops me.

"I'm going to see him!" I yell into his face.

Matthaeus turns around, looks at me and nods to the soldier who steps out of the way. I push the door open. It creaks on its hinges. Still no doorknob. Dante is lying on top of the bed. He's shirtless. His boots are off but he's still wearing the same jeans he'd worn when he'd left. They're dirty. Filthy with dark stains that I'm pretty sure are blood. I wonder how much of it is his.

I walk toward the bed, see the fresh bandages on his shoulder, the bruises beginning to color the skin of one arm. He's badly scratched.

I shift my gaze to his face. His patch is still on, the other eye closed. His chest rises and falls with his breaths.

As lightly as I can, I brush hair back from his face. It's sticking to his forehead. He's sweating.

I walk into the bathroom and retrieve one of the washcloths stacked on the shelf. After wetting it with cold water from the tap, I return to the bedroom to sit on the edge of the bed, wiping the sweat from his forehead. I also try to rid him of some of the dried blood on his shoulder.

That's when his arm shoots out, hand like a vise around my wrist.

I gasp and he hisses. I look to his face, see he's looking at me. I can't help but think how beautiful he is, even with the scars, the leather patch. Maybe more so for them. There's a darkness about him. Like an angel fallen. One who broke when he hit the ground.

He shifts his gaze to my wrist then and loosens his grip before finally releasing me.

"Mara," he croaks. I think he wants to say more but I don't know if it's the drugs they gave him but his head rolls back on the pillow so he's looking at the ceiling again.

"You're not dead," I say.

He chuckles, the eye without the patch closing.

I set the washcloth down and glance at the door. It's closed as much as it can be without a doorknob, and I can see the soldier standing just outside through the hole. Do they think I'll do something to hurt him?

I don't care about them, though. I look back down at Dante. His big, broken body. Broad, muscular shoulders and arms, a dusting of dark hair on his chest, scars on olive skin, the ridges of muscle cutting across his stomach. The concentrated dark line of hair that disappears into his jeans.

Something stirs inside me at the sight of him like this. He had stripped to his boxers the night before but like this, he's somehow more naked. And the sensations I feel looking at him make my heartbeat kick up a notch. It's a strange and foreign reaction.

I decide to lie down beside him, pulling the blanket up a little although we don't need it. He's already hot with fever. I move his unhurt arm, tucking myself into his side. It's warm enough this way. I lay one arm across his belly and feel his hand come up around me, closing over my waist. I look up at his face but he's still asleep so I close my eyes, too, and listen to his heart beat. The faint hint of his aftershave is still there beneath the blood, sweat and man smell. It's that last one that has me shuddering in spite of the heat radiating off him. That and the memory of him earlier. When he had me pressed up against the wall. When he promised he'd come back to me.

And I say a thank you to whoever or whatever it was that protected him. That helped him keep his promise. Because it's impossible that he's here. That he walked out of that cellar. That he's alive at all.

I DON'T REALIZE I'VE FALLEN ASLEEP UNTIL A SOUND wakes me. I blink once, twice, slow to remember where I am. It's fully dark now, the streetlamp only offering the faintest light.

"Get her out!" Dante orders and I lean up on my elbow looking down at him. I shift my gaze over my shoulder to the door thinking he's giving an order. Telling one of his soldiers to remove me. But there's no one there.

Sweat covers him and he feels hotter than earlier. I touch a hand to his forehead, and it comes away slick.

He blinks rapidly, his agitation obvious. He's dreaming.

I should get Matthaeus. He'll know what to do. But Dante is talking again, words I can't make out. His forehead wrinkles, hands fisting then relaxing again and again as he tries to grab for something but only catches air.

"Wake up," I try, noticing the gun on the floor on his side of the bed. It's not his. This one is smaller.

"Get her out. Now!" he snaps, and I try again.

"Dante?" I sit up. "Wake up."

He mutters a string of curses, switches to Italian, his arm reaching as if for the shoulder holster, the gun he keeps there.

I lean across his body and push the pistol out of reach just in case. It goes sliding across the floor to stop in the middle of the room.

But it's the wrong thing to do because the next thing I know, he's got me by my arms, and he flips me onto my back. He's not gentle. He's above me, straddling me, one hand closing around my throat.

"Dante!"

He's strong. Too strong even as I wrap both of my hands around his forearm and try to pry him off. I can't speak. Can't make any sound at all. He's crushing my windpipe. And when I try to move my legs, to kick, he tenses his thighs, squeezing painfully against the brand. All the while he's looking at me but it's like he can't see me. Like he's still trapped inside his nightmare.

I twist, slapping one hand against his chest, his face when I can reach it, kicking my legs as much as I am able and as my vision begins to fade along the edges, he finally blinks.

He looks at me for a long minute, gives a shake of his head, loosens his grip around my throat. I cough, rub my throat. In the next instant, he's lying on top of me, some of his weight on one of his elbows, the arm without the bandage on his shoulder. But much of his body is on me as he looks down, eyebrows furrowed, gaze dark so the green is only a thin circle around his dilated pupil.

It feels good to have him like this. The weight of him crushing me feels strangely safe even as it stokes those feelings of earlier, as if fanning the flames of a building fire inside my center.

He searches my eyes, pushes my hair back from my forehead, touches my cheek. The expression on his face is unreadable. He brings one big hand to the back of my head, cupping it, and it all happens so fast. He leans closer, without a moment's hesitation, and his mouth closes over mine.

It's not a kiss. It's a devouring. A hungry, starved beast feasting.

My mouth opens for him. I taste him, feel the intensity of him. His muscular, hard body, the weight, the heat of our kiss. His tongue in my mouth, mine meeting it. It's not just a kiss. It's more.

It's everything.

He grinds his hips against mine and I moan at the sensations his hard cock pressing against me through his jeans sends through me. He shoves my sweater up roughly to press himself against me, against my clit. Bare chest against bare chest.

My nipples harden and he draws back, watching me as he grinds his hips. His breath is short, like mine. And that hand on the back of my head shifting now as he closes his mouth over mine again, kissing me like he's starved. That hand moves between us, and he lifts himself up just a little, just enough to slip his fingers inside my panties.

I tense for a moment. He senses it. But this feels different than ever before. It feels good. And when he closes his fingers around my sex, I let out a sigh, a deep, guttural sound, an exhale contained for too long. His hand is rough and big and so good. So, so good.

He draws back to watch me, and I bite my lip as his thumb moves over my clit. I glance between my open legs at the thick length of his erection pressed against his jeans.

Tension builds inside me, something tightening, tightening, being rung out. I can't catch my breath as he moves his fingers over me, inside me.

I watch him, too, and this feeling isn't just between my legs. It's spreading through me, from my core out through my stomach, my chest, arms and legs.

"Oh, God," I mutter.

He kisses me again like he'll swallow my words,

my breath. Like he'll have it all. And all I can do is open my mouth to let him. To give it to him.

I moan into his mouth as he pushes a finger inside me once, twice, then draws it out, smears my arousal over my clit. When I arch my back, his touch takes me over the edge, and I come undone. He watches me and I can't look away, not when he's looking at me like this. Not when I'm feeling this thing. This pure, electrifying sensation.

Not when I'm coming for him.

I'm breathless when it's over and my body goes slack as he draws his hand out of my panties. He doesn't speak, just looks at me. But then something changes. He blinks hard. His forehead wrinkles and after a very long moment, he shifts his gaze away.

"Fuck."

He pushes off me, stumbles from the bed. Glances back once before taking two steps away and needing to grab the edge of a nearby chair to stay upright.

"Fuck!" he roars.

I sit, pulling the blankets up, my heart racing, a panic replacing that euphoria of moments ago. That strange calm I barely registered. The rightness of things.

Boots rush down the hall toward the bedroom and the door slams against the wall, as Matthaeus and another man stand in the doorway. They look at him, then at me, then back.

Matthaeus rushes to Dante. "Help me get him back in the bed!" he orders the soldier.

I scoot out of the bed as they haul him back into it. Dante is fighting them like he doesn't recognize them. Matthaeus curses when they finally hold him down enough that he can feel Dante's forehead.

"Keep him down," he tells the other man who has a knee on Dante's chest and his hands on his shoulders. I can see the bad one is bleeding again.

"You're hurting him!" I cry out, going to the soldier, trying to pry him off. Another one enters then, and I'm yanked off, held at the opposite end of the room, my struggles having no impact on him.

Matthaeus opens a black medical bag I hadn't noticed before and takes out a syringe and a small vial of clear liquid.

"What are you doing?" I yell as he fills the needle then pushes the plunger to get rid of any air bubbles.

"He needs to sleep," he tells me without looking at me.

"No!" I scream, propel myself forward, but the soldier won't let go.

He moves to Dante's side and grips his arm hard so Dante can't move. He pushes the needle into Dante's arm and the stuff works almost instantly before my eyes. I wonder if it's the same thing they gave me.

"What did you do?" I yell, struggling against the

soldier holding me back as I watch Matthaeus work on Dante.

"It'll help him relax. We need to get his temperature down," he says calmly to me, in complete opposition to my panicked words. He takes the dressing off Dante's shoulder. "Shit."

"You're hurting him!" I managed to slip free and grab Matthaeus's arm, but I'm caught again in the next instant.

"Get her out of here," he tells the man at my back when he's done.

"No! You're hurting him! Let go of me!"

Matthaeus turns, comes to me, his eyes fall to my throat.

I stop fighting, reach up to touch it. It's tender. I'm sure it's red and I wonder if he can make out Dante's fingerprints.

"Did he do that?" he asks.

I don't answer.

"What happened?" he asks.

"He was having a bad dream. I tried to wake him—"

"Don't do that. Don't touch him when he has those dreams, understand?"

"Why?"

"Just don't." He turns to the soldier. "Take her inside. Make her some tea."

"I don't want tea. And I don't want to go inside. I'm not leaving him."

"You shouldn't be in here. He needs to rest. Recover."

I look at Dante who seems to be sleeping peacefully now. But then Matthaeus turns back to him, presses against his wound. Dante winces because even in sleep it hurts as a line of blood streaks his arm.

"Why are you hurting him?" I kick my heel into the soldier's shin. He mutters a curse and as soon as his grip loosens, I lunge for Matthaeus.

He spins, grabs me. He's fast. They're all so much faster than me. He shifts my arms behind my back and holds me tight, jerks me once.

"You need to leave this room. Now. I don't want to have to make you."

I glance beyond him to Dante, then back, registering what he means by making me "You can't. I..." Fuck. Fuck, fuck, fuck. "Let me go!"

Matthaeus sighs, walks me out of the room, not letting his grip loosen once. "Mara," he says once we're inside and he directs me to one of the kitchen chairs. He keeps his hands on my shoulders and leans down so we're at eye level. "You need to calm down and do as I say, or I can't help him. Understand?"

"You're hurting him."

"I'm not hurting him. I wouldn't hurt him. Ever. Do you need something to help you sleep?"

I exhale, my lips tight, forehead wrinkling. I shake my head.

"Drink a cup of tea. By the time you're finished, I'll be done, and you can see him. All right?"

After a gesture from Matthaeus, the soldier who'd held me moves to make the tea. He takes a mug out of the cabinet and pours hot water in it from the boiler on the tap. He then opens another cabinet and takes out a box with a few tea bags in it. He glances at Matthaeus who nods.

"You don't need to look at him. Look at me. Do you understand what I'm saying?"

I turn back to Matthaeus. "I don't want any drugs."

"You'll sit here and drink the tea, understand?"

"I want to be in there with him. He needs me in—"

"You will sit here and drink the tea. Am I clear?"

I press my lips together and glare at him. I hate him.

He raises his eyebrows.

"Fine. Just until I drink the tea."

"Good."

The soldier sets the cup in front of me.

Matthaeus is slow to release his hands from my shoulders, but he does, waiting until I pick up the mug to take a sip. "Good. When you're finished you can come back inside."

I nod and I'd drink it faster, but the liquid is

scalding hot. Matthaeus leaves the soldier with me and hurries back to Dante's bedroom. I look up at my companion who is leaning against the counter watching me with his arms folded. I don't know his name, but I'll remember which one he is. I drink another sip, blink, my eyelids feeling heavy. The room grows a little fuzzy. I look down at the mug. The tea is half gone. When I look up at the soldier, he hasn't moved. He's still watching me.

I take another sip, tasting something strange.

"What is this?" I set the mug down, but when I try to stand, my knees give out. He's at my side in an instant, catching me. "What did you give me?"

"Nothing," he says. "Nothing bad."

My head lolls against his chest as he carries me down the hall. I pass out before I can even say another word.

17

DANTE

When I open my eyes, I'm alone.

I turn to the window. It's dark outside and I wonder how long I've been asleep. I move, wince at the pain at my shoulder. Two bullets will do that to you. Matthaeus has bandaged it up, but I can see the pink smear of blood. Lower on my arm is the healing scar from where the soldier's bullet grazed me just days ago. On my chest is the entry wound of the one that saved Cristiano's life. On my side and stomach are various lines and scars where the doctors did their best to stitch me back together after the explosion. It's not pretty to look at. Worse to touch.

But I did it. I killed Petrov.

One down, two to go. For starters.

I need to get back to the club and end his sons. I

don't even care at this point which of them touched her. They'll both die.

I lay back down because something else comes back to me then. Last night. The fever. The drugs that should have kept the nightmares at bay but only seemed to enhance their clarity. Like I was living it all again. The explosion. The pain. The thought that my brother was dying. That I was dying.

And then something else.

Her.

Mara beside me in my bed.

Mara *beneath* me in my bed.

I swallow hard, breathe in a tight breath.

A fever dream. That's all that was. It's all it can be. A fucking fever dream.

But even as I think it, I know it's not. I fucking know. I bring my hand to my nose, and I smell the faint scent of her.

Fuck! What did I do? What the fuck did I do?

I sit up, drag my hands through my hair.

What did I fucking do?

The door creaks. "How do you feel?" It's Matthaeus.

I turn, draw a deep breath in.

"Dante?"

"Like shit. I feel like shit. Where is she?"

He looks at me for a beat too long before answering. "I put her in another bedroom. She's sleeping."

I wonder if he knows. I nod. "Good." She

shouldn't be in here with me. Not in my room. And certainly not in my bed.

"Do you know who got you out?" he asks.

"No." I get up, walk toward the bathroom. "I need a shower."

"Petrov's dead."

I look back at him. "You don't say."

"Viktor has a bounty on your head."

"Good for him." I can't think straight right now. In fact, all I can think about is her. About what I did. About how I lay my broken, ugly body on top of hers. How small and vulnerable she felt beneath me. All I can imagine is her skin on my skin. My hand inside her panties. Inside her.

And I remember how she looked when she came.

"Fuck." I scratch the scruff on my chin, walk into the bathroom and attempt to close the door. "Can you put the fucking doorknobs back on the fucking doors?"

"What's your problem?"

I stop but don't turn around. "I need a minute."

"Just fucking say so then." He walks out of the room. I switch on the shower, strip off my jeans and briefs and take off the eye patch before stepping beneath the warm flow. I decide I'm not going to acknowledge the part of me that wanted one more draw of her scent before I wash my hands.

But all that does is serve to remind me of her face. Her body. Her mouth.

Her moan.

And I find myself gripping my cock hard, jerking myself off in the fucking shower as I try to banish thoughts of her.

I wanted to fuck her. To bury myself inside her. And I can't think of anything more fucked up than that.

She was kidnapped. Trafficked. Kept as a prisoner and used in ways I'm sure she'd rather forget. What the fuck is wrong with me that all I can think about is how her mouth tasted. How she opened for me. Came for me.

How my cock would feel inside her.

"Shit."

I stop. Switch the water to ice cold. That takes care of my erection. Too bad I can't wash out the inside of my head.

After making myself stand under the icy flow for a full minute I turn off the water and grab a towel. I dry my face and wrap it around my hips, then pull the patch on before I have to look at myself without it.

I stand at the mirror for a minute taking in my reflection. I scrub my jaw. I should shave. I've got more than a couple days of growth, but I can't be bothered right now. I go into the bedroom, dry off and get dressed in jeans and a black, long-sleeved T-shirt. I push the sleeves up, look at my scraped hand and arm from when that fucker tossed me out of the SUV.

That thought in mind, I stalk out of the bedroom and into the living room, relieved when I don't see her. I need to figure that part out, but I can't think about it right now. Can't think about her right now because all I want to do is think about her. Imagine her like she was last night. Remember it.

No more than that.

I want to fucking relive it.

"Is there coffee?" I ask when I find Matthaeus watching me. Does he know? There's not much he misses.

"Same place it always is."

I grumble a curse, pour myself a mug and sit on the armchair in the living room. "Where are the guys?"

"Sleeping."

"Which bedroom did you give her?" They're all taken if the men stayed the night.

"Mine. You think I'd put her in with one of the men?"

"She's sleeping in your bed?" The thought makes some primal, irrational caveman-like part of me furious.

"Not that they'd touch her, because they're not animals."

"That's not what I meant." Because I'm the only animal here.

"And yes, she's in my bed. To sleep. Alone." He picks up his mug of coffee but doesn't take his eyes off me. "I'm not stupid you know. Or blind."

I pause at that and take care not to break eye contact. How much does he know?

"So, she just went to sleep in your bed?" I ask as memory returns. How she looked when I first realized what I was doing. Choking her. And then…after.

"Not quite," Matthaeus says as if he'd given me time to process. He sips his coffee, all seeing eyes on me.

I raise my eyebrows and sip mine. "What does that mean?"

"She got upset. I made her a cup of tea."

"You…ah fuck." I know Matthaeus's tea. It's not tea at all.

"I had to. She's…" he shakes his head as he glances away, searching for the words. "She's very protective of you, Dante."

Now it's me who doesn't have the words. But then my gaze catches on the card on the table. The one that makes my heart stop momentarily.

"Where did you get that?" I'd found a similar one in David's things when we were looking for Scarlett. Never did learn much about what it was and forgot about it eventually. But seeing it now brings it right back.

"Your pocket," Matthaeus says.

I pick it up, turn it over. This one has a phone number in the same gold lettering as the front. I put my mug down, pick up my phone which is on the coffee table—I had left it here last night—and dial.

Matthaeus shakes his head but doesn't interrupt.

"You get home in one piece?" comes the same voice as the man who walked me out of Red's last night. The man who probably did save my life.

"No thanks to you. What the fuck is going on?"

"All thanks to me, actually. Even if you did fuck me royally."

"I don't even know who you are."

"I'm the man who needed Petrov alive."

"Why?"

"Because you and me, Dante Grigori, we have a common goal. We both want Felix Pérez. And you just killed the man who would draw him out of the hole he's hiding in."

DANTE

Jericho St. James.

The St. James family has their hands in several ventures in the states and northern Europe. Some legal, some not. Jericho has no social media presence. No address on any record. All I know about him is that he's thirty-one years old. His past is spotty at best. And in the last five years, he has vanished like a fucking ghost. In fact, apart from his birth certificate, high school diploma and a Harvard law degree, he doesn't exist.

And I'm about to meet him.

Matthaeus and I walk into the large, noisy café of the posh hotel near the public library, and I spot the man immediately. Not that I got a clear look at his face last night. But I know it's him the instant I see him from the asshole-grin on his face.

And I already don't like him.

"Dante," he says when we get to his table at the farthest corner. He rises to his feet.

I recognize the man standing at his back, hands folded in front of him, wearing black from head to toe.

St. James extends his hand to me. I glance at it, note the ink of a tattoo extending over his wrist and onto the back of his hand. He's wearing a ring on the ring finger of his right hand. Left hand is bare.

I shift my gaze back to his. "Jericho St. James." I don't shake his hand. I just take the seat nearest me, and Matthaeus takes the other one. "Who the fuck are you exactly?"

"Something to drink, gentlemen?" he asks as he resumes his seat, and a waitress comes by. He gives her a smile meant to dazzle and it clearly does. The girl flushes, almost trips over herself to take his order for coffee for the table.

He's well dressed and the large ring on his finger bears an insignia I can't quite make out from here. He's as tall as me, built about the same but his face isn't fucked up like mine. Although I have a feeling when I delve a little deeper his hands will come out as bloody.

I lean toward him when the waitress leaves. "You threw me out of a moving vehicle."

"We slowed it down." He smiles, scrutinizing me all along.

"It was still moving, asshole."

He shrugs a shoulder. "I saved your life."

"You don't know that."

"Yeah, I do. I give you serious credit for taking Petrov out. That is no easy feat. But walking into his club afterward looking like you did, out of it like you were and dripping blood on their tacky marble floors, well, that was just stupid."

"Fuck you. What do you want?"

"What I wanted was for the meeting between Petrov and Pérez to take place. Flush out that fuck. But I guess that's out now."

"What's your relationship with Felix Pérez?"

"He has something I want."

"And that is?"

He pauses. It's just for a moment, but it's all I need to see that this is it. This thing that Pérez has, that he wants, it's his weakness.

"There was a meeting."

"And?"

"The night of the explosion."

Now it's me who stops.

"Just before you and your brother started shooting up the place."

"You were there?"

"No."

"Then how do you know any of this?"

"Like I said, there was a meeting."

"You're just a fount of information, aren't you?"

"A meeting that Pérez recorded unbeknownst to the participants."

I lean back in my seat, fold my arms across my chest. It's my turn to grin now. "Sounds like an important meeting. Maybe I can get a copy of the minutes."

The waitress returns and he smiles at her, but I see how tight it is. Before he shifts his attention to me, he pours a spoonful of sugar into his coffee and stirs. I don't touch mine.

"He has another buyer lined up, you know," he says, clanking the silver spoon against the porcelain coffee cup.

I crack my neck. Flex my hands under the table. Another buyer for Mara? Doesn't make sense.

He watches me intently, dark eyes zeroed in so as not to miss the tiniest tell.

"And now that Petrov's out of the picture, he can move more freely."

"Doesn't add up."

He raises his eyebrows.

"That there would be a new buyer. Considering who she is, or more accurately who she isn't. Among other things." Not that I believed Petrov would actually return her. He'd more likely have killed her in front of Pérez and then killed Pérez.

"I'm just sharing information I've vetted. It's true."

"Who is it?"

"That I don't know. Whoever it is is keeping a very low profile, but he wants her specifically."

"Why?"

He shrugs a shoulder. "Your guess is as good as mine."

I draw in a breath, study the enigma sitting across from me. "What do you want, St. James?"

"I want Pérez, like I said."

"For the recording."

He nods.

"What's on it?"

He doesn't reply but I watch how his eyes darken. Whatever it is, it's very personal.

"Why am I here? Why make sure I walked out of Red's last night?" I ask.

"The girl. You've got her well-hidden."

I grit my jaw. Matthaeus signals for me to remain calm as I do the math.

"I need to borrow her," the bastard continues.

"No."

"I promise to take excellent care of her. You have my word."

"Your word means shit to me. No."

"He won't be able to resist coming for her. I know the deal he's struck is worth well over a million dollars and he's already been paid half."

"What part of no is confusing to you?" I push my chair back and stand. "Find your bait elsewhere." I turn, take a step.

"What that recording shows will be just as valuable to you as it is to me, Dante."

I pause.

"To your brother. His family."

I glance at Matthaeus.

"You don't want it known that your uncle was involved in, well, less than savory business."

At that, I spin, return to the table, and slam my hands on the surface. He doesn't even blink.

I lean in close. So close I can see that his eyes are actually different colors. One a dark blue, the other deep gray.

"I don't give a fuck what my uncle was involved in. And you should have done your homework before you came to me if that's all you've got." I straighten.

"Oh, I did," he says, standing. He takes a moment to button his suit jacket, but I don't miss the shiny metal of a pistol holstered on his belt. I get the feeling he doesn't need the soldiers standing just behind him. "I know you wouldn't want your true parentage getting out."

My jaw tenses.

"Or how that parentage came about."

He looks at me straight on, eyes unblinking.

"I am not your enemy, Dante. But I do need what I need."

"Who the fuck are you exactly?"

"Sit."

I don't.

He takes a breath in and sits, gestures to my vacant chair.

"Dante," Matthaeus says. He lays a hand on my shoulder.

I want to kill this man in front of me. I want to wrap my hands around his neck and choke the life out of him.

When Petrov goaded me about David, about him being my father, I didn't care how he knew. How he could have found out. All I was thinking about was Mara. What he'd done to her. What I'd do to him. It was necessary for survival, and it worked. I survived.

But this. This man knowing so fucking much, it gets to me.

"Sit down, Dante," St. James says. "Please."

I sit.

He reaches into his pocket and sets the same card he'd slipped into my pocket on the table. I don't shift my gaze from his.

"My client, this organization here, has a serious stake in getting that recording back."

"Who are they?" I remember I found the same card among David's things.

"Just a group of wealthy, interested and influential people. A society, of sorts."

"What did my uncle have to do with them?"

"Nothing good. And he wasn't *with them*. It's not

something you can buy into. You're born part of The Society or you're not."

I look at him. "And you?"

"I have ties."

"Vague is your middle name, isn't it? Give me something solid."

"He thought to use The Society to shield himself, ultimately, and there were some in the order who may have allowed more than they should have. It was damaging and will be more so if that recording gets into the wrong hands."

"My uncle was dead by the time that meeting took place."

He studies me. Does he know it was me who did the killing? At this point, I would be more surprised if he didn't.

"His name was mentioned. Along with your brother. Yourself. The cartel your sister-in-law is associated with."

"And what will you do with Pérez if you succeed in flushing him out?"

"I will hand him over to you once I ensure the recording is destroyed."

"What makes you think he'll destroy it? Are you just going to ask nicely?"

"He wants the girl back. He's desperate in fact."

"You don't get it, do you?" I ask, standing again. "The girl is not on the table. Period. You and I may have a common goal to find that fuck, but you're not using her to do it. So, if you want to try to blackmail me, you're welcome to fucking try, but you're wasting your time. The dead are dead. I'm not keeping up appearances. And I don't like being threatened. So why don't you go fuck yourself?"

Anger makes his jaw twitch. "I'll be here for a few days more."

"Not interested."

"You're making a mistake."

"Won't be my first."

"He'll come for her. He'll come with a fucking army because you taking Petrov out allowed him that." He stands again, buttons his god damned jacket again. "It was a stupid move. An emotional one."

I study him. He's right. It was definitely emotionally charged. But I'd do it exactly the same way if I had to do it over again. Maybe take more time to carve the fucker out.

But I wonder how far St. James is willing to go. Because he's not telling me everything. I know that much. Hell, I don't blame him. But he's not using Mara. No one is.

19

MARA

I wake up slowly but the difference this time to the last time is I remember exactly what happened. Matthaeus drugged me after Dante said he wouldn't do that again. Although he didn't say exactly that. He said he didn't want to drug me again. One word that makes all the difference.

It takes my muscles a little time to catch up to my brain's order to move. To get out of this bed. I'm not in Dante's bed even though I can tell from the room itself that I'm still in the warehouse.

The quiet around me is so complete, I wonder if I'm alone. I peel the blanket back and see that I'm still dressed. But I didn't expect not to be. These men aren't that type. They wouldn't touch me like that.

But Dante did.

I pause at the memory. I imagine how he felt on

top of me. How we were skin to skin. How he looked when he kissed me. How his mouth tasted.

And when he put his hand inside my panties... I close my eyes, my stomach fluttering. My body remembering.

When he put his hand inside my panties, I wanted it. I didn't want to cringe away. Didn't want to close my eyes and pretend it wasn't me, pretend my body wasn't mine. Didn't want to *not* feel it.

And I came. I had my first orgasm. It was amazing. More incredible than I could have imagined.

I've never come before. Not alone. Not with a man. Never. I pretended when Petrov made me. It was over quicker that way. And I've never touched myself. Never wanted to.

Now as I lie here, I close my eyes and imagine him like he was, as I slide my hand down over my stomach between my legs. I touch myself gingerly over top of my panties. Not inside. And I imagine his fingers there. Imagine how I felt to him.

Just then a noise from inside the apartment startles me.

I turn to the closed bedroom door. Hear someone laugh. A cold shiver passes through me at that sound. Because I know it.

My legs finally get the message from my brain to move, and I push the blankets off. Sitting up I swing my legs over the bed. There's carpet on the floor here. A small, scratchy circle with an ornate Persian design. Better than the concrete.

Another noise comes from one of the other rooms. Glass breaking.

I get up, go to the closed door, put my ear to it. It's thick but I can make out some sound. Men. More than one. But it doesn't sound like it did with Dante's soldiers.

I gasp when someone curses loudly and something shatters. Not a glass this time. This is too loud for that. I turn the lock on the door and jump at the next crash. Inside this room is a large bed, a proper nightstand, and a dresser. At the far end is a large window but this one has the small squares of glass. It's not an exit. This room is only half the size of Dante's and there's no attached bathroom. Nowhere to hide.

On the nightstand is a small lamp, a cheap, plastic thing. It won't do me any good if whoever is tearing up the place out there comes in here. And they will. It's just a matter of time.

I open the first of two drawers. Inside is a book, worn like it's been well read. That won't help me either, so I close it and open the next one. Here I find balled up socks, and when I rummage through, I close my hand over the cool, bumpy surface of a Swiss army knife.

I sit on the edge of the bed and look at my prize.

Helga used to have one similar to it. I took it from

her when she died but Petrov took it from me before we even got into his SUV that same night.

This one, though, is better. It's a pocketknife. The bright orange handle is solid. It fits perfectly in my palm. And the blade is sharp. Deadly.

I close it as I hear footsteps come nearer my room.

"Maaaaraaaaa," someone calls out, drawing out my name. "Come out, come out wherever you are," he sings.

My heart races. The blood inside my veins turns to ice.

No. No way.

It can't be him.

I know that voice though. Know his taunts. I know the man it belongs to. I haven't seen him in five years. I'll never forget him because he terrifies me.

I get to my feet, walk around the bed and back away from the door as the handle jiggles.

"Empty," another man says I guess of another room.

Someone pounds their fists against the door, and I jump with the violence of it. That pounding of fists will always make me jump. I feel my shoulders hunch, my body curling around itself.

I'm scared.

God. Will I ever not be scared?

And then it happens. The crash against the door, the wood creaking. It comes again, a kick making the door rattle, splintering the wood. The third kick sends his boot right through. I hear him curse then yank his leg out.

I don't scream when he bends to put his face in the hole. I don't scream when I see his eyes. His leering grin.

"There you are, sweetheart."

Sweetheart. It makes me sick when he says it. Makes me want to vomit.

He reaches his arm through, feels for the lock. It seems like a silly thing, that little lock. He could more easily kick the door in altogether. But he turns that lock and pushes the door open. I grip the knife hard, keeping it hidden in the palm of my hand.

He's tall. Not as tall as Dante but taller than me. And I know how solidly he's built. There's no getting around him.

He stops when he's a few feet from me, his fatigues dirty, a splatter of bright red on his chest. Some of it on his face.

"Well, aren't you all grown up," he says after looking me over.

Sweat slides down the back of my neck. I press myself against the cold, rough brick wall. He takes a step toward me, grinning all the while. I remember his breath. How stale it always smelled. Remember his yellowing teeth.

He cocks his head to the side. "Aren't you going to say hello?"

I swallow hard, see the two men move into the room behind him. Felix's men. I know because Miguel, the one in front of me, is one of Felix's most trusted soldiers.

"Well, we've got time to get reacquainted," he says, checking his watch as he steps toward me and takes me roughly by the arm.

I don't even think then. I can't. If he gets me out of this place, he'll take me back to Felix. Or back to another man like Petrov. And I can't do that again. I'd rather die than do that again.

So when he tugs, I let him, and I propel myself into him hard opening the blade and positioning it as I slam into his chest.

He's surprised. Confused. I can't tell. Maybe both.

And then comes a loud bang from inside. A door crashing open, boots of what sounds like a dozen men. Miguel's soldiers turn to look behind them, but I don't care about them. I push the small blade of the Swiss Army knife harder into Miguel's soft belly.

He looks down between us, puts his hand over mine, pulls the knife out and squeezes my wrist. The knife clatters to the floor. When he opens his palm, it's bloody. And when he looks back up at me it's with a rage in his eyes that I recognize.

But he's still got me, and I can't run.

"You stupid little bitch."

He shoves me backward, but he's injured, and he

stumbles into me. My scream is muffled by the sound of gun shots. I fall to the floor taking Miguel with me, his grip still a vise around my arm.

I can see the knife with its bright orange grip. I reach for it but can't quite reach it. Miguel kneels up over me, trapping me between his thighs and I scream when he makes a fist to punch me. I scream and close my eyes, covering my face, remembering how much his fists hurt.

But the blow doesn't come.

It doesn't come and a moment later, his weight is gone, and I open my eyes to find Dante standing over me. The look on his face fierce and furious. An avenging angel. He throws Miguel backward against the wall hard and advances on him as I scramble away. Dante draws his arm back and punches Miguel in the face with a ferocity that makes me scream. Miguel's head snaps back. Dante doesn't look at me when I scream. And he doesn't stop. He does it again and again and again until both men are on the floor. Miguel is on his back, arms at his sides, legs unmoving. His head at an unnatural angle. I wonder if the first hit didn't break his neck.

Dante keeps beating him, though, pummeling him. And I realize he's saying something as he punches him. Curses muttered under his breath, as blood from the dead man splatters up onto his face, as he slows down, worn out. Miguel is unrecognizable when Matthaeus finally comes into the room and forces Dante off.

Matthaeus looks at me, at the blood on my hand. At the dead man.

I watch Dante as he leans against the bed, knuckles red and raw, blood and sweat steaking his face.

I watch him as his gaze moves from the dead man, to the discarded knife, to me. And I can't read him. Can't read what I see on his face. But I do see how fury darkens the green of his visible eye.

Matthaeus moves toward Miguel's body. Dante never looks away from me, his gaze growing more intense, more charged. More angry.

"No ID. Nothing," Matthaeus says.

I'm the first to break the lock of our eyes. I look at Matthaeus. "He's one of Felix's soldiers. Miguel Alvarez." I shift my gaze to the dead man. "He's the one who killed Lizzie." God. To say it out loud.

The room somehow grows colder.

Dante gets to his feet, uses the back of his hand to wipe his face. It just smears blood and sweat though. He comes to stand in front of me and I'm reminded again that he's not the boy I knew, but a man. This man. This hardened killing machine.

I shudder.

He crouches down, puts his hands on my jaw and turns my face a little. He looks at something then brushes my cheek, I guess wiping away blood, before tucking a strand of hair behind my ear. He takes both of my hands inside his, looks at the back of them, then at my palms. With his thumb he smears Miguel's blood across one.

"Okay?" he asks.

I nod.

"We need to wash your hands."

I nod again and he helps me stand.

"We should move," Matthaeus says. "I don't know how they found us, but we need to go."

"A minute," Dante says, walking me toward the bedroom door.

"Wait!" I call out.

He stops and I slip my hand from his and go back to pick up the bloody Swiss army knife.

I feel Dante's gaze on me when I wipe it on Miguel's pant leg. When I straighten, I look down at his dead body once more. And I kick it. Kick him hard in the shins, then his thighs and finally between his legs. I kick and I kick and I kick. And it feels good. It feels so fucking good to hurt him.

I don't realize I'm screaming until powerful arms wrap around me. I'm lifted off the floor, legs kicking at air as Dante carries me out of the room and into his bedroom, to the bathroom.

My heart pounds when he sets me down in front of the sink and stands behind me. His arms locked around me. When I squirm, he only tightens his hold on me.

"Shh."

He's so close we're touching. His big, hard body at my back.

"Be still."

I can't though.

He leans his mouth to my ear. "Be still," he commands. "I have you."

I nod. Quiet as I take a deep, shuddering breath.

He runs the tap and checks the temperature before taking the knife from my hand and letting it fall into the sink. He picks up the bar of soap and washes my hands. I can only watch as he does it. His hands calloused and rough, mine small and soft, disappearing inside his. He scrubs away the blood and I watch the pink water run over the knife and down the drain.

I look up at our reflection. At us together. I'm surprised to find him not looking at our hands, at the task he's performing, but watching me. The line between his eyebrows deepens and I see the gray hairs at his temples. He's too young for gray, isn't he?

He has blood on his face, too. I wonder if he's seen it. I don't think so because he's not looking at anything but me. His gaze is so intensely locked on mine that it makes goosebumps rise along my flesh.

He blinks, finally looks down and he switches the water off. He sets his hands on the counter on either side of me, arms like steel bars. Not that I'd run. There's nowhere I want to be but here. He switches his gaze back to mine and I feel it in the pit of my stomach. That fluttering, like butterflies inside me. He still hasn't cleaned the blood off his face.

I turn inside the cage of his arms and reach up to wipe away the splatters of red with my fingers. His skin is rough with several days' worth of stubble. There's gray here, too, sprinkled through the dark. I like it. I look at his lips and remember them on mine. Remember how he tasted. And when he swallows, I watch his Adam's apple bob. I think again how beautiful he is. My broken avenging angel. The man who has saved me twice. The one slaying my dragons.

"Dante," comes Matthaeus's voice from inside breaking the spell. "We need to move."

"One minute," Dante calls out, not moving, not shifting his gaze.

I want him to kiss me again. I want to feel his lips on mine. Taste his taste. Smell his smell. I put my hands against his chest, move over solid muscle as I take them over his arms and wrap them around his shoulders. I feel his strength. And even when he winces as I touch what I realize is the bullet wound, he doesn't move. Doesn't pull back.

I climb up on tip toe and I touch my lips to his.

All I can think is how right this is. How this is exactly where I want to stay. Right here. In this moment in time. And when I move my lips, opening them to him, I feel his open too. Feel his body shudder as he draws me into him, kissing me.

My body melts against his and I feel myself relax. Then, in the next instant, everything changes. His lips tighten and he stiffens. His hands close around my arms, drawing me away.

"No," he says. Just that one word and it makes my world go dark again.

I look up at him, confused. I try to kiss him again, but he stops me.

"No, Mara."

Heat flushes my neck and face. I drop my gaze to the floor, to his booted feet, to my bare ones.

He keeps hold of one arm as his other hand creeps up my spine to cup the base of my skull. His fingers weave into my hair and tug, making me look up at him.

"I shouldn't have done what I did. I shouldn't have touched you."

I can't look at him. I'm embarrassed and hurt. How could I think he'd want me? After all that's happened, all they've done to me. It's stupid, really. Who would want me after that?

I feel my lip quiver and I bite back the pain, swallow down the hurt.

"It won't happen again," he continues. "I wouldn't be any better than the rest of them if I allowed it. Do you understand?"

I turn misty eyes up to study him, see how the

green of his eye is darker as if with the weight of his words, the feeling inside them. But I don't care about that. I don't want to hear this. I harden myself. Lock away any emotion.

"No," I tell him. And I grab my Swiss army knife, turn, and walk away, out of the room, needing to be away from him. Needing to figure out these strange new feelings. To manage my disappointment at his rejection.

20

DANTE

Fuck.

This is my fault.

I watch her walk away, wondering what the fuck it is I think I'm doing. Bringing her in here, standing so close, looking at her the way I did after what happened that night.

No wonder she's confused.

I adjust the crotch of my pants. Because I meant what I said. I can't let what happened the other night happen again. There's a very delicate line that divides me from the monsters. I've been toeing it. I need to step back because my cock got the wrong idea having her pressed up against me like that and I almost obliterated that line.

But now isn't the time to analyze this. Because inside, one of my men is lying on the kitchen floor with his head half blown off. They ambushed us.

And I wonder what Jericho St. James had to do with it. Because it's fucking convenient that I was with him when it happened. Convenient what his last words to me were.

Mother. Fucker.

I walk out of the bathroom, grab the duffel bag from under the table of clothes, stash a pile inside. In the kitchen I find Matthaeus laying a blanket over the body. I walk toward him, crouch down to help. I lay one hand on the dead man's chest. Micah. A kid. I close my eyes for a moment, apologizing, saying a little prayer even though I don't believe in any god. Such a cruel world could not have a god.

"I've already called to get someone in here to pick him up, but we should go."

I nod. "Where are the others?"

"Outside."

"Mara?" I find I have to look away when I ask him.

"Getting changed. The clothes you'd ordered had come. Someone had carried them in."

"How did they find us?" I ask as we straighten, and a bedroom door opens. We both turn to find Mara walking out wearing a pair of dark skinny jeans, a black sweater, and a pair of combat boots. Suddenly she looks older. Not so much like the lost girl I know she is, but like a woman. I wonder if she realizes her appeal and think maybe I should have bought her baggy, oversized clothes. But I chose these on purpose. Wanting her to feel safe, secure, in command of herself. I wanted her to feel like a woman. Not a lost little girl. Not under anyone's control. Even if there is a deviant part of me that wants her under mine.

She stops mid-step when she sees me, and I swallow hard. It takes a moment for my mind to shift from remembering how her ass felt pressed against my hardening cock to remembering what I said. Because I meant it. If I touch her, she will yield to me. And then I'd be just like the rest of the monsters who have ruled her life for fifteen years.

And so, I straighten, narrow my gaze, and cut off any emotion, any warmth. I tell myself it's for her own good.

Her face morphs from neutral to confused, to hurt and then finally, goes cold. She takes a step toward us, gaze locked on mine, and I see how the sapphire of her eyes has turned to ice.

Good. It's what I want. What we both need.

I clear my throat, shift my gaze to the large shopping bag in her hand. More clothes.

"Ready?" Matthaeus asks.

She nods to him.

Matthaeus goes first and I wait for her to pass me. I don't speak a word when she does. And I don't let my gaze fall to her ass for more than a split second as I follow her out.

Matthaeus opens the trunk of his waiting SUV

and puts his bag in. I reach out to take Mara's bag but when our hands touch, in that brief instant, there's a spark of energy, an electrical current passing between us. Before I can remind myself that electricity kills, she pulls her hand away, clutching it like it's been burnt. I get it.

I load her shopping bag into the trunk and watch as she climbs into the backseat and Matthaeus closes the door. Once she's inside he turns to me.

"You being careful?"

"What do you think?"

"She's vulnerable."

I face him squarely. "Do you think I don't know that?"

"You're closer to this than I am but you can't let your emotions get the better of you."

I grit my jaw, force myself to breathe in deeply, force myself to the matter at hand. I glance at her, seeing only her profile through the tinted glass. "How did they find her?"

"I don't know," he says, eyes on the two men smoking outside the warehouse. "It's not our men. I'd bet my life on that."

"Agree."

"What's the plan?"

"We get her back home where she's safe. Out of reach. We figure out what the fuck was said at that meeting that St. James needs kept quiet. And we find

Felix Pérez and take him out. Apart from the first part, the rest can happen in any order."

He snorts.

"Let's find a hotel near the airport. I'll call Charlie to arrange a flight."

I take my phone out and dial Charlie. Matthaeus climbs into the driver's seat. I take the passenger side and we ride in weighted silence.

21

DANTE

We spend the next few hours in a hotel room. Mara doesn't say a word to either of us. She just sits in the small nook at the window of the fourth-floor room looking out at traffic on the highway below.

Later, four hours into the flight to Naples, she's asleep and I'm still watching her. It's all I can do. I think about her life. How she has lived. How did she spend her days? Was she locked in a room? Waiting for them? Locked in a cellar?

Christ. I run a hand through my hair. The thought makes me sick.

I remember how she looked when she was kicking that asshole on the floor. Remember how she sounded, a mad, screaming, wild woman so different from the quiet, sleeping girl in the chair across from mine.

She's messed up. I knew she would be going in, but I didn't feel the extent of it in my gut like I do now.

She moves, muttering something as she turns over, her forehead creasing. Something slips from her hand and hits the carpet with a soft thud.

I look down. See the orange handle of Matthaeus's Swiss army knife. One I'd given him a few years ago. The blade is open. I stand, bend to pick it up. She must have been holding it under her blanket. Waiting for the next attack.

Fuck.

I close it, take the seat beside hers.

The instant I do, her eyes fly open and for a moment, they're panicked. Like she doesn't recognize me. Is it always going to be like this?

"It's me," I say. "You're safe."

She takes a moment to adjust her features, to put on the mask of cool detachment. She shifts in her seat and the blanket falls away. I catch it before it slides all the way off, adjust it over her.

"It's not safe to keep this open," I tell her, holding my hand out to her, palm up, the now closed knife there for her to take.

She reaches out, snatches it, careful not to touch me. "Did I kill him?"

"No. That was me."

She nods, shifts her gaze away. "But Felix will come for me."

"He's not going to get to you. I'm going to make sure of that."

She looks down at the bracelet on her wrist. "Samuel knew Felix too."

"Samuel?"

"My friend."

That's right. "What do you mean he knew Felix?"

"He used to work for him before he worked for Petrov. I had known him since I was little."

"The guard who gave you the bracelet? You knew him?" What. The. Fuck.

She nods.

"Petrov hired him knowing he worked for Felix?" I ask. That makes no sense.

"Petrov didn't know. I never said anything."

"When was this that he came to work for Petrov?"

"A year ago, I guess. He shouldn't have died." She trails off and I can almost hear what she's thinking. Hear the guilt she feels over his death.

"It wasn't your fault. Petrov killed him. Period. That wasn't on you. You know that, right?"

She shrugs a shoulder. But I've got another question.

"Can I see that bracelet?"

"Why?"

"Just let me see it."

She holds her wrist out to me. I take hold of it, feeling her soft, warm skin. Remembering how she felt the other night. I clear my throat, banish the memory and remind myself how small she is. How delicate. I turn her wrist over, the underside seeming even more vulnerable, and unclasp the bracelet.

"I want it back," she says.

"You can have it back. Just one minute." I study the thing, look at the gold square plate. See the tiny screws holding the two sides together. "Matthaeus," I say. He's got his eyes closed but I know he's not sleeping. He gets up and comes over to us. "These screws, let's get them off."

"Why?" Mara asks.

Matthaeus takes the bracelet and sits back down in his seat. He sets the bracelet on the table in front of him and unzips his computer bag. From inside it he retrieves a small case of screw drivers. He chooses one, tries it then replaces that one and takes another.

"He's breaking it," Mara says. She pushes the blanket off to stand but I put my hand on her knee.

"Stay."

She looks down at my hand then up at me. I hold steady, not letting her go. Because thing is, I don't want to let her go. I don't want to pull my hand away. No matter what I said, no matter the right thing, I know what I want.

She sits back and turns to watch Matthaeus as he takes the screws out. They're tiny. He sets them on the table.

"But he's going to ruin it. It's all I have left," she says.

"Mother fucker," Matthaeus says and holds up the small chip. He brings it to me and drops it in the palm of my hand.

It's quiet for a moment before Mara speaks. "What is that?"

"It's how Felix found you." He must have been tracking her for some time. Why would he do that? "And when I got you out, when I took Petrov out of the picture, he made his move."

I look at her, see the tears in her eyes. See how the skin around them reddens when she's about to cry. See how the dimple on her chin deepens when she bites her lip to stop the tremble. And all I want to do is wrap her in my arms. Tell her that none of those men matter. Because I'm going to send them all to hell.

Tell her I'll take care of her. I'll never betray her.

But then her face hardens, and she's shut herself off again. And it takes all I have not to pull her to me. Not to hold her tight.

"He lied to me too."

I don't say anything because it's true. He did.

"And he paid for it," she mutters. I think it's more to herself than me. She closes her eyes, turns her head away. "I'm glad he paid."

22

MARA

I watch the sun rise out of the airplane window. It's so pretty up here. I wish I could stay up in the air forever. I wish I could just keep flying, chasing the sunrise for the rest of my life up here in the air where no one can touch me. No one can hurt me. Betray me.

Below the sea sparkles crystal blue. We're descending. I see the mainland. We're too far to see the island but I know it's there. I know that's where he's taking me. My heart beats a little faster, my hands growing clammy.

The captain comes over the intercom telling us we'll be landing in fifteen minutes. To make sure our seatbelts are buckled. I doubt not having a seatbelt buckled would make much difference if the plane took a nose-dive into the water, but I do it anyway.

Fifteen minutes.

I close my eyes, my hand automatically coming to the wrist where the bracelet used to be. The gift Samuel had given me. He'd told me he'd had it since he was little. Said his mother had given it to him when he was just a child. He gave it to me after a particularly bad night, so I'd know I wasn't alone. I remember how I'd felt. How his words had made me cry, made me sadder than I already was.

But I know now his words were lies. His friendship just another betrayal. He'd been working for Felix all along. Felix had been tracking me that last year. Why? And when Petrov found out, he'd made it seem like it was my fault they'd sawn off Samuel's hand. It was my fault that he'd been killed. But that, too, was another manipulation. Another game. Another way to fuck with me.

It should be easier thinking about Samuel's death now. Knowing he wasn't my friend at all. But it isn't. It somehow hurts more.

A tear slips down my cheek, but I make sure I'm facing out the window, so no one notices. I wipe it away quickly. Steel myself as I finally see the small dot that is the island. I take a deep breath in and grip the arms of the seat, closing my eyes for the rest of the flight. I'm going to need to get better at this. At shutting myself off.

Why did he bring me here? Back to this place where it all began. Why would he do that to me?

A few minutes later, the plane touches down, the

landing thankfully soft. I open my eyes to meet Dante's ever watchful gaze. He's broken too. It's so obvious.

The captain's voice comes over the intercom as the plane slows to a stop. Matthaeus gets to his feet and stretches.

I shift my attention to undoing my belt. Dante stands, reaches for our bags and slings one over his shoulder. The other he holds in one hand and gestures for me to go ahead of him.

The attendant unlocks the door and it's opened, the stairs lowered onto the tarmac. The sun is bright in the clear blue sky, the air crisp and in that moment before my brain can step in and remind me of my reality, in that one small stitch in time, I feel something I haven't felt in a very, very long time. I feel it deep inside my belly.

Excitement.

A feeling of wanting to be out there. Wanting to take the steps that will lead me out under that sky, into that sunshine. Wanting to breathe in the air and exhale and just be.

It's the lightness of freedom.

Of home.

But my mind is quick to correct. And I clear my throat, take a step. I can see in my periphery that Dante saw it, though. Whatever that was must have played out on my face. Or he's just so in tune with me. But that's wishful thinking. I remember his rejection earlier. The hard *no* when I'd kissed him.

Heat flushes my face at the memory. How stupid I am.

I hurry after Matthaeus who exits first and watch him shake hands with the man standing beside the SUV that just came to a stop near the plane. They hug briefly before Matthaeus moves and the man turns his attention to the top of the stairs where I'm standing.

My breath catches in my throat, the gasp audible.

I hesitate, turn to find Dante at my back. He wraps his hand around the back of my neck, and I feel his warmth, his strength. His thumb rubs the hollow at my nape. He leans in close.

"It's okay. You know him."

I do.

I turn to the man who is smiling. He's trying to hide the worry in his deep blue eyes that the furrow between his brows gives away.

It's Cristiano. Dante's older brother.

"It's okay, Mara," Dante whispers again.

I nod, take a deep breath, and fumble for the handrail. My hand is shaking. My legs too. But I take step after step, focusing on my feet, not on the man waiting.

Dante stays close behind ready to catch me if my legs give out. When I step onto the tarmac, Cristiano walks toward me but is careful to keep distance.

They're all so careful with me. Like they're scared to spook me. Don't they know I can't be any more spooked?

I look up at him. See the warmth in his gaze. See the gray at his temples. The lines around his eyes. The boy is gone. Again. Just like Dante. Cristiano is a man. A stranger to me.

"Mara." He glances over my shoulder to Dante and when I follow his gaze, I see Dante give a small shake of his head. Cristiano steps back giving me more space, room to breathe. "Welcome home."

He's as tall as Dante. Built the same. He doesn't have the damage to his face that Dante has though. When the brothers hug and I see them together, I remember something. Laughter. Warmth. A happy family.

They both turn to look at me again, Cristiano cautiously smiling, Dante watching. Always watching. He doesn't even try to hide the intensity of his gaze or the darkness of his thoughts.

"Your grandmother, Scarlett, and even Noah are anxious to see you, Mara," Cristiano says. I think he's trying to make me feel relaxed. I know he is. But all it does is increase my anxiety.

I look up to Dante, my throat tight. Why did he bring me here? Here of all places.

Someone closes the trunk, making me jump. Dante is beside me again, standing close enough for our arms to touch. Cristiano looks like he has something to say but doesn't. Instead, he climbs into the passenger seat of one of the three SUVs with their darkly tinted windows.

Dante does that thing again, his hand on the back of my neck, and I turn to him.

"Are you okay?"

Why did you bring me here?

I want to ask it, but I don't. Instead, I nod and climb into the back seat of the SUV. I scoot to the other side as Dante gets in beside me. A few moments later, we're moving.

The coast is beautiful. Even in winter, even though it's cold, there's something almost magical about this turquoise sea. All I can do is stare out the window at it as we drive. When our procession comes to a stop at a port, the men step out. Dante and Cristiano talk briefly in Italian before Dante turns to me, holds out his hand.

"We'll take the boat from here. You and me together. Okay?"

I nod but I'm starting to feel sick. It will be good to have a break before we get to the house. Good to get myself ready. This should feel good, right? I think about this as I squint against the sun, making my way across the lot to the boats bobbing in the water. But the truth is, I can't remember the last time I dreamt of being rescued. Of coming home.

Home.

No.

The island isn't home. Not really. I lived with my grandmother although I guess we spent much of our time on the island. I don't remember my mother and never knew my father. Is he out there somewhere? Does he even know I exist? Does he care? No because if he did, he'd have come for me. I don't have any siblings that I'm aware of. My mother died before I could even form memories of her. I am alone.

As that thought settles over me my gaze falls on Dante and something inside my chest aches.

No, I won't fool myself.

I. Am. Alone.

I make myself repeat it.

We reach the boats. Dante climbs onto one, then reaches a hand to me. Cristiano is nearby, Matthaeus beside him.

"I can't swim," I say when I look down at the boat bobbing in the water.

"Well, we're hopefully not swimming today," Dante says with a smile. "But just in case, I'm a strong enough swimmer for the both of us, okay?"

I don't answer.

"Give me your hand," he says, his smile gone when I don't respond. "I won't let you fall, Mara. I'll never let you fall."

I hear his words. Think of all they can mean. Think how stupid it would be for me to trust them no matter how much I want to. How desperate I am to.

But then Samuel comes to mind. His deception. My stupidity. It helps. And when I place my hand into Dante's, I don't let myself think about how it feels when he holds it, how he feels when I'm close to him. I step onto the boat and sit down where he directs me inside the little cabin. He starts the engine and a few moments later, we're moving, the sound deafening, our speed exhilarating.

It's cold but I don't care. I get up, make my way outside. Salt air blows my hair, droplets of water hitting my face.

"Go back inside. It's too cold."

I shake my head, sit down at the front, turn my face into the wind. It feels wonderful. God. I feel alive.

He makes a sound and I glance at him to find him smiling. And when he shifts his attention to steering, I watch him. I watch his dark hair blow in the wind, watch how he stands so strong and straight, unyielding to the cold. Stronger than any man I've ever known.

And there's that feeling again. Home.

But I'd better be careful with that. Careful to guard my heart.

As the island comes into view and he slows the boat, any exhilaration dissipates, replaced by an anxiety so deep I feel like I'm going to be sick.

Because there it is. The hulking house on the island. The safe haven that turned into something so opposite, so gruesome.

The place I watched my best friend murdered.

The place I saw them all dying.

Dead.

The place my nightmare began.

23

DANTE

She leans over the edge and throws up as soon as I dock the boat.

I rush to her, wrap a hand around her arm when she leans too far out. When it's over, she looks up at me, her red-rimmed eyes shiny making the blue look like shards of glass. She wipes her mouth with the back of her hand.

I could chalk it up to travel. Time differences. Jet lag. Lack of sleep and sea sickness but I know that's not what this is. And as much as I wish I could tell myself all of those things, her words quash any hopes of that lie.

"Why did you bring me here?" she asks.

I see the door open over her shoulder, see Lenore rush out but stop. See little Alessandro and Scarlett behind her. She turns to follows my gaze too, but I stop her, take her arms and rub.

"Your family is here, Mara. This is where you belong."

Her eyes mist with fresh tears, sadness softening her features. "I can't do this," she manages, her voice barely a whisper before it breaks on a sob.

I pull her to me, and she lets me. For the first time since I found her, since I carried her out of that penthouse, she gives herself over to my embrace. She lets me carry her full weight, hugging her arms tightly around my middle and pressing her face into my chest as if she can burrow inside, disappear there. If my heart hadn't already broken when I first saw her, saw what they'd done to her, it is surely and wholly split in two now as I hold the trembling remnants of what was once a beautiful, vibrant girl in my arms.

I gather my own strength. Collect my rage. Build it like a weapon around all the pain, all the loss and my arms wrap tighter around her.

I will kill the men who did this to her.

I will tear them limb from limb.

I walk with her around the island first. Cristiano and the others go inside. I see Lenore watching from the window. See her face as she takes in her granddaughter, a woman now. A stranger. She hasn't seen her in fifteen years. I don't know what she expected. A happy reunion, maybe. It was naïve if she did. Wishful thinking.

We walk for more than an hour along the beach, climbing the cliff to a midway point. I avoid the top. The mausoleum. She knows it's there, but I get the feeling she's avoiding it too.

She doesn't talk. Neither of us do. Her arms stay wrapped around herself and I know I should give her space, but I don't. I can't. I stay close. She has to know I won't let anything else happen to her. Because I still remember those words she spoke to me in the beginning.

"Dante would never have let what happened to me happen."

I will never forget them. Forget how she sounded when she said them. Forget how she looked at me then.

When we're back down on the beach around the back of the house we stop, and she sits in the sand. I sit beside her.

"Do you remember what I told you?" I ask.

She doesn't look at me. Her gaze is fixed on the water, fingers digging in the sand. I get the feeling she's holding on by a thread. Her anxiety is a living, breathing thing.

"I'm never going to let anyone hurt you again. You're safe here, Mara. Safe with me."

She turns to me, opens her mouth to say something but just then comes a bark from around the corner of the house. We both turn to find Cerberus charging toward us at full speed, a giant beast of a dog.

I get to my feet, ready to grab him before he can get near her and scare her half to death. Who the fuck let him out here?

After he gives me a cursory lick on the face, I pull him away, only to see her extend a hand to him, letting him sniff it, then laying it on his head to pet him. He seems to understand to be gentle as he licks her hand, then her arm. I loosen my grip as he brings his face to hers, sniffing loudly before nuzzling his cold, wet nose in her neck. This makes her close her eyes and giggle when she lets him tackle her to the ground and lick her face excitedly.

I stand back and watch in awe. Her eyes are closed against the onslaught of affection from my brother's would-be beast who is a gentle giant at heart.

And when I hear footsteps, I turn to find Noah, Scarlett's younger brother, walk casually toward us, a smile playing on his lips at the sight. I look at him. He's twenty years old now. Mara's age. Still a kid in my mind but not really, not if I look at him in this moment. He's a man. Like me.

Mara sits up when she sees him and something about her expression rubs me the wrong way. It's not the reaction she had to me or to my men. She doesn't cringe away, getting to her feet, looking to me for guidance. Hiding behind me. No, she remains as she is and watches him come toward us, her gaze curious. I feel something in my gut that is the opposite of what I should feel.

"He's not a puppy but I figured you still loved dogs," Noah says in English. We speak English at the house mostly for Scarlett and Noah, although they both speak Italian fluently now. I still don't know how much Italian Mara remembers but her English is perfect. She even has an American accent. I know Helga wasn't American according to Scarlett and I wonder if she had American teachers.

But I don't much care about that right now.

Right now, I'm watching this strange interaction playing out before me.

Noah greets me with a nod. He still isn't my biggest fan after what happened five years ago. Talk about holding a grudge. I nod back and watch him take a seat beside Cerberus and Mara. He throws the ball out into the water and Cerberus goes after it. Noah has been working out, bulking up his skinny frame. I only now realize how much bigger he is, although nowhere near as big as me.

He switches his gaze to watch the dog, but Mara keeps hers locked on the side of his face. And as she watches him, there it is again, that tightening in my gut, the energy in my hands as if they want to fist. To attack.

"Noah," she says.

He turns to her, gives her a smile that's not quite a man's smile just yet. He nods. "Wasn't sure you'd remember me."

She smiles at him and I see a warmth in that smile that she's shared with no one else. Not even me.

My jaw clenches and it takes all I have to keep my hands from turning into fists.

Cerberus comes running out of the water, drops the ball and shakes off, sending water all over us. Mara and Noah laugh. I mutter a curse as a cloud crosses the sun stealing its heat.

"We should get inside. I'm sure your grandmother wants to see you," I snap. I'm talking to her but looking at him and wondering what the fuck is wrong with me. This is what I want, right? Her home. Her relaxed. Her feeling safe. Normal.

This is exactly what I want for her.

So what the fuck is my problem?

"Okay," Mara says and when I shift my gaze to hers, she's looking at me again. But the moment I meet her eyes, she blinks, swallows, stands up a little taller as her gaze grows a little more distant, a little more closed off.

She's steeling herself. It's not against me, I tell myself. It's against what's to come.

But when we head to the door, I notice she falls back to walk beside Noah, not me, as we enter the house. They're all waiting, like they were watching,

Lenore wringing her hands with worry, tension high. Then Alessandro charges around the corner, pulling his eye patch in place as he crashes into my legs. His greeting is warm and welcoming, a reminder to get my head out of my ass and be happy that she remembers Noah. Be happy of her instant connection with him.

Because what the fuck is wrong with me that I would feel like this.

Fucking jealous.

24

DANTE

Mara smiles at Scarlett first, recognizing her from the night at the house in the Netherlands. She looks at her rounded belly. My sister-in-law glows with the pregnancy. She's beautiful already but like this, happy, she's almost too bright to look at.

I want that for Mara.

I want her to glow with happiness.

They hug and Scarlett rubs her back then draws away to look at her. Mara's about an inch taller than Scarlett but so much younger. Not only in age but in every way.

"It's really good to see you again," she says. "I was so worried about you. We all were."

Mara smiles. I see the effort it takes. "I was worried about you, too."

Lenore sniffles and we turn to her. She has tears

streaming down her face. Mara's eyes fill up and she glances at me momentarily before letting Lenore hug her so tight I'm afraid she's going to break her.

"Darling girl," Lenore says. "I never thought I'd see you again."

Mara's eyes are huge, she's got her arms around Lenore but she's not crying. I can't tell what she's thinking.

Lenore draws back, looks her over, then hugs her again, telling her she's made all her favorite foods. I wonder what they could be considering she was five last Lenore saw her. I have no idea what her favorite food is. I wonder if she even has one.

Cristiano hangs back. I can see she's a little more leery of him. Like she is with me in a way. She glances at him then quickly away and I bend down to pick up Alessandro.

"And this is Alessandro," I tell her.

He extends his arm to shake her hand. She smiles at him, taking in the eye patch. She shakes his little hand.

"It's nice to meet you, Alessandro. How old are you?"

"Four." He holds up four fingers, double checks that it's only four, then adjusts his patch which in his rush he's gotten twisted.

"Let me fix that there, little man," I tell him, setting him down and crouching to take off the patch then put it back on. He's watching Mara.

"I hear you're going to be a big brother soon," she says.

"Yeah. It's going to be a girl though," he says, not hiding his disappointment.

"Hey. Girls are fun."

"I guess. I'm helping get her room ready." He glances at Scarlett then leans closer to Mara. "If it wasn't for me everything would be pink."

"Well," Mara starts with a smile. "It's good you took care of that."

He nods.

Scarlett rolls her eyes over his head.

I straighten as a door opens and Charlie comes out of Cristiano's study. "Sorry, I had to wrap up a call," he says, eyes on Mara.

She stiffens as he approaches but her reaction to him isn't what it was to Cristiano, my men or me. Still, he stops a few feet away. "It's very good to see you, Mara. Welcome home."

"Thank you," she says, then turns to me and I see the plea in her eyes.

"I'll take Mara upstairs. We're all pretty tired."

"I made up her room at the far end," Lenore says, clearly a little disappointed by the reunion. Cristiano puts a hand on her shoulder.

"I'll show you which one it is," Noah says. "It's right next to mine."

Mara smiles at him and I watch him lead her to

the stairs. I turn to Cristiano. "You have a room for Matthaeus?"

He nods. Matthaeus has a house on the mainland. His family home. But he usually stays here when he's in town. I get the feeling he doesn't like being in that old house with all its ghosts. The ghosts in ours aren't his. They don't bother him.

I turn to Lenore. "She just needs to adjust. It's all a shock."

"I know," Lenore says, eyes misty.

Cristiano rubs her back and Alessandro takes her hand. "Make me a snack?" he asks. He's a sweet kid and instinctively knows to distract her.

I pick up my duffel and Mara's shopping bag and walk up the stairs. After dropping my bag in my room, I walk down the hall where I can hear Mara and Noah talking. I notice Mara's room is just a few doors down from Lizzie's old room. I wonder if that was a great idea but with all the guests, we're running out of space. Lizzie's room has been turned into Alessandro's room in any case.

The door is open, and I see the pair of them standing at the window. Noah is pointing something out. I clear my throat and they turn.

"I'll take it from here, Noah."

He hesitates, then nods. "Sure thing." He walks out of the room. I close the door and go to her.

"Are you okay?"

"I'm not sure. I barely remember my grandmother. I mean, I don't. Not really."

"You were five. That's understandable." I open a dresser drawer, see the clothes inside. Scarlett took care of buying clothes for her so everything would be ready. She did it before I even went to get her never doubting that I'd bring Mara home.

Since all that happened with her brothers, Rinaldi, her own uncle, she's been working with trafficked women all over the world. Helping to get them home and reintegrated within their families and society. Mara has always been top of mind for her. I wonder if that's because it was her brothers who took her to begin with. I wonder if Mara's put that together yet.

"There are clothes. Everything you need." She nods and I go to her. "Listen, why don't you have a shower then get some rest. You don't have to come downstairs yet if you don't want to. You just take your time. We all just want you to feel okay. All right?"

"What happens now?"

"What do you mean?"

"Felix. Why did he come after me? Why does he want me back?"

I consider how much to tell her, my mind split between here, her and what I need to do. I need to talk to St. James. Figure out if he had anything to do with the attack at the warehouse. I need to talk to Charlie and Cristiano about what went down and find out about this new buyer. Tell them what St. James said about this alleged recording. There's so much to do but taking care of her, making sure she's okay, it's the most important.

"He's going to sell me again, isn't he?"

Fuck. I wasn't going to tell her that. "It doesn't matter what he thinks he's going to do."

"Was he planning to get me back all along? With Samuel giving me that bracelet, he's known my location for a long time."

"Don't worry about Felix, Mara. I'm not going to let him near you."

"You don't know him. You don't know how determined he can be."

I brush a hair behind her ear. She looks tired. "Try to relax. Get some rest."

"What are you going to do?"

"I head back tomorrow," I say, knowing she won't like it but biting the bullet and getting it over with. "Matthaeus and I."

"What?"

"You'll stay here."

"Here? Without you?"

"You'll have Noah," I can't help but say.

She looks confused. "You can't leave me here. I don't want to be here."

"This is your home. This is where you're safest."

"No, you said...You said I'd be safe *with you*."

She shakes her head, panic making her eyes wide and bright. "And this is where it happened. Where it all started. This is where…just…" she stops, squeezes her eyes shut for a long moment as she drags in a deep, shaky breath. "Down the hall, a few rooms away, it's where they did it. Where they…"

I take her arms, rub once, hold tight. "That's over. Years in the past. It's safe here now. *You're* safe here, Mara. There's life in this house again. Laughter. A life for you."

She shakes her head violently and tries to pull free of my grasp. I don't let her go. "I can't be here. Not without you. I won't."

"You will," I say with a finality that surprises even me. "You don't have a choice."

She shoves against my chest. "Let me go."

I do and she takes two steps away. "You drugged me again."

No luck she'd forget that. "That was a mistake," I say, no sense in mentioning it was Matthaeus, not me.

"What if I hadn't woken up in time. What if he'd—"

I go to her, take her arms again. Squeeze. "He didn't. And you did wake up and we got to you in time. You're safe. No more what-ifs."

"I'm not safe! Don't you get it? I will never be safe again!"

I give her a shake. I can't help it. "You're tired. Overtired. And stressed—"

"I'm stressed because you brought me here!"

"I brought you home!"

"This isn't my home. I don't have a home!"

"Fuck, Mara." I take a breath in, count to ten. I shift my gaze over her head. I need to be patient. I know that. "You need to fucking help me out here. I'm doing the best I can."

"The best you can?" She snorts. "You wouldn't abandon me here if you were doing your best!"

"I'm not abandoning you."

"You promised you'd take care of me. You promised you wouldn't let anyone hurt me again."

"And I won't."

"You said I'd be safe with you!"

Fuck. "Cristiano will protect you."

"I don't want Cristiano. I want you!"

Her anguish hits me harder than a kick to the chest.

"If you're dead, you won't be able to keep your promise," she finally says, losing a little steam.

I look down at her, feel her small hands against my chest. "I'm not going to die. I'm going to keep my promise to you."

"Don't you think you've used up your lives?"

"What?"

She turns pitiful eyes to mine. "Please take me with you. I want to be with you."

"I'm no good for you, sweetheart."

"You don't get it. You're the only one I can be with. Don't you want me?"

Fuck. Fuck. Fuck. I run a hand through my hair, turn away momentarily, then back to her. "What we did, what happened between us, I shouldn't have let that happen. That's my fault, not yours. I took advantage—"

"You didn't."

"I want you to have a life, Mara. I want you to be happy."

"Just not with you."

I sigh. "Not with me. That can't be."

"Do you have someone else?"

"What?"

She searches my face then lets her head drop. "Never mind. Nothing. I'm tired. You're right."

"Mara."

She sits on the edge of the bed, rubs her face. She won't look at me, but I can tell something has shifted for her. Like something else has broken. And this one's on me.

"Hey," I say, crouching down, taking her wrists, and pulling her hands away from her face. I don't know what I want to say. What I should say. My feelings for her, they're strange, wrong. Mara was a part of my life from the moment she was born. Lenore took over her care almost immediately after her birth. We don't know who her father is, and her mother had died before she'd turned one. She's always been a part of my family, too. And I love her.

But that love, those feelings for my sister's best friend, for the girl stolen when she was too young to even start her life, have changed. And none of it makes sense, not to me. Not right now.

All I know, all I can focus on, is that she is safest here.

Without me.

My life is forfeit. And she deserves a good man who will love her without adding any more baggage. Not some monster. Because she was right when she told me only monsters enjoy the feel of blood on their hands. I do. I like the kill. And going after Felix is, in a way, exhilarating. That rage I feel, it's what makes my heart keep ticking.

And I won't let her waste the life that she has just gotten back on someone like me.

"I'm tired," she says again before I can say anything, so I nod, pausing once more before rising to my feet. Not sure this is where I should leave it. Not sure I shouldn't explain to her. Make her understand that I have to let her go because I do want her. God, how I want her.

And it's more than that. I feel more than that.

But I can't have her. So much has been stolen from her already. I won't steal a love I don't deserve.

25

MARA

I pretend to be asleep when my grandmother brings up a tray of food hours later. I can't sleep though. I've been trying but it won't come. There were nights Petrov used a drug that knocked me out completely rather than leaving me conscious but paralyzed. Sometimes I'd wake up in a different place not even sure how many days had passed. In a strange way, I miss that oblivion now.

It's fully dark but for the moon. I look up at the ceiling, see how the moonlight reflects on the colorful glass of the Venetian lamp hanging there. The house is quiet. I heard Noah go to bed a few hours ago. And when Dante came to check on me, I didn't move. Didn't even breathe.

My heart hurts when I think about him. The feelings I have are strange, confused. I've never before felt what I'm feeling with him. Never wanted or needed to be so close to someone. Never felt the need for touch. The opposite, actually. I repelled it. Over the years my mind trained itself to shut down. To drift away. Be anywhere but there when it was happening.

Thinking about it now makes my throat close up. How did I survive all those years?

I learned about Petrov when I was eleven years old. It could have been years before that that he'd made the deal. That he'd bought me. Well, Elizabeth. He'd thought he'd bought Elizabeth. He'd required a certain education of me. I was never to speak Italian again. Never to speak Spanish either although I did learn that. I lived in Mexico too long not to. In a way I guess I should have been grateful to him. It was because of him that I wasn't sold earlier. Wasn't used up even if I was used. They were careful not to get caught. Not to take my virginity which Petrov paid for. But there are other things, other ways, and no one will ever know just how used up you are.

And I learned to disappear in those years. I sang Flora's song in my mind and floated away. Flora was one of the women who was kind to me. She was a cook and a part of my life for several years. I'll never forget her.

It didn't always work but it was the best I had. And now, with Dante, everything is different. I think I love him. No, I don't think it. I know it. From before, from when I was little. He was always different to me. Special. I didn't understand it then but now that he's back in my life, now that we're older, I get it.

Dante and I are destined to be together. Like our souls are linked. We belong together.

And no matter what he says, he feels it too, I know it. But it still hurts.

Frustrated, I push the blankets off. I won't be able to sleep. Not here, in this room. In this house. There are too many ghosts. Strange how I can forget my grandmother but that night? The night those men came into this house and massacred the Grigori family? That I still feel deep inside. And it's not just memories of Lizzie, of the moment of her death. Of how she died. It's more. It's like all their pain, their screams, their terror, it's been swallowed up inside me, like it's alive inside me. A part of me.

And I need to get away from it. From here. Because everything is so much louder here.

I slip my arms into the sweater I'd found in one of the drawers. I'm wearing a pair of loose-fitting pajama pants and a tank top. I go to the window, open it. A cool breeze blows in, and I hug my arms around myself. But it feels good to breathe in the fresh air. This house is stifling. Suffocating.

On the desk I see a stack of pretty, flowery paper. I pick up the pen lying on top and write a note. Because I don't want my grandmother to hurt any more than she has. Any more than I've hurt her, even today, when I couldn't be who she wanted. Who she expected. I don't want to hurt any of them.

I write three words. That's all. Because there's nothing to explain.

I am sorry.

And I am.

I open the bedroom door and half-expect half-hope Dante to be sitting outside keeping vigil. My guardian angel. But he's not there. No one is. I don't let myself feel the disappointment that creeps up at the realization.

Sconces cast a soft light along the corridor. The house looks different than it used to although that could be my memory. I make my way quietly down the hall. If there's one thing I'm good at it's being quiet. Weightless. Soundless. Like a ghost myself.

I don't let myself even glance at Lizzie's room a little farther down the hall. I can't. But when I get to Dante's door, I stop. Because maybe I knew all along how this would go.

I stand there for a long minute. I think if I concentrate hard enough, I can smell his aftershave. I know it's just my imagination though. I put my hand against his door, then lay my forehead on the cool wood. And it takes effort to keep quiet.

But exhaustion helps and I am exhausted. Exhausted of these unending, constant tears.

He will be sad, I think. Will he think I betrayed

him? After he saved my life. After he risked so much and lost one of his men.

But I can't do that. Can't go there. My life is forfeit and I think some part of him knows that as well as I do.

I steel my spine, swallow down the tears, and turn away from his door. I go down the stairs without making a sound. So strange, after all these years, the house smells the same. Stranger still that I remember that detail when I've forgotten so much.

Downstairs is as dark as upstairs. No guards inside. But I see two smoking outside of the front door, so I head toward the kitchen. I remember the layout. Even some of the paintings are familiar, the one of Lizzie's mom the most prominent. I pause in front of her. I remember that she was kind. Remember how we always thought she was a magical princess become a queen. She was so beautiful. Lizzie would have been as beautiful if she'd lived.

I turn and continue to the kitchen. It's dark too and I'm only surprised when, before I get to the door to exit the house, I hear a small whine. I turn to find Cerberus, the hulking German Shephard, in his bed in the corner.

He lopes toward me, tail wagging even though his steps are slow. I woke him.

"Hi," I say, crouching to pet him. He licks my face, lays his head in the crook of my neck and I find myself laying mine on his. "You're so sweet," I tell him, and am reluctant to stand, feeling a chill when I look down at him staring up at me with those huge brown eyes. It's almost like they know.

I turn and walk to the door. When I hear a single bark behind me, I don't look back. I just step out into the breezy night and only when my feet touch the cool rocks do I realize I never put on shoes.

But it doesn't matter anymore. Nothing does.

In a way, I feel at peace. More at peace than I ever have. I let my feet carry me up toward the cliffs to the one place Dante tried hard to avoid earlier.

The Mausoleum. And then beyond.

26

DANTE

I can't sleep. I didn't expect to, but I could have used at least an hour or two of oblivion.

A glance at the clock tells me it's a little after two in the morning. I push the blanket off, pull on jeans, a hoodie, and a pair of boots then step out into the hallway. All is quiet, the hallway deserted. Cerberus gives a whiny bark from the kitchen. It's out of place, not like him, but I ignore it and head toward Mara's room.

Strangely, I can almost feel her presence here.

I pause at her door to listen but hear nothing. I don't want to wake her, so I don't knock. Instead, I turn the doorknob and peer inside. It's dark, the curtains mostly drawn but not completely so moonlights filters in.

And something feels off.

The bed is empty, blankets pushed back. But the

bathroom door is closed. Maybe she's in there. Although I don't see a light from under the door.

Cerberus's low whine registers in the background of my mind as a strange sense of foreboding twists my stomach. I cross the room to the bathroom.

"Mara?" I ask, knocking once. When there's no answer, I open the door.

It's empty, though, and the memory of the last time we did this, repeated this exact scenario, returns. My heart rate accelerates but I stop, take a breath in. I look around the room, see the tray Lenore had brought up for her. It's untouched. I knew that, though, from when I checked on her before going to bed myself. She'd been asleep. Probably too exhausted to eat.

Cerberus barks loudly.

I stop and listen. And that urgency I'd felt moments ago burns inside my gut. I hurry toward the door, but something catches my eye as I pass the desk.

A note.

Three words.

Three. Fucking. Words.

I am sorry.

I fly through the house and into the kitchen where I find Cerberus barking at the door. I don't bother pulling on a jacket but open the door. The instant I do, Cerberus bounds out, and I hurry after him, taking in the cool breeze as I scan the beach for her. She's not here though. And as Cerberus picks up her scent and runs toward the cliffs, I realize where she's gone. The one place I tried hard to avoid all day. Tried so hard to shield her from.

The wind picks up as I climb the rocky cliffs, the ascent growing steeper and steeper. Cerberus disappears over the peak and the ground levels out a little as I reach it. I can see the marble wall of the Mausoleum as rocks slip under my boots.

I should have seen her by now. Cerberus had only just started barking. Or had I missed the sound before? Did she write that note hours ago and slip out to come to these cliffs? To the one place she was always afraid of when she was little.

"Mara," I call out once I'm standing in the face of what is fierce wind up here.

Something creaks, the sound eerie as wind propels clouds from the moon, letting that silvery, ghostly light shine on the marble walls.

That creak comes again. I walk to the building, enter through the open door. The Tabernacle lamp burning inside.

But if she was here, she's gone now.

Cerberus barks a single, sharp bark. I rush out of that dank mausoleum and follow the sound. The sea roars below us as I near the cliff's edge, slowing my steps as rocks slide out and over the edge.

"Mara!"

Nothing.

But it's when I get around the bend that I see her and simultaneously, I feel relief and utter terror at the sight.

She looks like an apparition. A blur in the dark. Clothes and hair blowing in a wild halo around her. A ghost already.

"Mara," I say, walking toward her.

Cerberus is lying on the ground, head on his paws, whining. I'm not sure she realizes we're here. She's so intent on the sea. Her face to the wind. Hair whipping it while she stands still as stone.

I navigate the steep decline toward her. I don't want to spook her. I'm so close. But it would take one step for her to slip away. For her to be gone for good this time.

And when I'm almost within reach of her, I hear her. She's singing a tune. Something in Spanish. Something sad.

"Mara."

She startles, turns, eyes vacant for a moment before surprise registers on her face, her mouth freezing in an O.

"What are you doing, sweetheart?" I ask.

But she doesn't answer. She doesn't get a chance to when she shifts her position and loses her footing, letting out a scream as rocks slip out from under her bare feet and the ground gives way beneath her.

27

MARA

I feel my feet go out from under me and it's in that instant that I realize something.

I don't want this.

I don't want to die.

My scream rips through the night, louder than the wind. Sharp rocks cut into the bottoms of my feet. When I look down, I see the sea, black now in the darkness, black without the light of the moon as clouds obscure it and rain begins to fall. Black but for the churning white as it crashes against the cliff wall.

That sensation of falling sends my belly into my throat. This is it. I will die on this island after all like I was meant to all those years ago.

But then I'm jolted to a stop, the vise like grip on my wrist threatening to pull my arm from its socket.

I look at my feet dangling naked and pale above the water, look up into Dante's terror-stricken face.

I want to tell him that I'm sorry. That I didn't mean it. But there's no time for that as he moves and more rocks spill over the edge. I'd scream if I could find my voice. Scream as I watch those stones bounce off my feet and into the white cloud of water disappearing into the vast, raging sea.

And when I feel a tug on my arm, I lift my gaze up to his again. To his face as he shifts his position, anchoring himself.

"Give me your other hand!" he calls over the wind.

I reach my other arm up to him. It takes two tries, but he catches it and tugs hard. Knife-like rocks tear my clothes, cutting my chest, my stomach, and thighs. But he has me. He's pulling me to safety.

Another tug and I'm wrapped in his arms, my feet still not touching the ground as he carries me away from the cliff's edge and back toward the mausoleum, holding me so tight it's hard to breathe. At the mausoleum where just a little while ago I'd paid my respects to the dead, he stops, puts me down. His hands come to either side of my face, thumbs brushing back wet hair and raindrops, grip a little too tight, gaze a little too dark.

He opens his mouth to say something, closes it again, teeth tight, jaw tense. And I see that he's raging too. Angrier than both sea and wind as he mutters a curse then bends to pick me up. He hauls me over his shoulder and begins a hurried descent back across the beach to the house, Cerberus barking, running alongside us.

The knowledge of what I've done hits me when we're in the house. I shudder.

"Good boy," Dante tells Cerberus, petting him before pointing to his cot.

The dog obeys after a glance at me. I feel guilty even looking in his eyes.

I expect Dante to put me down. I expect him to rail against me. To let loose his rage on me. I deserve it.

But he doesn't. Not yet. Not as he stalks up the stairs and into his room. Not as he locks the door and carries me dangling over his shoulder into the bathroom where he sets me down in the shower stall and pushes my back to the wall.

He's furious.

Too furious to speak.

I open my mouth, but he puts up a finger. "Shut up. Shut. The. Fuck. Up."

He switches on the water, and I yelp at the sudden momentary cold before it warms up. He shifts his attention back to me, hands on me, angrily ripping the clothes from me before pushing me fully beneath the flow. Only when I'm trapped in the glass enclosure does he release me, his body blocking the exit. He strips off his shirt, pushes off his boots then his jeans and briefs and steps into the shower with me.

28

DANTE

I am furious.

I take hold of her face, one hand on each side, and make her look up at me. She blinks against the spray of water, but I don't care. I pull her to me, hug her tight. Because if I don't, I'm going to shake her. Because all I can think is how close I came to losing her again. To losing her finally this time.

I push her away.

"What the fuck were you thinking?" I ask.

She winces at my tone.

"What were you fucking thinking?" I demand.

"You shouldn't have brought me here!" she cries out.

"Where should I have taken you then? Where?" Christ. The urge to shake her is back. I want to fucking rattle her bones. Jolt some sense into her.

"Just leave me alone!" She tries to force my hands from her, but I shift my grip to her arms, hold her tight, look down at her. Water runs over the planes of her body, soft, full breasts, hard nipples. Her too-flat belly. She's scratched up from the rocks.

She looks at me, too, and I let her. I hold her there and I let her. And when she meets my gaze again, I realize I don't care about anything but this moment. Her. I can't not kiss her. Can't not have her.

I cup the back of her head, pull her to me and close my mouth over hers. I kiss her hard, water pelting the back of my head as I devour her. I want her. I have never wanted anyone like I want her. As wrong as it is, I fucking want her.

Her hands come to my chest, my biceps. I draw back, lift her up, press her back to the glass wall. She wraps her legs around me and I'm at her entrance. And all I can do is look at her as I decide.

Because this is the moment to decide. The line is clear. I'm toeing it, have been since day one.

Now, my cock at her warm entrance, I have to decide.

And I do.

I already have. Hell, maybe I had since day one.

I thrust in hard and watch her gasp. Her hands wrap around my shoulders, and she opens her eyes, looks at me.

I draw out and thrust again. And fuck. Fuck, she

feels good. So good. So tight. So fucking perfect. Perfect for me. As if she was made just for me. I don't bother switching off the water when I carry her out, her legs still wrapped around my waist. I lay her dripping wet on my bed, tug her to the edge and grip her ankles to push her legs wide, opening her, looking at her. And then I'm inside her again, fucking her, fucking the past out of her.

And I know this is right. I know this is the only thing right in this fucked up situation. This fucked up world.

Her. Here. In my bed.

Mine.

Fucking mine.

I lean closer, needing to kiss her again, to taste her mouth, suck on her tongue. And when I do, she wraps her hands around the back of my head and gives me everything. Her breath, her body, her fucking soul. Because I will have everything. Every part of her.

And when that breath catches, I draw away to look at her, watch her come undone, face tensing, mouth open, eyes dark, black pupils ringed with a fine line of the most beautiful blue.

"Dante," she gasps, biting her lip, fingers pulling my hair as she closes those eyes and turns her head a little. The walls of her pussy pulsate around my cock, taking me to the edge of oblivion. I call out her name and make her look at me again. I need to see her eyes again as I empty inside her, laying claim to her, taking her for myself.

Because she belongs to me. She has always belonged to me.

29

DANTE

It's only when I pull out that the reality of what we've done, what *I've* done, sinks in. I look down at her, see her soft, relaxed face. I slowly release her legs.

She lies still, spent, but I see her pulse beating at her throat.

"Did I hurt you?" I finally ask, my voice sounding strange, grainy like sand, not my own.

She shakes her head, reaches up a hand to brush hair back from my face. I'm not sure if it's wet from the shower or sweat.

Relieved, I nod, walk into the bathroom because I need to be away from her for a minute. Away from those eyes. I switch off the still running shower, clean myself off, then hold a washcloth under warm water and carry that and a bath towel back into the bedroom.

She's lying exactly where I left her, legs dangling off the bed, her expression soft, sleepy. Her body boneless. She blinks as if her eyelids are too heavy, her eyes tracking me as I cross the room. Looking at her like this, lying naked on my bed, makes my cock stir again. I push one leg open, and she doesn't resist when I clean her. I notice a little smear of pink on her thigh and shift my gaze back up to hers as guilt settles in my gut.

"I did hurt you. You should have said—"

"You didn't."

It's not her words that silence me. More her tone. Different than usual. More sure.

I finish cleaning her then dry off what's left of the water from the shower. I look at the cuts on her chest, stomach and thighs, then pick up one of her feet to see the cuts on the bottom. I shift my gaze up to hers.

"Why?"

A shadow darkens her eyes, and she looks away momentarily. "I'm sorry," she finally says.

I raise my eyebrows. "You're sorry? You're fucking sorry?"

She swallows, sits up at this change.

I shake my head, walk across the room to my dresser and drag on a pair of sweats before going into the closet to pull out one of my button-down shirts. I hand it to her.

"Put it on."

She does and I return to the bathroom to get the first aid kit, then backtrack to her. She's leaning against the headboard buttoning up the shirt.

"Leave it. I need to clean those cuts."

She looks down, drops her arms. The shirt barely covers her nipples. I think how much I like how she looks in my clothes again. And I think about how she's a woman now. No longer a girl.

But then I imagine her out on that cliff, steps away from plunging to her death and something inside my chest twists. I take a breath in.

"Why?" I ask again, sitting on the bed and taking her feet on my lap to clean the cuts with alcohol.

"I don't know. Being back here, in this house, my grandmother, Noah. Lizzie's room so close. It's all just…it's too much. I told you on the boat. I can't do this. It's too hard."

I bandage the worst of the cuts as I process her words and only when I'm finished with both feet do I look at her again. "After all this time, I didn't find you only to lose you again."

"If it makes a difference, when I saw you up there, I didn't want to do it anymore. I didn't want to die."

I study her and I don't think she's lying. I'm not sure she's capable of lying. She's somehow managed to hold on to her innocence. After everything, all those years, she's still innocent.

That knowledge makes my chest ache. She lived

with monsters for so long. Alone and no match for them for too fucking long.

But the thought of almost having lost her returns. It hardens me. "Good. Because if you try anything like that again and I will never forgive you. Do you understand me?"

Her neck and cheeks flush red, eyes growing wide and a little frightened.

Good. I want her scared of this at least. I raise my eyebrows and she finally nods.

"Lie down. Let me look at those."

She obeys wordlessly and I open the shirt. My dick is hard again as I lay her out, taking in her perfectly round breasts, puckered nipples. I want to take one in my mouth. Suck it. Bite it. Make her come again. Take my time and hear her call out my name when she does.

It takes all I have to shift my gaze away, to clean the cuts on her stomach, chest and thighs. They're not as bad as her feet, so when I'm finished, I set the first-aid kit aside and look at her.

Her eyes move from my face to my bare chest, lower. I wonder what she thinks when she sees the scars. The patch covering the place my eye used to be.

"I came," she says when she meets my gaze again.

"I know."

"No, I mean, I've never come. Before you."

"What?"

Her cheeks go red again. "I've never had an orgasm."

I guess I hadn't thought of this. I remember what Petrov said but I'm sure he was lying, trying to get under my skin. But never before?

"Not even when you touch yourself?"

"I don't."

I am speechless.

"I didn't want to. Not after—" she stops abruptly and her expression darkens, some of that anxiety creeping back into her face.

"Open your legs," I tell her, wanting that softness back. Never wanting to see her anxious or afraid again. "Open them for me. I want to see you."

Without shifting her gaze, she spreads them open.

I move between them, look at her. I lean toward her to kiss her, taking my time, tasting her. Her pupils are dilated when I draw back, so I bend to take a nipple into my mouth. It hardens instantly and I tease it, suck and nibble it before repeating on the other side. I'm hard as I straighten, spread her legs wider and look at the pretty pink lips of her sex.

Leaning down I smell her arousal. I close my mouth over her sex, licking the length of her, clit to ass and back. I do it two more times and when she lets out a moan, I close my mouth over her clit and suck hard. It's moments before she's bucking beneath me again, coming on my tongue. Her fingers are woven into my hair as she grinds herself against my face. I cup her ass cheeks, pull her open, lick her from clit to ass again, then start all over. Devouring her, my dick so fucking hard it hurts.

I want to take her again, but I can't. I'd hurt her. She's tight and I'm not small. The one thing I do not want to do is hurt her. So, I tug her to the very edge of the bed and push my sweats down just enough to fist my cock. She watches in fascination as I rub it between her folds, moaning a deep, throaty moan as I smear her come over myself. Her eyes lock on my dick as I pump hard and come all over her tits, her stomach, her pussy, wanting to cover her with my scent like some animal. As if marking her as mine will ward off the evil in her life.

But that's not what I'm thinking about as I shudder with orgasm. It's not that when I tuck myself away and lean down to kiss her again. To take her offered tongue in my mouth. I'm thinking about something else. The one thing that is the only thing. The only way forward. And it's so clear. So fucking obvious. Like it was always meant to be. Like *we* were always meant to be.

30

DANTE

She sleeps the rest of the night. When I slip my arm from beneath her the next morning, her eyes flutter open for an instant, a smile just barely playing on her lips before she's out again.

I tuck her back into the bed, have a quick shower and head downstairs where my brother and Charlie are already in his study when I arrive.

Cristiano checks his watch. "Since when do you sleep much less sleep in?"

"Jet lag," I lie as I pour myself a cup of coffee from the silver carafe Lenore left for us. Knowing when they find out, when Cristiano hears that I took Mara to my bed, he will lose his shit.

"What happened last night? I heard Cerberus bark but when I got downstairs, you'd taken him out."

"Not exactly. I went to check on Mara around two in the morning. Just had a weird feeling."

"Mara?"

"She'd gone up to the cliffs."

There's a moment of stunned silence, although can any of us be stunned considering?

"Fuck," Charlie finally says, running a hand through his hair and shaking his head.

Cristiano's face is stone. "You got to her in time."

"Yeah," I say even though it wasn't a question. I sip my coffee. "Just barely." I can't think about what would have happened if I'd been just a minute later.

We sit in silence for a long moment.

"Will she do it again?" Cristiano finally asks.

"I don't think so."

He studies me, eyes so much like our mothers it's eerie. He nods. "Okay." He takes a seat on one of the armchairs and I join Charlie on the couch. "Let's talk through what's going on. Make a plan."

I nod and start. "We have a few players. Jericho St. James."

"Still digging into him. He's a fucking ghost," Charlie says.

"This IVI secret society or some shit. He supposedly is working for this organization. Claimed to have ties to it when I asked if he was a member. It's the same card David had in his luggage."

"I remember," Cristiano says.

"Says there was a meeting Felix recorded and it's why he's after the son of a bitch."

"What meeting?"

"Not sure but apparently there could be implications for our family. Although I'm not sure he wasn't feeding me a line of bullshit to enlist my help."

"What implications?"

I swallow too hot coffee before answering. "What David did to our mother for one."

Cristiano's eyes narrow and I see how he clenches and unclenches his fist. I wonder if he's even conscious of it. "That's on him. What else?"

"I don't know if he was involved in human trafficking himself, I'd guess yes, but somehow you and me, our family, even Scarlet, were allegedly named during that meeting."

"Allegedly." Cristiano doesn't seem worried, and I get it. I'm not worried about this recording either because chances are Jericho is full of shit.

"But it's not going to matter anyway if I talk to St. James and learn he had anything to do with the attack on the warehouse. I'll kill him myself," I say. "And then there's Felix Pérez and some new buyer. Which I don't get."

"What new buyer?" Charlie asks.

"I don't know. If St. James knows, he's not letting on. But apparently money has changed hands and this person wants Mara specifically. Not Elizabeth as far as I can tell since word is out that she isn't Elizabeth. I'm guessing this deal's been in place for about a year. It's when Pérez infiltrated Petrov's home via a guard who befriended Mara. He gave her the bracelet with the tracking device hidden inside. It's how they found the warehouse and her."

"A year?" Cristiano asks as confused as I am. He turns to Charlie. "Any idea how we can figure out who the buyer is?"

Charlie's forehead is furrowed. "I can see about money having changed hands. I'll start there if I can get access to Pérez's account. See if we can work it backward."

"It's a start," I say. "And when I meet with St. James, I'll see what I can get out of him. It may have to do with this IVI."

"They're like a vault."

"And I'll be dealing with Petrov's sons."

"Forgot about them," Cristiano says. "From what I hear you did the older one a favor taking dad out."

"Still, I doubt he'll send me a thank you card unless it comes with a bullet."

"What do you want to do about them?"

"Kill them."

"Are they important enough?"

I look at my brother. "He shared her."

Cristiano's jaw tightens.

"He shared her with at least one of his sons. He wouldn't tell me which, so I figured I'd take them both out."

My brother mutters a curse. "I should be there with you."

"You've got Scarlett and the baby coming, not to mention Alessandro."

"I can—"

"No, Cris. Just no," I tell him.

"We can provide support from here," Charlie offers.

I nod.

"I don't like this," Cristiano says.

"I've already arranged more men and a house," Charlie adds. "A property in Todt Hill."

"Staten Island?"

He nods. "It has quite some acreage and is surrounded by a twelve-foot stone wall. Our men are already there setting up and the previous owner had decent security in place."

"Perfect."

"When are you going back?" Cristiano asks. I know he doesn't want me going back without him at all, but this is mine. It always has been.

"Tomorrow."

"Does she know?"

Just then the door slams open, and we all turn. Cristiano and I both on our feet instantly, hands on our weapons before we see Noah.

He doesn't even scan the room. His eyes land instantly on me.

"You fucking asshole!" He stalks toward me, slaps

his hands against my chest to shove me. He doesn't budge me, but I take a step forward to get in his face.

"What the fuck is your problem?" I ask.

"Noah?" Cristiano says, trying to come between us.

"What the fuck is *my* problem?" Noah starts. He's foaming at the mouth. Like a rabid dog. "What's *your* problem?"

"What's going on?" Charlie asks as Cristiano steps between us.

"He hasn't told you?" Noah asks almost spitting the words, gaze burning between me and my brother. "Hasn't mentioned where Mara slept last night?" He tries to shove past Cristiano again, but Cristiano blocks him. "I saw her, you fucking asshole. Saw her coming out of your room!"

Cristiano's gaze shifts to me. I'm looking at Noah, but I see him in my periphery. Periphery is a thing I took for granted before I lost my eye. Now I'm much more aware of where I am in a room, positioning myself to see.

"Get out of the way," I tell my brother.

"I'm sure there's an explanation," Cristiano says tightly. I see the 'there better be a fucking explanation' look on his face. "Sit down," he tells Noah and shoves him into a seat. "You too," he tells me and closes the door. But before we even hear the click of it, Noah's on his feet, hands gripping the collar of my shirt.

"You don't want to start this with me, kid," I tell him. I still haven't touched him. I will, though. If I have to.

"How could you do that to her? After everything she's been through?" Noah asks.

"Relax," Cristiano tells him, yanking his hands from my collar. "She went up to the cliffs last night. Dante brought her back."

Noah looks at him and there's a moment of heavy silence while he processes her intention. "Fuck."

My brother turns to me. "She slept in your room?"

I don't owe him an explanation. He doesn't know this version of Mara. The rescued woman. He still sees her as a little girl. Lenore's granddaughter. Lizzie's best friend.

She's not those things anymore, or not only those things.

"She did."

He must see something on my face that gives me away then. Something that has him turning on me like Noah just did. He comes to stand nose to nose. "In your bed?"

I suck in a breath.

"Brother?" he presses.

When I don't answer, he fists my collar. "Everyone out," he tells the others without turning away from me.

"I'm not—" Noah starts.

"Out!" he commands, and I hear Charlie talking to Noah. See them walk out of the room. Hear the click of the door closing behind them.

Cristiano slams me against the wall the instant it does. "What. The. Fuck. Did. You. Do?"

I shove off the wall and get in his face. "You think I'd hurt her?"

He grips my collar and we're nose-to-nose. "I think you'd better have kept your dick in your pants."

He must see on my face that I did not because he shoves me again and I knock a lamp to the floor.

I glance at it, hear the crunching of glass under my boot when I step toward my brother. "Do I need to remind you what you did with Scarlett?" I ask, shoving him back. "Forcing her into your bed."

He draws his arm back, hand fisted. "I didn't do what you're thinking." He swings but I block him and push him away. This time it's him who sends his desk lamp crashing. "And this is very different." He straightens, steps toward me so we're toe-to-toe. "This is Mara we're talking about. Lenore's granddaughter for fuck's sake. You'd better not have forced her into your fucking bed." As if the thought burns through him, he swings again, this time at my gut.

I twist my body, take the brunt at my side. I straighten, shove him against the wall and press my forearm to his throat.

"You really think I'd take a woman by force? You think I'm like him? Like my fucking father?" Cristiano opens his mouth to say something, but I'm too far gone. Because isn't this what he's thinking? What they all must be thinking? "Fuck you for thinking it, asshole."

I swing.

31

MARA

I can hear the fighting through the closed door of Cristiano's office when I get to the bottom of the stairs. Scarlett and Alessandro, wearing his eye patch, come out of the kitchen. Noah stands from his chair next to Charlie in the living room, looking pissed off.

They all seem surprised to see me and I remember how quiet I can be. I smile but it's awkward because in that instant, something slams in the office. Something big. Like possibly one of the brothers.

"I'll see what's going on," Scarlett says, leaving Alessandro with Lenore as she steps toward the study.

Charlie blocks her path. "Leave them." He glances at me and suddenly, I know they know what happened last night. I know it's me they're fighting about.

Scarlett follows his gaze over to me. "What's going on?"

"Just leave them, Scarlett," Charlie repeats. "They will work through it."

For a moment I'm not sure she will but then we hear the sound of a boat, and she finally exhales, relenting. She comes to me, smiles. "Are you doing okay this morning?"

"Yes. I'm hungry, though," I say, turning to my grandmother. It's strange to call her that or even refer to her as that in my mind, but I have to. If not for myself then for her. And somehow things feel a little different this morning. A little better.

"That's good," Scarlett says as the door opens, and Matthaeus walks inside with a soldier. I wonder where he was. His hair is windblown, and droplets of water have collected on his shoulders. He's carrying a thick folder in his hand.

After a quick greeting to the room, he turns to Charlie. "Study?" he asks.

"Yeah," Charlie answers just as something—more likely someone—crashes against the door, rattling it.

Matthaeus's eyebrows rise high on his forehead.

"I think they need a few minutes," Charlie says.

Matthaeus glances at me and nods. "I'd kill for a cup of your coffee, Lenore."

Strange choice of words, I think, but no one seems to bat an eye.

"Everyone come to the kitchen," Lenore says, cautious eyes on me as she opens the kitchen door. I head in with Scarlett and sit beside Alessandro at the table.

"You're wearing your patch again," I say.

He leans in. "I don't want my uncle to feel like he sticks out," he whispers conspiratorially.

"That's very thoughtful of you."

Scarlett smiles at him proudly and we spend a few minutes talking about the pregnancy as Lenore serves food. She joins us then, sitting beside me. I feel Noah's gaze on me and get the feeling he's angry.

Breakfast is tense, considering. Charlie and Matthaeus are busy looking at whatever it is Matthaeus brought with him.

When I'm having the last sip of coffee, Cerberus whines at the door.

"Mara," Noah says, standing. "Walk Cerberus with me."

I look up at him, nod, get to my feet. I'm glad for the distraction although something is going on with him.

My grandmother is up, too, and taking a jacket off the rack to put it over my shoulders.

"It's cold out today," she says, and I look at her. She's about three inches shorter than me and I can see she's been crying. When she brushes a strand of hair back from my cheek, I think she's going to cry again.

"Nonna?" I ask, wanting to head that off.

That stops her and the ghost of a smile appears on her lips.

"Nonna," I say again, feeling the word on my tongue. It came naturally. Memory. I'm glad. "Thank you." I reach down to hug her, but when I pull her tiny frame to myself, I feel a choked sob against me. I cringe at what I'd almost done last night. "I'm back," I whisper. "I'm back. Please don't cry."

She nods, draws away while wiping her eyes with a handkerchief she takes from her apron pocket.

Cerberus whines.

"We'd better get this guy out," Noah says and opens the door.

I button the jacket and follow Cerberus out, Noah at my back.

Cerberus runs off to take care of business and Noah and I walk quietly along the beach. The wind is cold, like last night, and when we get to the edge of the house I glance up at the cliffs and shudder.

What I did was selfish.

If I'd succeeded, I'd have broken their hearts twice.

"I saw you," Noah says.

I turn to him, thinking he saw me last night, not sure how to explain.

"This morning." He doesn't quite look at me when he says that part and I realize what he means.

"Oh." I'd slipped back to my room when I thought no one was in the hallway. Not that I was hiding, I just didn't want to make things awkward or difficult. "Oh," I say again. "Is that why…" I glance at the windows I know are Cristiano's office windows.

Noah nods, eyes cast to the sea watching Cerberus carry a big stick out of the water.

"I…it's strange being back here. Last night was really hard."

He turns to me, wraps his hand around mine. I freeze, remembering Samuel. Remembering what happened to him. But then I tell myself that he was a liar. Even if he didn't deserve what he got.

I look up at Noah and I swear I can still see the little boy from all those years ago. We couldn't understand each other at all, and I wouldn't stop crying. I couldn't. Joseph had put me with Noah, told us to play as if that would fix everything.

"What happened to Joseph?" I ask.

Noah's expression darkens. "He's dead."

"Good."

"Listen, Mara, if Dante hurt—"

"Dante didn't hurt me. He wouldn't. He saved my life." In so many ways.

"If he—

"Stop. He didn't. I don't want to talk about this."

He studies me as if to be sure and then finally

nods. Cerberus drops the giant stick at our feet for Noah to throw.

I stand back, smiling at them, liking the simplicity of this, us on the beach playing with a dog.

But that simplicity feels so far off for me. Like I'm an imposter here in this house, this life. They all are in a way. There is nothing simple about the lives of anyone in this house.

32

DANTE

My brother and I haven't fought like this in years. By the time we slow down, Cristiano's office is a mess of shattered glass, a laptop in two pieces, a crack in the window where my head collided with the glass. It's that that stops us.

"Tell me is that it?" I ask finally. Because what the fuck? "You're worried David's genes got into me and I —"

"Fuck. Christ! No! Never! Just... fuck!" Cristiano steps back and slams his fist into the wall instead of my face.

I feel the slow trail of blood along my temple and when he looks at me, he shakes his head, takes a tissue from his desk, and holds it against the cut.

"No, brother. That's not what I think. What I ever thought," he says.

I nod, taking the tissue as I turn to look out at the sea.

After the rain last night, the day is overcast, the water a deep charcoal. I run my hand through my hair, remember what she'd said about monsters. Remember what I'd said when I'd still had some fucking self-control. Am I that? Am I no better?

"But fuck, Dante. What did you think you were doing?"

"It's not like you think."

"Then how is it?" he asks.

I turn to him. He's worried. I see it behind the fury in his eyes. Hear it in his voice. "Explain to me how it is."

Fuck.

I look away from my brother to watch Noah and Mara from the window. Cristiano comes to stand beside me. I'm not sure he understands this thing with Mara yet. I'm not sure I do. It's too strange. Too fated.

"She's easy with him," I say. "Different than she is with me or most men as far as I've seen."

"He's not threatening to her."

"All men are threatening to her."

"Not him. She must remember something about him from when she was little."

Noah wraps his hand around hers and they stop to talk. A tightness builds in my gut at the sight of it.

"Relax," Cristiano says, hand on my shoulder. We watch them silently.

"I'm taking her back tomorrow."

"You sure that's a good idea?"

"I think bringing her here was a bad one. And she won't stay here without me. I don't think she can, and I won't risk her going up to those cliffs again. I can't."

Cristiano nods. "Lenore will be upset."

"I'll talk to her. She'll understand. It's better for Mara. And once everything is sorted, once Felix is dead, things will be different. She can start to heal. I don't think she can do that until he's gone because she isn't convinced he won't get to her."

"Dante," Cristiano says, and I turn to find him studying me. I grit my teeth and wait as I take in the look in his eyes. See how he's processing, understanding what I can't quite say. Because what I want to do is keep her. But it's the worst fucking idea I've ever had.

My brother puts a hand on my shoulder. It's a gesture of understanding. Of acceptance. And in this moment, I find myself so grateful, so fucking grateful he didn't die the night of the massacre. So grateful he survived David.

"Take Noah with you," he says.

"Why?"

"She trusts him. And I trust him."

"And Scarlett?"

"I'll talk to Scarlett. He's not a boy anymore. She needs to let him go."

"He's trained?"

"Trained but untested. And young but determined. He hates Felix as much as we do. And I know he wants Mara safe."

The pair turn and walk back into the house. I look at them. Both young. Somehow still innocent in their own way.

"She'd be better off with him," I say, I don't know why.

Cristiano studies me. "I don't think so. Maybe before I'd have said yes, but no. Not anymore. No matter what, her brain works a certain way now. And as little as I like the idea of you bedding her, I can see she needs you. You saved her life. More than once and in more ways than one. She can lean on you. You're solid. She looks to you when she's unsure. She needs a man who's not afraid to make her face her demons. Noah is not that man. Not yet anyway."

"So, what you're saying is she needs an asshole."

"Exactly," he says with a grin and pats my back. "And you fit the bill."

"Fuck you," I say in jest but as I watch them out there, there's a part of me that still wonders if she wouldn't be better off with Noah. Or someone like him. If I shouldn't walk away now even though I'm not sure I can.

33

MARA

I'm sitting beside Noah in an SUV on our way to a house in Todt Hill on Staten Island. I'm relieved Dante didn't leave me behind and glad he let Noah come. I guess after what happened last night, he wasn't taking any chances. But I meant what I said. I don't want to die.

"Word is out," Matthaeus says, reading something on his phone. Dante takes a turn onto a winding, tree-lined street with fewer houses than the last, twelve-foot walls surrounding each property. "She's Grigori property."

I should probably be offended by that but I'm not. Not very modern of me, I know, but I want to be Dante's. Because he's mine. He was always meant to be mine. I catch his eye in the rear-view mirror and feel a tremor go through me. I want to be alone with him. I want to feel his weight on me. His mouth on my mouth. Him inside me.

My neck and face flush with heat.

He shifts his gaze back to the road, but I don't miss the slight grin on his face. I wonder if he knows what I'm thinking. If he's thinking it too.

"St. James?" he asks.

"Still at the hotel."

"Because he's waiting for a visit. If he knew about the attack, I'm going to kill him."

I know this isn't just talk. I know Dante means every word and when I see the image of him beating Alvarez to death, I shudder.

"This one is ours," Matthaeus says, and we pull onto a driveway where the tall gates slowly open. Two armed guards stand just inside the property. From here, I can't see the house. The place seems big and from a quick count of soldiers, well protected.

Dante glances at Noah in the rear-view mirror. I know Noah doesn't like him. He then shifts his glance to me momentarily before shifting it back to the road.

"You two will get settled here. There are more than two dozen armed men on the property. You'll be protected. Eat something. Relax. Get some sleep. You didn't sleep at all on the flight."

"What about you?" I ask.

"Matthaeus and I have an errand to run."

"Visiting that man. St. James."

He doesn't reply, just slows the car to a stop. He doesn't kill the engine. After climbing out he opens my door and helps me, then closes it. We stand, me with my back pressed against the SUV, him leaning on one arm, hand directly over my head. The other hand closes over my pelvic bone.

"Promise me you're going to eat something." I'm too skinny. I know.

"I'll eat. Thanks for letting Noah come."

"That was Cristiano's idea."

"Why don't you like him?"

He glances over the top of the SUV I guess at Noah. "I don't dislike him," he says when he looks back at me.

"Word play." I don't look away from him. I feel like every time I see him could be the last time. "I'm scared for you."

"I'll be fine."

He leans in close, tilting his head, scruff of his jaw against my cheek as his breath raises goosebumps along the nape of my neck. I feel him inhale, feel his lips on the underside of my jaw just below my ear and that sensation goes right to my core. I wrap my hands around his shoulders, reassured by the sheer strength of this man.

"You do things to me," he whispers, the words almost a rumble rather than sound.

My nipples tighten as they brush against his chest, too many layers between us. His hardness presses against me and butterfly wings flutter inside my stomach. He draws back a little, dipping his head to touch his forehead to mine, and looks at me.

"Come back to me," I say.

"You're dramatic."

Not dramatic but realistic. "Promise me. Promise me you'll come back to me." I wonder if he realizes how much I mean this. How much I need him to come back. How much my own life depends on his. Because I don't want to die. But I also don't want to live if he dies.

He kisses me and I close my eyes. It's a tender kiss, not hurried but like a promise itself. The start of something.

When he draws back and I open my eyes, he brushes his thumb across my cheek. It comes away wet.

"I promise," he says. "I'll come back to you. Always."

I blink again, unable to hold back the fat tears that drop heavy onto my cheeks. I hug him, press my face into his chest and squeeze my eyes shut to inhale his scent so deeply there's no room for anything else but him. Just him. And then it's time to go. Someone clears their throat and Dante's hands come to my arms, unwinding them from around his neck. He touches his forehead to mine one more time, then kisses the tip of my nose. He takes my hand and walks me to Noah who is standing nearby, jaw tense, eyes narrowed on Dante.

Dante's expression changes. Cocky Dante surfaces.

"Don't look like that," he says to Noah and ruffles his hair like he's a kid.

"Fuck off," Noah brushes his hand away, fixing his hair that is now standing up in all directions. He makes a point of taking my hand and giving Dante a rebellious grin. I think what he really wants to do is flip him off. A few moments later, Noah and I are inside the double front doors and a trio of SUVs heads off the property.

34

DANTE

I watch her in the rearview mirror until she disappears. When I see Matthaeus studying me, I clear my throat, focus on the drive into the city. Matthaeus goes over what he'd managed to dig up on St. James which isn't much. No criminal record. No social media profiles. No links to any organizations apart from IVI which he's disclosed. One family home in his name that he doesn't live in, in New Orleans. No other known address.

"Where has he been for the last five years?"

"No idea. Can't find a damn thing. It's like he disappeared from life."

"No. There has to be something. We're just missing it. Any other family?"

"A brother, but he appears to be clean. At least on the surface."

"I doubt that."

IVI itself is interesting. A society begun centuries ago by educated, wealthy men whose descendants to this day are active members. There are thirteen founding families from all over the world, the majority from Europe and North America, and the information available about them is vague at best. But I recognize some of those names and I'd be more surprised if things weren't vague. Money and power like that buys silence and influence. They have compounds in most major cities around the world and at least some presence in many less-cosmopolitan areas.

They appear to have some sort of outdated caste-like system—elitist if you ask me—with a judicial branch they call The Tribunal.

Now that is one of the most interesting pieces. IVI, or The Society as they're called by members, has a Tribunal in most locations. They seem to operate separately of any legal courts and there are rumors about sentences that go as far as execution in rare instances. The last was only a few months ago in the New Orleans faction.

I'm intrigued. And I want to know what David thought he was doing trying to buy into something like this. I mean, I get it. Money and power. Those are the things that rule men like him. Well, that and vengeance. I want to know who he worked with. If he had a contact within the organization. Who that contact is and if they had anything to do with the trafficking of women. Of girls like Mara.

My head is fully in the game as I pull up to the circular drive of the posh hotel where I met St. James the first time. I drop the keys into the waiting hands of a valet. Matthaeus and I enter through the glass doors that slide open as we approach. Two men flank us as we step onto the elevator. The others will remain in the lobby. As I watch the doors slide closed, I remember the last time we did this at a different hotel. It was only days ago but feels like a lifetime.

He's taking up the entirety of the thirty-second floor so when the elevator doors open, we are greeted by two men in suits who I'm sure are armed beneath their jackets. One stops us, the other comes forward to search us. They relieve us of our weapons even finding the switchblade I'd put in my boot before leading us to the double doors directly in front of the elevator. They open the doors, and we enter, my men stopping just inside as Matthaeus, and I move into the room.

It's a large, circular space, the building itself circular. And very modern with minimal furnishings and floor-to-ceiling windows for walls. Everything is white. White marble floors veined with gold. White leather furniture. White furs draped over chairs. White counters in the kitchen.

"Blood has to be hard to get out of the rug," I say,

observing the thick carpet beneath my boots that spans the whole of the sitting space. I stop, unbutton my jacket. Matthaeus takes his place to my right.

Jericho St. James has his back to the room as he watches out the window. He turns to us, sips from a crystal tumbler as he looks us over. From what I can see, he's not surprised by our visit.

"Gentlemen," he says, noting the two men I brought. "Welcome back."

I don't like his face. I don't like his smug grin. I take a step toward him, and a large man instantly steps between us, hand firm on my chest to stop me.

"That's not necessary," St. James says to him. "But you didn't need to bring soldiers," he adds for my benefit.

"I lost a man. I should have brought an army."

"I'm not the one you lost your man to. Sybil, get my guests a drink."

I turn to where Sybil is standing. She's petite, young, attractive, wearing a very short maid's uniform. I raise an eyebrow as she places a bottle of whiskey and two tumblers on a tray, carrying it to us. St. James has now taken a seat on one of the three leather armchairs. Again, white. It's a fucking eyesore.

When the woman bends to put her tray down on the coffee table her skirt rides up. She's not wearing anything underneath. She takes her time in that position as she pours for each of us, and I see the glint of a butt plug between her cheeks.

I catch St. James's eyes on me. He smiles. "For later," he says, and I like him even less.

"Sit. Please." He gestures to the chairs and Matthaeus, and I sit down.

"I lost a man," I say again.

"Like I said, you didn't lose him to me. I didn't have anything to do with the attack on your warehouse," he says, then tilts his head like he's confused. "You were living in a warehouse?"

"Your warning was convenient." I don't bother answering his question.

"My warning was common sense. Any idea how he found her?"

"Tracking device in her bracelet." I'm sure they were watching the warehouse, waiting for an opportunity.

"I hear Felix is pissed he lost one of his best men."

"You hear a lot of things. What are you playing at?"

"I'm playing at trying to get you on my side. We have a mutual interest in finding Felix Pérez sooner rather than later. He's met with some high-profile people over the last forty-eight hours. We're running out of time."

"How do you know this?" Charlie hasn't been able to turn up any information on his whereabouts.

"My sources are better than yours."

"Then why haven't you moved in?"

"I'm not a killer."

"So, you want me to be your muscle."

He shrugs a shoulder, sips his whiskey.

"I'm not looking for a job," I say.

"I know where he'll be on Saturday night."

"Where?"

"You agree to help me, and I'll tell you."

"How do I know you weren't behind the attack on the warehouse?"

"I don't work with pigs like Alvarez." His lip curls with distaste and I see how his eyes narrow, a muscle twitching in his jaw. "I know the kind of man he is. The things he's done." I remember what Mara said about him being the one who killed my sister. My five-year-old sister. Fuck. "I'm not that sort of criminal," St. James must still have been talking but I'd tuned him out.

"But you are a criminal," I say, forcing myself to focus.

He shrugs casually like he could give a shit.

"I need proof you're not going to fuck me over," I say.

"Proof such as?"

"You're a smart guy. I'm sure you can think of something."

His gaze is narrowed but he never takes his eyes off me. "The Petrov brothers."

"They'll do." This is what I'm hoping for. He somehow has an in with them. I don't know the extent of his relationship with the Petrov family, but I don't like what I'm seeing.

He finishes his drink, sets his glass down. "Clear the room," he tells the soldier who stopped me advancing on him.

The man gives the order and a moment later, it's just the three of us and his bodyguard, my own men sent to the hall.

"Viktor is the one you want."

"I want both."

He shakes his head. "Sacha wouldn't have touched your girl."

"And you know this how?"

"He doesn't like girls. And I know for a fact he didn't want to have anything to do with what he called his father's and brother's *dirty habit*. Petrov was married to his mother at the time he took Mara. Viktor and Sacha are only half-brothers, you know."

I didn't. I didn't much care who he was married to or the exact details of their bloodline.

"He's very close to his mother. Always has been. Viktor has assumed control of the family, the finances, the businesses. Everything."

"What does that have to do with me?"

"Sacha would prefer he did not have control of any of it. He's the…more intelligent of the two. Definitely the more reasonable."

"I'm sure he can hire a Russian hitman to take out his brother."

"It's not that simple."

"What's your relationship with Sacha Petrov?"

"We've done some business together. I'll be honest, it would be profitable for me, too, if Viktor was out of the picture. And here we have something else in common. You and I would both prefer Viktor dead."

"First you're pissed that I took out the father and now you want the son executed too?"

"Considering the circumstances, I adjusted my plans."

Silence as I study him.

"He raped her. But you already know that," he says casually.

My jaw ticks. This asshole knows exactly what buttons to push and how to push them. He sees my weakness. Probably has from day one.

"There's a dog fight." He reaches into his jacket pocket, takes out a folded piece of paper. He probably planned this all along. "Tonight. In a few hours in fact. Viktor will be there. He'll likely be drunk. And too trusting of soldiers he shouldn't be trusting of."

I reach to take the sheet of paper, unfold it, read the address. I hand it to Matthaeus who quickly sends the location to Charlie to check.

"Is this sufficient to start to build trust between

us? Coupled with the fact I saved your life the other night."

"I'm curious what you were doing inside Petrov's club in the first place. Quite the coincidence."

"There's no such thing as coincidence, Dante."

He knew I'd be there. How? Was he taking a chance I'd succeed in killing Petrov? Hedging his bets.

"No, there isn't. What were you doing there?"

"Sacha Petrov mentioned your…appointment."

So I'm right. He's working every angle.

"And he knows you're giving me this information about his brother. What is this some elaborate back-scratching scheme?"

"Business. That's all. I need something. He needs something. You need something. A show of faith is what I'm giving you tonight. Access to one of the men who hurt Mara."

I narrow my gaze. "If you're lying, if this is some sort of ambush—"

"It's not."

"I'll kill you," I say as if he hasn't spoken at all. "I'll do it slowly. The way I like." I look around the white space. "The hotel will have a hell of a cleaning bill."

He clears his throat, stands. "If you're finished threatening me, I'd like to get back to Sybil. She's had that thing in her ass for a couple of hours. Can't be comfortable, poor thing."

I stand. Someone opens the door, but we remain where we are, St. James and I have our eyes locked. And I'm more curious about him than ever.

The bodyguard clears his throat.

I smile. "Well," I start, taking one last look around. "Happy fucking then."

35

DANTE

The dog fight is taking place about an hour-and-a-half outside of the city in some beat-down, forgotten neighborhood in an abandoned warehouse that looks like it's been out of use for about a hundred years. There are no lights in the parking lot, but judging by the number of trucks, the event appears to be well attended. Sick fucks.

I drink a big swig of whiskey and pull on a baseball cap. Matthaeus and I walk to the building. I can already hear the voices of men and barking of dogs from here. Two men stand sentry at the entrance. They're big and have a general don't-fuck-with-me look to them. The one remains sitting on his stool assessing us while the other stands, gives a nod of his head as if to ask what our business here is.

"Can I help you?" he asks, giving us the once over.

"Hear there's some fun to be had," I say, reaching into my pocket for my wallet. "Money to be made."

"This is a private event," the man says.

I make sure he sees the bills I take out, fold over. Sees the money still left inside my wallet.

He drags his gaze from the wad of cash to me. "Like I said, private."

I sigh, take out another two hundred-dollar bills.

His colleague clears his throat. The man takes my money and gestures us in.

It's just the two of us going in although four men are waiting nearby. Bringing soldiers would only draw attention. And if St. James is right—and he'd better be fucking right—Viktor's soldiers will look away when I take him out.

The sound is amplified inside. It bounces off the large, cavernous space. The place was an old paper factory and although some equipment remains, it's mostly been gutted. The windows are all but gone and there's a chill in the air. Although I don't feel cold. I'm too amped up.

A makeshift bar stands along the edge of the crowd with kegs of beer at the ready. The space is dimly lit but brighter as we pass the bar and make our way to where most of the crowd has gathered. I'd guess there to be over two hundred people, mostly men, but a handful of women too.

A dog barks and there's a joint cheer from a group deeper in the circle. We push our way through, passing the place where caged dogs anxiously await their turn. I admit I'm not a dog lover per se, but this is just fucking wrong.

Matthaeus and I split up looking for Viktor Petrov. As I get closer to the pit I stand back and watch two men drag a Pitbull by its hind legs. It's a sickening sight. The dog is mangled. He's been mauled to death. And as I move around the crowd, I see the dog that did it. A big, mean looking thing.

Made mean by men, I remind myself.

I make out Viktor's soldiers pretty easily. They don't look like the others in here. Too well-dressed even in casual clothes. Most of these others look like they crawled out from some hole just to attend tonight's event.

Matthaeus is across the room. He gives a slight nudge of his head and I follow the direction to find Viktor Petrov crouching by the cage of a dog, talking to another man, the dog's owner, I'd guess. The dog is caged and leashed but when he lunges at Viktor, Viktor still stumbles backward, falling on his ass, spilling his drink before he gets to his feet, laughing.

He's clearly drunk. And stupid.

One of his men comes to his aid but Viktor shoves him away, turns back to the dog's owner and nods.

I pull my baseball cap down to hide the patch, grateful for the shadows, the lack of lighting. If he caught sight of me, would he recognize me? The eyepatch may make him look twice but would he know me?

A PA system comes on, screeching before someone taps and asks if *this thing is on* then laughs. The next fight is announced and Matthaeus walks toward the pit as the crowd divides to let the man Viktor was talking to lead his animal through. The dog is on a tight leash, and he snaps and growls at anyone who gets too close. I wonder how many men lose fingers or whole hands at these events. The stupid ones are drunk enough.

Viktor follows behind him holding a wad of cash up in the air, fist pumping it like he's already won.

I move into the crowd, losing sight of him momentarily as the other dog, the one that mauled the last losing dog, is brought back into the ring. Bets are placed and the man over the loudspeaker eggs them on, talking about the new fighter, about his victories. About how the current champion was just warming up for this, the biggest fight of the night.

Someone knocks into me as I weave through the crowd and beer splashes out of his plastic cup. He turns to me, expression pissed like he's about to start a fight himself. I straighten to my full height. He's almost as tall as me.

"You got some on me," I say after a glance at the few drops on my sleeve.

His gaze shifts between my eye, the scar on my

cheek and the patch. There's something to be said for wearing an eyepatch. On someone like me, it can be scary.

"Sorry, man," he says and backs away.

I turn, Matthaeus at my side now. The fight is about to begin.

Viktor is laughing, drinking sloppily out of his plastic cup. Only one of his soldiers is nearby. The others are standing outside of the crowd. I get the feeling they like this about as much as I do.

The dogfight begins and the crowd swells forward to watch. Viktor laughs. I notice how high-pitched the sound is. Like that of a crazy man. I'm close enough to see his hands now. They're dirty. Black under his fingernails. The wad of cash crumpled like it's passed through a thousand hands tonight alone.

I think about Mara.

Innocent Mara.

I think about his hands on her. Him forcing her. She's not even half his size.

That same fire that coursed through my veins the night I sat opposite Ivan Petrov in that cellar burns through me now. It makes my heart beat faster, dulls the sounds around me as it pumps hard and fast in my ears.

From the holster on my belt, I take out my dagger. Feel the cool weight of it in my palm. I step closer.

The crowd cheers, Viktor with them as the dog he's obviously bet on injures the champion. Well, the soon-to-be ex-champion. Matthaeus glances around, gives a nod. No soldiers have come forward apart from the one standing closest to him but just as I get close enough that I can almost touch Viktor, that soldier turns his head, and our eyes meet.

We remain like that for a moment.

Now is his opportunity. Now is the time to pull Viktor away. Protect him. It's his job. And I think about what I'll do if that happens. I think about my promise to Mara that I'd come back to her.

I won't leave here without killing Viktor Petrov no matter the cost.

I can't.

Even if it means breaking my promise to her.

I tighten my grip on the dagger's hilt, feel every curve of the design.

The soldier's eyes narrow and he turns away.

Neither Matthaeus nor I move as we wait to see if he's calling men over. More soldiers. But he doesn't. He just sips from his cup and keeps his back turned.

And I advance. Taking the two steps that will bring me to within stabbing distance of one of Mara's rapist.

I don't hesitate. And I don't bother to look him in the eye. He's not worth that. I just push my knife into his kidney, twist and tug it free, then repeat on the other kidney.

His body stiffens. There's a gurgling sound, then comes the stumble backward, his head turning, the remains of the idiotic grin on his face. Like his brain hasn't quite processed what just happened. Like his body has yet to register the pain. The meaning of it.

I catch him, keep him upright. Because I want him to know it's me, the man who killed his father come back for him. I want him to know that Mara is being avenged. Slowly but surely.

He turns just enough to see a glimpse of me, the eyepatch side of my face. His eyes grow huge. Good. He recognizes me.

I give him a wide grin as the cup drops from his hand. I hold him to me to push the bloody blade into his stomach. Not as soft as his father's but with just a little nudge, I manage. And, like I did with his father, I tug upward.

A choked sound escapes his lips, and his eyes roll back. Blood dribbles from the corner of his mouth. He's dead.

And every time I think I will feel some satisfaction. With each kill I think I'll feel a little better. But no wrongs are righted. No damage undone. I could massacre every soldier who ever had a hand in her captivity, and it wouldn't matter. Because she still lost fifteen years of her life. And she'll be lucky if it's only the fifteen. If she can make a life at all.

With a grunt I push Viktor off, turning to walk away as I holster the bloody dagger. Matthaeus is at my side and we're out of the crowd before the first scream comes. A man's scream. No one stops us as we walk back to the entrance, to the front doors of the place. Even the soldiers standing guard outside only nod, one making the comment that it's a short night for us.

I don't bother to respond. We get back to the SUV and I climb into the passenger seat, pick up the bottle of whiskey on the floor.

Fuck. I need a drink. Need to wash my hands. Viktor's blood feels too sticky and I have a sick feeling in my gut at the thought of her at that man's mercy.

I need to get back to the house. Back to her. Need to see her. Touch her. Feel her beneath me. Hold her. Take her. Banish all the memories of those years from her mind.

And I need her to do the same for me. To forgive me for leaving her on her own for so long. Forgive me for living my life while she was out there in the hands of monsters like this.

Forgive me for ever letting any of this happen to her.

36

MARA

I lie awake watching the hands of the clock tick through the minutes. It's late. He should have been back by now. Should have been back hours ago.

But then I hear it. The sound of tires crunching rocks beneath. I push the blanket off and hurry to the window. My room is beside the master, directly over the front entrance. I wanted to be in his room. I thought I would be. But the man who seemed to be in charge told me this was mine. Noah's, at least, is across the hall.

From here I watch three SUVs pull up to the house, but I don't breathe a sigh of relief just yet. I won't until I see him.

The vehicles come to a stop and soldiers spill out. I count. Four from the first two vehicles. Not Dante, though.

The driver opens the door of the last one and I hold my breath, but I know it's not Dante even from this distance. It's Matthaeus. But then the passenger side door opens and there he is. Dante.

I exhale and warm tears fill my eyes. I touch a hand to the window, laying my forehead against it, finally able to breathe again. He slams the door shut and I notice his steps are uneven. I know why when I see the bottle in his hand, watch him bring it to his mouth.

My heart races as he disappears into the house, and it takes all I have not to go running out of the room and down the stairs. It takes all I have to stand here at the window as I listen for him. Hear someone ascend the stairs.

A door opens. Closes. I watch mine all along. My back to the window.

A few minutes later, there's a rumble of voices outside. His.

"Why isn't she in my room?"

My heart races, my smile wide. He wanted me in his room.

"Fix it," he says just as my door opens and there he is. Standing in the doorway. Taking up all that space, the soft light of the sconces on the walls outside making a golden halo around him. My fallen angel. My broken angel.

He steps inside, his gaze sweeping over me in the dim light of the bedside lamp. He closes the door and sets the almost empty bottle on the nightstand to come closer.

I see then the stains that color the front of his jacket, the cuffs of his sleeves.

Blood.

I smell him. Sweat and whiskey and something else. Something dark. I push hair back from his forehead as he watches me, my beast.

He's careful not to touch me. When I look down, I see why. His hands are dirty.

I reach out to take them, but he closes them into fists.

"Don't," he says.

I glance up then down and I hold them, turn them. After a moment he opens them so I can see his palms.

"I need to wash," he says and moves to pull free. When I tug, he stops.

I trace a finger through the dried blood on his palm.

He captures my wrist and I'm surprised at the force of his grip.

"Don't," he repeats.

"Did you kill St. James?"

He shakes his head.

"Who then?"

"Viktor Petrov."

"Viktor?" I'm surprised.

He nods and I smile. My avenging angel.

I reach my free hand to touch his face, rise on tiptoe to kiss his mouth. I taste whiskey and I want more. I slide my hand down over his hard chest, undo the button of his jeans, push down the zipper just enough that I can slip my hand inside and cup him.

He sucks in a breath as I wrap my hand around the shaft, feel the smooth skin.

I slip my tongue into his mouth and he kisses me back, releasing my wrist to fist my hair and tug my head backward. The kiss grows urgent as I squeeze my hand around him, stroke him.

He groans, moves me to the bed and pushes me onto it. He sets one knee between my legs, looking down at me, hair disheveled, face dark with desire. The white gown I'm wearing is nearly translucent, the buttons undone at the top, so my breasts are available to him. He fingers the delicate lace trim then tugs it aside, and we see the smear of dark red on soft white at the same moment.

"I need to wash," he says, voice hoarse as if he hasn't spoken in a while.

I shake my head, reach out to touch him, to grip the waistband of his jeans to tug him toward me. "Fuck me."

He pushes my hand away. "After."

"Now." He watches me as I take his dirty hand and push it into the gown, over my breast. "Now.

With his blood on you. Fuck me with his blood on you."

It's sick, I know, but some part of me wants this. Needs it. A victory of sorts. My tormentor dead. His blood on me as I live.

"I need you to," I say.

He squeezes my breast, draws it out and grips the nightgown, ripping it partially. He looks at me as he finishes the task, the fine fabric slipping through his fingers as he rips it the rest of the way and takes me in. I'm completely naked. I hadn't worn panties. His gaze moves slowly over me, head to toe, pausing between my legs, then back to my face.

"Hands and knees. Ass to me."

My belly flips and I swallow hard as I climb to my knees and turn over. I know what he wants and I lower myself to my elbows. Arch my back. I want this too. A primal fucking. Like the animals we are.

He makes a sound from deep inside his chest. I don't think it's conscious as I look at his face, his gaze on my offering. I'm his. Doesn't he know that? All of me. Every part of me. I was made for him. I've always been his.

He discards his jacket, his shirt, then sets one knee on the bed, jeans still on. He pushes them down just far enough to fist his cock. With the other hand he grips my ass and spreads me open. He looks at me there. He can see all of me and I watch him as he does, feeling the trickle of my own arousal slide down the inside of my thigh.

He brings himself to my entrance and I arch deeper, closing my eyes as I feel him slide into me. Stretching me. Filling me.

"Hard. Do it hard."

"Mara—"

"I need it."

He grips both cheeks pulling me wide and drawing out.

My eyelids fly open, and I turn back to find him dipping his head to me, licking me like he did before from hole to hole and back.

"Oh, god."

He straightens, keeps me spread open. "I need to wash," he says, but I know he won't walk away. Not now. Not the way he's looking at me.

"I want his blood on me."

He studies me.

"Please."

He finally nods and pushes into me the way I want. I suck in a breath.

"Fuck, Mara," he utters as he takes me the way I need, hard and rough. I think it's what he needs too. To fuck the past out of me. To fuck all those other men out of me. He kneads my ass as he drills into me and soon, I'm lying flat on my belly, arms over my head, wrists inside his hands, his weight on me, breath at my neck.

"I'm going to come," I tell him as he shifts my wrists into one of his hands. With the other, he grips a handful of hair turning my head so I'm looking at him when my release comes. When the first wave takes me under, all I can feel is him. All I can breathe is him. All I want is him.

When I open my eyes again, I find him watching me, gaze intent. Dark. He draws out, turns me onto my back and reenters me. I'm spent, raw, but I still want and need so much. When he kisses me, it's all teeth and lips and I taste the copper of blood. I don't know if it's mine or his. He shifts his grip to my thigh and pushes it up, opening me wider. He draws back a little, just enough so he can watch us together, watch me take his cock slippery with my arousal, my come.

"You're so fucking beautiful," he groans.

I smile, arch my back, my clit rubbing against him.

"Perfect," he manages before thrusting one final time, a groan coming from deep in his chest as he throbs inside me, making me come again as he empties. And we are one. The way we were always meant to be but better. Fiercer.

Whole and broken at the same time. Together.

37

DANTE

I carry her to my room, into the bathroom where I fill the tub with hot water, bathe her and wash myself before taking her to my bed.

She looks up at me, sleepy-eyed. "I can walk you know."

I smile, tuck her in then climb in beside her.

The brand at her hip is healing. I don't want to bring it up now, though. I don't want to talk about any of that, but I will have to think of what to do with it. How to somehow cover it up so she doesn't have to see it daily, a constant reminder of the horror that happened to her.

No. I stop myself.

The horror she survived.

She is strong. A survivor. I should not forget that. She is a fierce warrior in her own right. *My* fierce warrior. She just needed my help to ascend to her rightful place. The place she always belonged.

"How did you do it?" she asks, eyes half-closed. She must be exhausted. She hasn't slept in twenty-four hours.

"A knife in his kidneys. In his gut."

"Bloody?"

"Very." She's dark.

"Did he know why?"

"Yes."

"Good."

"Was it only Viktor?" I don't want to say the rest of the question out loud. Was it only Viktor who touched you?

Her eyes shift away and she's momentarily that little girl again. But she collects herself and I can almost see her steel herself. She nods. "Sacha didn't like that I was there. He tried to stop Viktor once, but Viktor was bigger than him. Stronger."

She grows quiet, rests her cheek against my chest, fingers tracing a scar along my shoulder, slowly moving up to the one on my face. We lie like this for a long time and just when I think she might be falling asleep, she speaks.

"Do you think I'll ever forget?"

"No," I tell her. It's the only honest answer.

She's quiet for a long moment before speaking. "In a way, I don't want to."

"Why?"

"I don't know. I can't lose another part of myself, you know?"

I tug her closer to me. "You're a survivor. It takes strength to survive and you're strong."

She shifts her head a little and I can feel her looking at me as she begins to caress the scar on my cheek. "Do you want to forget all the things that happened to you and your family?"

"No. I only wish I could undo them."

"Do you miss them?"

I nod once.

"Is it strange that I don't miss anyone? Not even my grandmother?"

I turn my head to look at her then. "What do you mean strange?"

"I don't know. Do you think there's something wrong with me?"

"I think you did what you had to do to survive. Stop thinking about it. You can't change what happened to you. You can only move forward."

Silence again. And again, I think she's asleep but then she brings her fingers to the patch. The instant she does, I capture her wrist.

"Don't."

She gasps, not expecting that. "What's under it?"

"Nothing you need to see."

"Why? Do you think I'll find it ugly? Do you think I could find anything about you ugly?"

I switch my grip so I'm tracing a circle on her

wrist with my thumb and close my eye. "Leave it alone, Mara. Get some sleep."

"You know what happened to me. The things they did." Her eyes fill up. "Do you think I'm ugly?"

I look at her. "No. Fuck no. Never."

"Then how can you ever think I'd find anything about you ugly?"

"Sweetheart, I'm not worried about you finding it ugly. I just don't want to scare you."

She laughs outright. "Scare me? Dante, I've lived with monsters. I can't be scared by my angel."

I must look confused because she lays her hand softly on my cheek.

"It's what you are. An angel who fell and broke when he hit the ground. Who has now become my guardian angel."

"You mean your avenging angel. Or devil more likely."

She smiles again. "Angel for sure. My avenging angel." She grows quiet, the sad smile vanishing. "I love you. I've always loved you. You're like the other half of me. Always were all those years. I thought of you every day. You're the only person I thought of. How can I be scared by something that is so much a part of me?"

I just watch her, take in her honesty, her strength. And what I want to do is keep her with me forever. Spend the rest of my life slaying her demons. But there's a part of me that's torn. That knows why she thinks she loves me. That part that knows there's better for her. Better than me. Knows if I were a better person, if I were truly the angel she believes me to be and not a devil, I'd let her go.

"It's empty. Under the patch. I don't wear the prosthetic." I reach up, pull the patch off. I don't know what I expect. A gasp. A cry. Her hand covering her mouth. The disgust she'll try to hide.

But her expression is unreadable and a moment later, she leans in and kisses my eyelid. And I think how good she is. How much better than me she deserves.

38

DANTE

The next night I leave Mara in the kitchen when I get a text from Charlie to contact him right away. Matthaeus and I make our way to the study where my laptop is already set up to log on to FaceTime Charlie. He answers on the second ring. He's in Cristiano's office on the island.

"Matthaeus updated us on Viktor Petrov," Cristiano says.

"One more down. One to go. Plus, whoever Pérez's buyer is. Any word on that?" I hope that's why he's reaching out because it's late in Italy.

"No, but there is something else. I got my hands on a photo that I'm not sure what to make of," Charlie says. "It's old, I'm thinking five years."

"Five years?"

"I'll show you why I think that in a second. I can't be sure where it's taken but I'd guess Mexico, not the states." The screen flicks and I'm looking at a photograph where Felix is sitting on the couch. Behind him stand two guards. There's a couple beside them. The woman is heavily pregnant. But it's not her that has piqued my curiosity.

"Is that Jericho St. James?"

I peer closer, try to figure out what's changed because yes, that's him. But not. This man is younger, obviously. And his expression is happy. He has his arm wrapped possessively over the shoulders of the woman.

"Is he married? Is that his wife?"

"No, not married. At least not that I could find. And no kids. I'm doing more digging but look at the far corner. I'm going to zoom in."

I look and am again surprised. "Mara?" She's sitting across the table from a woman and they're rolling dough together. She's smiling at the woman, and it looks like one of her legs is mid-swing beneath the table. "She can't be more than fourteen, fifteen." Which explains the timeline Charlie came up with.

Matthaeus gets up, goes to the door, and instructs a soldier to get Mara. He returns with her a few minutes later.

"What is it?" she asks anxiously.

I turn the screen to show her the photograph. "Do you remember this?"

She walks to the desk, peers down. Her face is a little paler when she looks back up at me.

"That's Flora," she says, pointing to the woman sitting across from her. Tears fill her eyes. "She left a few weeks after that day. Just disappeared. Never even said goodbye."

I watch her, wanting nothing more than to go to her, take her in my arms and tell her it will be all right.

"I think he hurt her," she adds.

Fuck. I hate this. I hate this so much.

"Do you know this couple?" Matthaeus asks as if sensing my reluctance to bring her any more pain.

"I don't know them, but she was nice. She let me feel the baby kick."

"Any idea who she is?"

"Kimberly. It's what he called her. This man." She points to Jericho St. James. "I think he was her husband."

"Was?"

"She died soon after that day."

"How do you know that?"

"Felix told me when I asked if I'd get to see her and the baby. Kimberly had said I could visit. She thought it was going to be a girl but wasn't sure."

Listening to her, I hear how young she is in so many ways. How inexperienced even given what she's been through. She has been almost sheltered in her captivity and at the same time, so not. Guilt gnaws at my gut. She shouldn't be here. She should be home. Out of harm's way. It was selfish of me to bring her.

But I shove those thoughts aside and something else nudges at me. I ask a question I'm not sure I want the answer to.

"Did Felix have anything to do with her death?"

She shifts her gaze to me, and her eyes darken. "I don't know why you need to ask. He had everything to do with it."

39

DANTE

Jericho St. James is visibly put out when he walks into the living room of the penthouse suite. His hair is ruffled like he's been running his hands through it, and he's dressed more casually than I've seen him before. He's in jeans and a white button down, the sleeves of which are rolled up to his forearm exposing a full sleeve dragon tattoo on one arm and the tail of a twin dragon creeping out from under the sleeve of the other. Along with his watch I notice a bracelet of worn wooden beads. Prayer beads. The tattoos fit. So does the watch. But that bracelet? Not so much. It's not his. I don't know how I know it, but I do.

"Have you come to thank me in person for providing Viktor's whereabouts?" he asks, drawing my gaze to his face as he tucks his hands into his pockets. "Or anxious I don't bail before giving you Pérez's location on Saturday night?"

I grin, take out the folded sheet of paper from my pocket, unfolding it and holding it out to him. "I'm here to ask you about this." It's the photo Charlie had found.

For a split second, I see the expression of surprise on his face. Of shock, even. His eyes lock on the grainy 8x10 printout. It takes him a moment to school his features but when he shifts his gaze to mine, I see his Adam's apple work as he swallows. See something in his eyes as he tries to appear indifferent.

"Drink?" he asks, turning to walk toward the sideboard where a decanter of whiskey stands. His posture is stiff, shoulders tight. I wonder if his hands are fisted in his pockets as he crosses the room on wooden legs.

Without waiting for a reply, he pours two glasses of whiskey and carries them to the sitting area. He makes a point of not looking at the picture I've set on the coffee table as he hands me one of the tumblers.

"What's the real reason you want him?" I ask.

He swallows the whiskey and takes the same seat as last time, gesturing to his bodyguard to leave.

"Are you sure?" the man asks.

"It's fine, Dex," he says. "Just bring me the bottle before you go."

I watch him as he finishes his drink. The giant of

a man, Dex, sets the decanter on the coffee table before he leaves.

St. James puts his glass down and instead of pouring himself another, he pulls the printed photograph closer and picks it up. I'm not sure I'm imagining the slight tremble of his hand. For a long moment, he studies the printout, his face partially obscured by the paper. He then folds it over, sets it back down and looks at me.

"Do you think she's safe with you?" he asks.

"What?"

"Mara. Do you think she's safe with you?"

I narrow my gaze, sip my drink.

"I'm asking you a question. Do you think now that you have her in your possession that she's safe?" There's something urgent in his tone. Something hard and old.

My jaw tightens. I know where he's going. "No," I answer.

"Then you are wiser than I was." He leans forward to take the bottle and pours himself a hefty glass full.

"Who is she?"

"Who *was* she," he corrects and drinks a long swallow. "Kimberly." His reaction isn't what I expect. I don't know if it's the surprise of seeing that photograph or what. He's rattled. Visibly upset. And he isn't quite looking at me.

"Who was she to you?" I push.

"My fiancée."

"The baby—"

He doesn't answer but I see the tightening of his jaw, the twitch of his eye.

This isn't the same man I'd met days before. He's not the asshole who saved my life then threw me out of a moving vehicle. Not the same cool, collected dick dismissing us to fuck his maid as he casually gave me the location of a Russian mobster to kill. This man before me is simply human. And I see the cracks of his humanity. The brokenness of him.

But I steel myself. His pain has nothing to do with me. And this is about saving Mara. So, I reach for the photo, open it, study it. "Too bad. She was good looking," I say. Dick move, I know.

He doesn't comment. Just drinks.

"You all seem like you're having a good time while a kidnapped girl sits just a few feet from you."

"I didn't know who she was. And I didn't know Felix Pérez. Hell, didn't realize there was a photograph. I'm guessing a still taken from a video."

It does look that way. But like his pain, I don't give a shit. "You didn't know him? Because you seem chummy to me. What were you doing there if you didn't know him?"

"Business that doesn't concern you," his tone is firm, the mask of that other Jericho St. James back in place.

"Anything having to do with Pérez concerns me."

"Not this."

"What about Mara? You saw her and did nothing?"

"She didn't seem distressed."

"No? So, she didn't stand out at all as not really belonging there?"

"Like I said, I didn't know anything about her, not until after."

"After what?" I ask, tossing the photo back onto the coffee table making sure it's face up, so he has to look at it.

His eyes lock on it and there's that crack in the exterior again. "She was eight weeks from delivering." It takes me a moment to realize he's talking about the pregnant woman. "She was so excited. So happy. It was all she could talk about." He takes a sip of whiskey. "But she never got to experience any of it. She was killed not a full week after that ill-fated visit to Pérez."

He's quiet, his pain palpable and immense. He then shifts his gaze to me and again I see the slight difference in the color of his eyes, the deep gray of one and dark blue of the other. How whatever is going on inside him makes the one go darker and the other lighter.

"My meeting with Pérez was on behalf of a client. I used to practice law but I'm sure you know that. Kimberly and I were traveling at the time and, well, I regret having brought her. If I'd left her at the hotel..." he trails off, shakes his head. "But I was naïve then." He swallows more whiskey. "Stupid even. And she paid for it."

His eyes lock on the woman and I see his regret.

"We were at a café a few days later. It was the morning we were due to return to the states. Just having breakfast on the beach. She wanted to feel the sand between her toes one last time, she said." He smiles a rueful smile at that. "We had thought about building a house there. Beachfront. Made plans and even looked at some land." He looks at me, face hard again. "Never make fucking plans. Never," he advises.

"What happened?"

"I went inside to pay the bill. She was gathering up her things. I realized when I got to the counter, I'd left my wallet on the table and returned. She must have noticed it before I did because she was walking toward me as I got outside, flip-flops in one hand, a big smile on her face," he pauses here. "She got in the way," he finally adds. He shifts his gaze away, pushes his hand into his hair like he's going to pull it out. "Fuck. She just got in the fucking way."

He collects himself after a moment and turns back to me.

"You were the target?"

He nods.

"It was Pérez?" I ask.

"Not personally, obviously. I'm honestly not sure

he's ever actually killed a man. Just gives the orders. Piece of shit." He swallows a big swallow of whiskey.

"Why did he do it? Who are you to him?"

"He was hired. He didn't know me from Adam. I need to confirm who it was that hired him."

"Confirm. So, you know?"

"I have my suspicions."

I put two and two together. "And the meeting that was allegedly recorded will confirm your suspicion?"

"Not alleged and yes." His gaze shifts and he's studying me now. "Betrayal by those closest to you burns hotter, don't you think?"

"Are we bonding?"

"Fuck you."

"Where will he be?"

He tilts his head infinitesimally to the side. He's got the upper hand on this one. He has the information I need. "You'll need to bring the girl."

"No."

"Then you're wasting my time."

"Tell me where he'll be. I'll be there. I'll get you what you need."

"You need to bring the girl. It's the deal."

"Why? What deal have you made with him?"

"If I tell him she'll be there, he will come."

"So tell him she'll be there."

He breathes in a deep breath.

"This is my offer. Tell him what you need to tell

him to get him there and I'll get you what you want." I put my glass down.

"I held her as she died, you know," he says, his gaze is on that sheet of paper. That sliver of history. "I know what you've seen," he continues. "What you've been through. But let me ask you something. Have you felt the life slip away from someone while you watch? While you cradle their body against you begging the god you once believed in to spare them? To take you instead?"

I clench my teeth and shift my gaze away.

"I can tell you it's not something you ever want to experience. Never want to see or feel." He closes his eyes, and when he opens them again, the look inside them is different. Like there's an infinite sadness locked inside there that this memory has unlocked. "Their eyes change as the soul slips from the body, do you know that? The good ones, at least. The innocent ones. You and me, we don't have souls left to lose but the innocents? You see the light go out." He picks up the bottle of whiskey and refills his glass then downs the whole thing. "So, if you're smart, Dante, you'll be rid of Mara for her own sake. Get her a new identity. Make her disappear. It's the only chance she'll have at a life."

40

MARA

Dante doesn't come home until after four in the morning. I've drifted off to a restless sleep when the crunching of gravel beneath tires wakes me. I push the blanket off, get up and go to the window. By the time I get there he's inside.

I wait for him but when the clock just keeps ticking and twenty minutes have passed, I pull a robe on over my naked body and walk quietly down the stairs.

I can hear a couple of soldiers in the kitchen, but the study is quiet. The strip of light underneath the door and the sound of music tell me he's probably inside, so I knock. I don't get an answer and I wonder if he can hear me, so I push the door open and peek my head in. Dante is sitting in near darkness behind the large oak desk. The only light comes from the dim lamp on his desk. It casts a shadow over half of his face as he lifts it from whatever it is he's looking at. When he sees it's me he doesn't say anything. Just sits back and watches me slip inside and close the door behind me.

I walk around the desk. He picks up the glass of whiskey and swallows what's left inside. I notice the bottle is nearly empty and can smell the whiskey on him.

"You drink too much," I tell him as I undo the belt of my robe.

He pushes his seat back a little and takes me in, the robe split open. I watch as his dark gaze slides over me, pausing at the slit of my sex before returning to my eyes.

"You should be in bed," he says, licking his lips as he leans his head back and watches me kneel between his spread legs. When I reach for his belt, he doesn't stop me. I undo the buckle, then the button and zipper of his jeans.

"Mara," he groans but it's half-hearted.

I take him out and he is already getting hard. I stroke the smooth skin of his cock and bring my tongue to the very tip, lick the salty drop there.

He sucks in a breath and closes his hand over the back of my head. "Fuck."

I dip my head down to take him into my mouth, hearing the rumble of a moan inside his chest. I wonder if he needs this as much as I do. This closeness. Wonder if he needs me as much as I need him.

"Stop," he says half-heartedly, fingers caressing the back of my head, doing the opposite of what he's saying.

I turn my gaze up. Slide my mouth over him.

He watches me, something sad in his eyes as he closes his fingers in my hair, his cock growing thicker, harder. I taste him, the first salty drops as he guides himself deeper.

I curl my hands around his thighs and relax my throat as he takes control. He's slow at first, watching me as he guides me over him. But as the urgency grows, his fingers pull at my hair and his breathing changes. The muscles of his thighs tense beneath my hands as he begins to fuck my face. He's slow at first until he can't anymore. He rises to stand, bracing one hand on the edge of the desk as he leans over me, gripping a handful of my hair, keeping me still as he watches me take him. Watches me catch my breath every time he draws out. Watches me swallow his cock as he pushes deeper and deeper, thrusting faster. But all the while I can see he's fighting with himself. This urgency, this desire to take. To fuck. To own. Fighting this thing. Fighting us. When I choke at the next thrust, he curses as he pulls out, abruptly releasing me.

"You should go," he says, his voice gravelly, thick, not sounding like him. "You shouldn't be here."

"I can do it," I say, thinking he stopped because he thought he was hurting me. When I try to take him into my mouth again, he grips my hair again, pulling my head back. He looks down at me with that tortured look on his face. "Let me try again. Please," I say.

His eyebrows furrow. It's as though in his head he's in another world. He drags me up to my feet. I stumble, reaching out for his chest to steady myself and there's that look again, that broken thing deep inside him surfacing. A thing that can't be fixed.

"Fuck, Mara," he says, and he pulls me to him, kissing me hard. "Fuck."

Before I can ask what it is, what's going on, he shifts his grip to lift me up. He sets me on the edge of the desk and opens the robe to look at me. I set my feet on the armrests of the chair behind him and his gaze drops between my spread legs.

"I'm yours," I say. I am. I'm only his. Only ever been his. I don't understand why he's resisting the pull between us.

He drops his head, shakes it, then moments later kisses the space between my breasts before licking one nipple, taking it between his teeth and sucking.

I cry out, wrapping my hands around the back of his head, feeling every sensation like a live electrical wire starting at my center and spreading out inside me. I want to come. I need to come.

"Please," I gasp when he draws back, my nipple

hardening in the sudden cool of the room with his warm mouth gone. He gives me one glance before taking the other nipple, my breath catching as he brings his mouth to mine and presses his cock against me.

"One more time," he says, cupping the back of my head with one hand as he lays me down gently on the desk. "Just once more."

Once more? I don't understand but before I can ask, before I can say anything, he's inside me, stretching me, gaze locked on me. His thrusts are barely controlled, and I wrap my legs around him, arching my back, wanting to get closer, closer, needing to.

"Christ. Fuck." He takes hold of one thigh and bends my knee back, shifting my position a little. I moan because, like this, I feel him deeper inside me.

"I'm going to come," I manage, my eyes closing as he leans down to kiss me, both hands on my face now as if he's imploring me to open my eyes, to look at him. And when I do, what I see breaks my heart. Even as my body bucks beneath his, and ecstasy washes over me, my heart splinters as it does. As I hear his words, understand their meaning. "I love you!" I cry out, desperate.

He leans his head against mine, stopping for a moment, sweat slick between us. He holds me tight, mutters a curse, and resumes his thrusts more powerful than before as he groans his release, emptying inside me.

And I think this is it. I know it is. The last of him. The last of us.

I close my eyes and wrap my arms tight around him, feeling the agony after the ecstasy. I cling to him as he shudders with his release, his weight heavy on me, his breathing hard. He's spent. Like he's given me all he can give me.

He straightens and I feel cold as I sit up. He tucks himself into his jeans, buttons them. Doesn't bother with the zipper or his belt. His gaze is heavy as I sit up and he closes the robe around me, tying it.

"Dante?" I want to ask what's happened, but I'm afraid. I don't want to hear. To know. I'll hold on to this illusion as long as I can. Because for all that's happened to me, I'm not sure I've felt my heart break quite like this.

"You should go to your bed," he says, voice taut, tone sharp. He walks away with the bottle of whiskey in one hand.

I don't miss the wording. "Come with me."

He doesn't answer. Just sits down on the couch where the light barely reaches him, leaving his face in shadows. But even then, I know he's watching me.

"You drink too much," I tell him again.

I slip off the desk, feel the warm wetness between my thighs. Something drops off the desk and I turn to pick it up. That's when I see what he was looking at. It's a folder full of photographs. I bend to pick up the few that have slipped to the floor, sitting on his chair to look at them. I spread them out over the desk. The photos are torn and they're all of one man. I know him. And I don't like him. It's his uncle.

"What were you doing?" It's as though he's taken every photo his uncle was posed in and torn him out. I don't know where the other halves are.

"Nothing."

"Not nothing. These are all ripped."

He drinks straight from the bottle.

"Dante?"

"You need to go, Mara."

But I am not ready to hear that. Because I know what he means. "What are these? What were you doing?" I ask instead.

It takes him a long time to say something. So long that I'm not sure he will speak at all. Then he finally does. "He's not my uncle."

"What do you mean?"

He shakes his head. "You're not safe with me. You'll never be safe with me. You know that, right?"

I close my eyes, shake my head. He can't do this. "Tell me about your uncle."

He takes a deep breath in and when he exhales it's a sigh. "You want to know why all this happened? Why my family was massacred? Why you were kidnapped and..." he trails off, looks away shaking his head. "Why what happened to you happened?"

I don't answer. I can't.

"Because you know, when you said a while back that the Dante you knew wouldn't have let what happened to you happen—"

"I was just—"

"No, you were right. You were actually more right than you could have known. But I was never that Dante. The hero. Because what happened to you, and to everyone else, happened because of me." He swallows three big gulps. "It all happened because I was born. And it's not finished. It will never be finished."

I stay where I am, glance at the torn-up photos then back to him.

"He's not my uncle. Well, wasn't. He's not alive anymore. I took care of that."

"What?"

"He raped my mother. Got her pregnant." He raises his arms into the air and in this strange half-light, a joker-like grin warps his features making him look strange and not like himself, not my Dante. "And ta-da! I was born. A bastard. A rape-child. A hate-child."

"I don't believe...your mother loved you."

"She did. The hate...it was for David. You see, my mother rejected him but kept his secret from my father. Or at least the man I grew up thinking was my father. If she hadn't, they'd probably still be alive. I may be dead, but they'd be alive. You'd have had a normal life. Grown up on the island, gone to school. Probably be at some university maybe, with Lizzy, dating boys your age and just living like a twenty-year-old should live. Not like this. Not in hiding from criminals. Not having lived as a sex slave to those bastards. Used and sold. And certainly not fucking someone like me. Because I am one of those monsters, Mara. It's in my blood. You knew it at the start. You know it in your heart. And as long as you're with me, you're not safe."

I can't quite absorb his words, his meaning. I get up, go to him. I don't sit beside him but kneel on the floor at his feet and lay my head on his lap.

"What happened tonight?" I ask. "What changed?"

He closes his hand over the back of my head, and I hear him swallow two glugs of whiskey.

"You're not a monster," I tell him when he doesn't answer.

"Yes, I am."

"And I'm only safe with you."

"No, sweetheart," he says, the expression on his face as he looks down at me, as he pets my hair, so sad and broken. "I wish it were true but no, you're not."

"It wasn't your fault. Even if your uncle...your..." I trail off.

"Father. The word you're searching for is father."

"No," I say, straightening, setting my hands on his thighs, and looking up at him now. "You're Lizzie's brother. Your father was her father, the man who raised you and loved you. Your uncle was the monster. Not you."

He snorts, brings that bottle back to his mouth, so I reach for it.

"It's enough, you've had too much already."

"Let go, sweetheart. I'll say when it's enough." He gets to his feet, easily shrugs me off and drinks as if to make a point.

I stand and when I try to take the bottle from him, he grabs my wrist.

"I said let go. Go up to your bed—"

"My bed? Not yours? Not ours?"

"There is no ours."

"I don't believe you."

"It's better for you. Safer."

I shake my head, try to tug free so I can get the bottle. "I'm not going without you."

"Yes, you are. And this thing between us, it stops. Now."

"No." I try to grab the bottle with my other hand, but he tugs me roughly away and forces me to sit on the couch.

"St. James is right," he says.

St. James. The man from the photograph. "Right about what?"

"You don't want to leave, suit yourself. I'll leave. But this is finished. I should never have started it in the first place. That's on me." He drinks the last of the whiskey, sets the bottle down and starts to walk away. "But I'll be damned if I steal one more thing from you."

"I want this. You can't steal what I freely give!" I'm on my feet and grabbing his wrist to stop him. He spins, has me by both arms and slams me against the wall. My head spins and it takes my vision a moment to steady. His grip is harder than it's ever been before. I forget how strong he is. But then he lets go and I wish he'd hold onto me. I don't even care if he bruises me. I can't be without him. Doesn't he know that?

"See. This is what I mean. Exactly what I mean," he says. "I can only ever hurt you."

He's drunk. That's what this is. It's the alcohol talking. "It's not finished. We're not finished. I'm yours, Dante. And you're mine. It's our destiny. Don't you know that? Don't you know anything?"

"Destiny." He shakes his head, laughs outright.

I slam my fists into his chest. "Yes, destiny!"

He grabs my wrists. "You're young. And somehow have held on to your innocence. I won't steal that from you either." He releases my wrists and takes a step back. "Haven't you had enough of monsters to last you a lifetime?"

"You're not a monster. Not *my* monster. It's what you said. You said—"

"That was before. This, what's happened between us, it's wrong. I can't be with you. I should never have started it. You should be with someone safe. Someone like Noah. Not a cold-blooded killer."

"You're not that!" My voice breaks and my eyes mist.

"I am, sweetheart. I am exactly that." He cups my face with one hand, fingers warm. His expression softens. "And you know it."

I lean into his touch. "I don't want anyone else," I say.

He shakes his head and walks toward the door. I find myself slumping, leaning my weight against the wall.

"I want you," I say so quietly I'm not sure he hears.

"Tomorrow, you and Noah are gone. Charlie's arranging a safe place for you until we can get everything worked out."

"What?" I'm not sure I'm hearing right, not over the shattering of my heart.

"You'll have a new identity. Start a new life. Then you'll be free, Mara. Truly free to have a life."

"Dante—"

"A life without me."

41

DANTE

It's Saturday night. I check my watch waiting for a call from Matthaeus. A text. Something to tell me it's done. She's safe. I haven't asked him or Charlie for Mara's location. I don't want to know because I'm not sure I'll be able to stay away.

Truth is that what St. James said scared me. Scared the fuck out of me, in fact. I can take all the shit life throws my way. I can deal with the low life pieces of trash of this world. But bedding Mara? It shouldn't have happened. I shouldn't have touched her.

She thinks she loves me. And what the fuck did I expect would happen? She's a girl. A girl who's been through hell and somehow survived it. I'm a man for fuck's sake. What did I fucking expect?

Noah was right that morning he stormed into Cristiano's office to beat the crap out of me. I only wish he'd been strong enough to do it. But then that would make him a monster too, wouldn't it? And she needs someone who isn't that. A protector who isn't a predator.

Is there such a thing? A coin has two sides.

No. That's bullshit.

I've been holed up in the study for two days. We've got eyes on Jericho St. James but so far, nothing. He hasn't moved from his location at the penthouse. But it's Saturday night. If anything is going to happen it's going to happen tonight. Charlie is working on tapping into his phone but again, nothing. The guy is locked down tight.

I twist the cap off the bottle of whiskey sitting on my desk but close it again. Mara's right. I do drink too damn much. I check my phone for a message from Charlie for the hundredth time. Pérez is here. It's why St. James is still in town. It's the only reason. He's a desperate man. He's been hunting for the killer of his fiancée for five years. This is his chance. He wants confirmation of who put the hit out, and the way to get that, is to draw the son of a bitch out and get the recording from him. Although if it were me and I had a suspicion, I'd trust my gut.

But then I think about what he said. About the betrayals of those closest to us being the hardest to bear.

I pick up my phone to call Charlie again, but a knock at the door comes and a moment later,

Matthaeus enters. He looks like he's had about as much sleep as me.

"Is it done?" I ask.

"Moved them twice, changed vehicles, men. She'll be safe."

"Good. How many soldiers did you leave?"

"Two in the apartment, two more in the building and constant guard outside."

I nod and ask the question I really want to ask. "How was she?"

"Upset. Put up a hell of a fight."

My jaw clenches.

He sits on the chair across from mine. I see how tired he looks but he studies me quietly. "You sure about this?"

"It's best for her."

"Is it?" he asks.

The image of Mara standing ghost-like on that cliff appears in my mind. "What do you mean? Someone's watching her, right? She's not alone."

"How long can you keep someone on her 24/7?"

"As long as it takes."

"I get it, what she's feeling. You saved her life."

"That's the point. She hasn't had a life—"

"Risked your own for her," he continues as if I haven't spoken. "You're probably the only man she can think of who hasn't hurt her."

"I've hurt her."

"Have you considered… When this is over, going back for her?"

I look down at the phone on my desk. Screen is still black.

"When Pérez is dead. When St. James is out of the picture," he adds.

St. James's words play in my mind. It's not just Pérez. Monsters crowd me at every turn. I can't cast my shadow over her. I won't. Not if I have a chance to give her what she deserves.

"You can bring her back. Keep her," he says, possibly confusing my silence for acquiescence. But I can't entertain that. I won't. This is hard enough without hope of something different. Of possibility.

"No, Matthaeus. I can't." I get up. "And I don't want to hear another word about it or her." I walk out of the study.

42

MARA

Noah and I are in an obscure hotel in a long-term stay unit on the outskirts of town. Two soldiers are inside the apartment with us, and more are on the property somewhere.

I look out of the window onto the pool which I can see inside the glassed-in space. People are swimming in this icy winter's night, the glass foggy in places from the heat and humidity inside.

"Hey," Noah says from the doorway.

I turn to find him holding a plate of toaster waffles. They smell good but I'm not hungry. "Hey," I say, returning my attention to the people at the pool as I hear the door close after he enters.

"Breakfast for dinner. You need to eat something."

"I have enough people telling me what I need to do. What's best for me. Please don't turn into one of them."

He comes to stand at the window beside me. The plate is gone. I guess he set it on the desk. He's quiet as he looks out onto the distant lights of the city.

I turn to look up at him. He's about as tall as Dante but built differently, more lean muscle than bulk. And he's just different. Not as hard as Dante. Not as broken. Even after everything he's been through.

He turns to smile down at me, and I feel a tenderness for him I don't feel for anyone else. I think it's from those first days in captivity. I was so young. And he'd been there, the same age as me, and scared too. Both of us so scared. We'd needed each other.

But then he speaks and ruins it. "He did the right thing," he says. "I didn't think he would."

"No, he didn't. He's under some illusion I'll have a life. That I'm better off without him–"

"You are."

"I love him."

"You *think* you love him," Noah replies.

"That's not it."

"And I get it, honestly." He walks over to sit on the edge of the bed. "He saved your life. He took a bullet for you. Multiple. And he's probably one of the few men who've been good to you."

I watch him, curious.

He shakes his head. "And in a way he's larger than life." He meets my eyes. "But he's dangerous, Mara. And men like him, trouble finds them."

"I don't care about any of that. It doesn't matter."

"You know the history. Who did it. Who betrayed them. You know the guilt he carries because of that. And as little as I like him, I also feel sorry for him. He's fucked up. I mean really fucked up. You'll never fix him. You can't."

"Do you think I don't know that he's broken? And who says I want to fix him?"

"Don't cry."

"I'm not." I wipe the back of my hand across my eyes to catch the few fallen tears. "I don't want to fix him, Noah. I just want to be with him. He's the only person I feel...I don't know...like he knows me. I don't have to hide or be anything."

"I know you too. You don't have to hide with me. Or be anything with me. And Scarlett too. And Cristiano. And your grandmother. There's a longer list than you're willing to accept. You just have to give us all a chance. Don't you think we deserve a chance?"

They do and he's right. I know. But this thing with Dante, it's just more. "I love him," I say finally. "I can't live without him." *I won't.*

"Don't say that."

"It's true."

There's a long moment of silence before he

speaks. "I know what you almost did. Going up to those cliffs."

I look away.

"You have me too, Mara. Always."

"You can't fix me, either, you know," I say without looking at him. "You should live your own life, Noah."

I put my fingertips to the cool glass of the window, see how the rain is turning to sleet as the temperature cools. Down below are all those people in their bright swimsuits just laughing and living, oblivious even to the fact that it's winter just beyond the vulnerable divide of the glass wall.

"If you're not going to eat the waffles," Noah starts, trailing off. I turn to glance at the plate then at him.

"Did you pour enough syrup on them?" I ask, forcing a smile as I make my way across the room and pick up a section of waffle.

It's then there's a popping sound. Then another.

"What—" I start but Noah's quicker than me. His gaze shifts to the closed bedroom door and in the next instant, simultaneous to the loud crash in the other room he's on top of me, throwing me to the floor, his full weight on me as I slam down hard. I'm dazed when I hear Noah's muttered curse. He lifts off me just as the door slams open and from my place on the floor, I see into the fog that's engulfed the other room and the outlines of the men who were guarding us lying on the floor as that fog begins to creep into the bedroom.

"Cover your nose and mouth!" Noah yells. I'm already coughing, choking on whatever that stuff is.

I roll onto my back to watch Noah lunge for the first man. But the man is twice as big as him, wearing a gas mask and armed. The one behind him, also masked, even bigger.

The man barely glances at me on the floor before Noah crashes into him. I can only watch as he rams his elbow into Noah's gut before slamming his forearm across his chest, sending him crashing against the wall and knocking the wind out of him.

I barely have time to scream, to tell them to stop, or to pull the Swiss Army knife from my pocket. It all happens so fast. Noah's down and it's a miracle he isn't knocked out by the force of that hit, but he's coughing, choking.

The second man looks around the room as the first one comes for me, bending to haul me up to my feet by my arm. I sway, the room spinning.

"Hold your breath," he says. At least I think that's what he says, over my hacking cough, my panic.

I glance once more at Noah, see his eyes flutter open, see them focus on me as the man throws me over his shoulder like a ragdoll, carrying me off. Out of the apartment where the soldiers who were to guard us lie in heaps. Out into the hallway where more masked, armed men dressed in black from head to toe wait.

The fire alarm is going off. A door opens, a woman almost steps out into the hallway, but is shoved back into her room, the door slammed shut by the man carrying me. We hurry down the stairs and all I can do is hold on to him as he carries me out into the sleet-soaked night. I can finally draw in a deep breath, still choking on whatever that gas was, my throat full, tears streaming down my face.

Outside the men pull off their masks. It doesn't matter though. I don't recognize any of them. We slow as an SUV with tinted windows pulls up.

"No!" I kick, pound my fists into his back. I can't let him put me in that SUV. I'm finished if that happens. But my fight has no impact at all. And soon he slides me off his shoulder as the SUV door opens. I just make out the silhouette of a man in the back seat and I try one more time, scratching at the face of the one who has me. My feet touch down as he curses, and he almost releases me. Almost.

But then the one inside the SUV grabs me by my arm and drags me inside. The door is closed, the SUV moving. He releases me as the locks engage and I push as far from him as possible expecting Felix Pérez. Terrified of seeing Felix Pérez again.

But it's not him sitting across from me.

It's not him at all grinning at me, casually checking his watch, the inky green of a tattoo creeping out from beneath his shirt sleeve.

43

DANTE

My phone rings, waking me. It takes me a minute to realize where I am. In my bedroom in the Staten Island house lying on top of the bedding fully clothed.

I fumble for the light, for the phone vibrating on the nightstand. It disconnects before I get to it but immediately starts to ring again. I answer on the second ring.

"Brother?" I ask, seeing Cristiano's face on the screen. He looks grave.

"We missed something," he says. "Something big."

I scrub my face, brace myself.

"St. James. I know why he's pushing so hard. Why he needs that confirmation so badly."

"Why?"

"We assumed when his fiancée was killed that

the baby died."

I feel myself go cold.

"He's been off the grid for the last five years. Disappeared like a fucking ghost."

"What the fuck are you saying?"

"The woman, Kimberly Barrett, she didn't die at the café. She died in the ambulance on the way to the hospital. But they were able to save the baby."

"What?"

"A little girl. No name. At least not that we know. Just the word of one of the medics who delivered her. There's no record of the birth otherwise. At least not at first glance. It's why we missed it."

"Jesus."

"St. James left Mexico two nights later with his fiancée's body. That was the last anyone heard from him. But it wasn't just her body he brought home. It was his daughter."

I push my hands into my hair. "Christ."

"He's kept the child a secret for a reason. Buried the fact of her existence. Maybe he's afraid the person who put the hit on him would go after her."

"He's doing this to keep his daughter safe." Fuck.

"There's one more thing."

"Fuck."

"He's gone. The penthouse is empty."

"What?"

"I don't know how he did it. Charlie's had eyes on the place since we've known about it."

"When?"

"I don't know."

"Fuck!"

"Is Matthaeus able to confirm Mara's location is secure?"

I open my mouth to answer but just then the bedroom door slams open, surprising me. I look up to find Matthaeus standing in the doorway looking like he, too, has just woken up, his hair disheveled. Shirt untucked from his jeans.

And I know from the look in his eyes the answer to Cristiano's question.

"I don't know how it happened!" He fists handfuls of hair, eyes wild.

"No." I feel the blood drain from my head and don't recognize my own voice.

No reply.

"No." I say again, my throat tight because I know what this is.

"Fuck!" He slams his fist into the wall.

I swallow as I hear Cristiano's curse.

"A team came in. Military precision. Masked. Ready. Gassed our men, no casualties. Noah's beat up—"

"Mara," I say, somehow not screaming her name.

"He took her. Left his fucking calling card."

"Who?" Do I need to ask though?

"Jericho St. James."

44

MARA

I know this man. He's Kimberly's fiancée. But he looks very different than he used to.

He smiles and I get the feeling he's trying hard not to look wolfish, but it's not working.

"Mara. You don't need to be afraid of me. I'm sorry about how that had to happen, but I had no choice. I can promise you though that no one got hurt. I made sure of that."

I remember how the soldier slammed Noah against the wall, though, and slip my hand into my pocket, feel the Swiss Army knife.

"I'm Jericho St. James. Do you remember me?"

"What do you want?" I ask, not bothering to answer his question.

"A few hours of your time. That's all. You'll be safe."

"I doubt that," I say, slipping the knife out and flipping it open.

One corner of his mouth quirks upward as he glances at the knife between us. He's not afraid of me. That's obvious. Entertained maybe, but not afraid. It pisses me off.

He shifts his gaze to mine. "That's not necessary, Mara. Put it away before you hurt yourself."

Why do men always do that? Belittle? I want to tell him to go fuck himself. "Stop the car. Let me out."

"I wish I could." He reaches toward me, and I jab the knife in his direction realizing the ridiculousness of the situation. Locked in this car with this giant of a man. At least I have the blade though. Even if it is small, it hurt Alvarez. It slowed him down long enough for Dante to get there.

But then I remember Dante isn't coming tonight. He sent me away. He doesn't want me.

He puts his hands up, palms facing me. "Just wanted to fasten your belt."

"I said let me out," I scream it.

"Put that away. Last time I'll ask."

"Go fuck yourself."

He smiles, not trying to hide anything now. The next thing I know, as swiftly as Dante did it when I took his knife from him, Jericho St. James makes his move. He's just as fast, his big hand closing around my wrist while the other relieves me of the switchblade. He releases me, checks the sharpness then closes it.

"Fasten your seatbelt," he says more firmly and tucks my knife into his pocket.

"That's mine."

"You'll get it back later. In fact, I may even give you an upgrade."

"What do you want with me? Is Noah all right? The soldiers?"

"They'll be fine. Like I said, I made sure no one would be hurt. Just knocked out for a while."

I'm not sure if I can believe him.

"As for what I want, I need something from someone you know, and I need you in order to get it."

I feel my blood run cold. Feel goosebumps rise along the length of my arms. Because I know what's coming. "You're taking me back to him."

His jaw clenches, face tightening. "You'll be safe."

"I'll be safe if you stop the car and let me out now."

"I'm sorry but I can't do that."

"You mean you won't. It's a choice. You're making a choice!"

The driver takes a turn, and we get onto the highway heading out of the city. I look out the back window as the lights of the town fade into the distance. I know the farther we go, the less likely it will be for Dante to find me. If he even knows I've been taken. If he even cares.

"Perhaps you'd like to meet the baby."

"Baby?" I'm surprised by this turn in tactic but am instantly suspicious. "Kimberly died. The baby is dead."

A shadow flicks through his eyes and it's as though he almost winces at my words. "No. The baby, well, she's five years old now. Not a baby anymore. She survived. You're right about Kimberly, though. She died. You can see for yourself once we arrive at the house. I know my daughter will be excited to meet you."

He must see the confusion on my face because he appears gentler in the next moment.

"Please put your seatbelt on. I wouldn't want you to get hurt."

"If you're so concerned about my safety then why would you give me back to Felix? He will hurt me."

"I've arranged things, so he won't get a chance to."

"Please."

"I'm sorry, Mara. But I need to protect my little girl."

We drive for almost an hour back in the direction of New York City but bypass the exits and eventually drive through the guarded gates of a secluded community. I sit up, watch as the driver takes turn after turn until we're on a cul-de-sac with a tall wall securing the only property. It's reminiscent of a few days ago when we drove up to the Todt Hill house, the gates that open similar, the armed soldiers indistinguishable from Dante's.

Lights shine in the windows both upstairs and downstairs in the mansion. Once the SUV comes to a stop before the front doors, Jericho St. James climbs out and closes the door. The driver remains where he is as Jericho walks around to my side of the vehicle. He talks to a soldier whom he dismisses as he opens my door.

"Out," he says, standing to the side to let me climb down.

I'm wet and cold and shuddering as I slip out of the vehicle.

"It's warm inside," he says as the SUV drives off and leaves us standing before the formidable house. "Come, Mara."

He takes care not to touch me. I know he can drag me in if he wants. It would probably take little effort but he's not. And I don't have much of a choice, so I climb the few steps up to the double front doors, Jericho following at a short distance. Two armed men stand outside, nodding to him as the door is opened. Inside is lit up warmly and I hear and smell the fire I can see in the oversized fireplace in the foyer. When he closes the door behind me, I look around, taking in the grand dining room, a formal living room. From beyond it is a door that's slightly ajar. The light is on inside and I can hear voices. A TV program. Singing. And a child's whispered voice singing along.

I turn to glance at Jericho who is also listening, who smiles a smile that lets me glimpse the man I'd seen five years ago.

"Come," he says. "Maybe you'll understand why I need to do this."

He doesn't wait for me to reply but heads through the living room and toward that door and as I follow the sound grows a little louder, the child's voice whisper-singing along with the song like she's done it a hundred times before. It isn't what I expect even though I know he's taking me to see his daughter. The sound is too soft. Too innocent and too vulnerable for the likes of this man.

I stop at the entrance and watch when Jericho enters. An older woman stands from the couch. She has her hair wrapped in a silk scarf and has a sickly pallor to her face. She smiles at me and nods her greeting to Jericho who nods back but his attention is on the child with a cloud of soft dark curls around her head. She's so captivated by what's on the TV that she hasn't noticed we've even walked into the room. She's holding a well-loved bear on her lap, rubbing his ear, and singing along, her tune a little off. It's the sweetest sound and my heart melts.

And I know my reaction is exactly what he wants. Why he brought me here.

The song ends.

Jericho clears his throat. The little girl turns to him and instantly, her eyes light up and she's on her feet, crashing into his legs.

"Daddy!" He lifts her up and she wraps her arms around his neck, that bear still clutched in one hand.

"You know all the words now," he says to her and hugs her tightly. I see how he's closed his eyes, how tightly he's holding her. It brings tears to my own eyes.

"I've been practicing," she says, and he draws back, sets her on her feet but keeps one of her hands in his as he crouches down.

"I think you've grown taller," he says. "You're almost taller than me."

She giggles. "Only when you're crouching." She hugs him again and he looks at me over her shoulder. He straightens, lifting her in his arms and facing me. Her expression is cautious.

Looking from father to daughter, I see she has his eyes and realize their color is slightly different, one blue and one gray. The little girl pulls a little closer to him.

"It's all right," he reassures her and walks toward me. "This is Mara," he says. "Mara, this is my daughter, Angelique."

DANTE

"How the fuck did he find her?" I boom.

"Just like we've been watching him I'm sure he's been watching us," Matthaeus says.

"You said you moved her twice. How did he do it?"

"I don't know. They're bringing Noah here now. The other guards are just starting to come around."

"No one was hurt?"

"No. Apart from Noah being a little beat up. He tried to fight off one of the men before he was knocked out.

"Noah?"

He nods.

With all those soldiers, it was Noah who tried to fight. "The card?" I ask.

He takes out his phone and shows me a screenshot front and back. "Noah's got it."

I take the phone, look at the back. The front has the same I.V.I. logo so it's useless to me. But on the back, he's written something.

"Faust. Box 4. Midnight."

"What the fuck—"

"The opera Faust is playing tonight. The show will be over by midnight. I guess that's when he'll bring her."

"Who's rented Box 4? Pérez doesn't strike me as the opera-going type."

"I'll see what Charlie can find out from here," Cristiano says. "It could be a trap, brother."

"I don't have a choice but to go. He took her. I need to get her back. I'll call you after," I tell Cristiano before disconnecting and turn to Matthaeus who is already on his phone getting soldiers lined up.

When he's finished, he slips his phone into his pocket and tucks his shirt into his pants as we walk out the door to one of the waiting SUVs. Soldiers are loading into the others now. He checks his watch. "We should be there in about forty minutes."

"Midnight. He timed it well." And kid or not, I'm going to kill the mother fucker when I get my hands on him.

46

MARA

I watch him with the little girl while she has a snack. She's five years old and small for her age, swinging her legs back and forth under the table. Jericho has to coax her to eat but she's clearly more interested in feeding her bear and watching me. I get the feeling she doesn't get many visitors.

When the woman, Angelique's grandmother, turns the corner pulling along a child's suitcase, his expression changes and he hurries to her.

"You should have let one of the soldiers carry it down," he tells her, taking the case from her.

"It wasn't heavy," she says. "I'm not that feeble yet."

"Still." He studies her. "You're tired."

She shakes her head. "No more than usual."

"Is it time for our trip?" the little girl asks.

They both turn to her. "Almost," Jericho says.

"Is Mara coming with us?" she casts a curious but shy glance at me and smiles. When I smile back, she hides her face in her stuffed bear's stomach.

"Part of the way," Jericho answers.

He's a different man with her. In a way, I'm glad to see it. I never had someone to protect me, not until Dante—for a few days at least—and little girls need protecting. I'm glad she'll have her father because if I think about what could happen to a little girl like Angelique at the hands of a Felix Pérez or Ivan Petrov, it twists my stomach.

Jericho stands, looks at me and my full plate. I guess he thought he'd feed us both a snack.

"You didn't eat."

"I'm not hungry," I say, standing too.

He nods, bends to kiss Angelique on top of her head and tells her he'll be back in a few minutes. Then he shifts his gaze to me.

"Mara?" he gestures to the stairs, and I walk ahead of him, unsure what to expect. "End of the hall. Last door," he says once we're on the first floor.

I pass six other doors before getting to the one he pointed out. This one stands ajar. I push it open and enter. He follows me in.

"Is that your mother?" I ask as I take in the pretty room. Obviously, not his. Not that I expected him to take me to his bed. He's not that type of man. I can see that much. Or maybe it's what he wants me to think. Why he wanted me to see him with his daughter.

The room is luxurious but unremarkable. The only thing that stands out is the long black dress lying on the bed and the pair of heels on the floor. Just what I'd need for an elegant night out.

"Yes," he says, answering my question.

I turn to face him. "She's sick."

He nods once.

"Do you want me to feel sorry for you? Is that why you brought me here? To see your daughter and your sick mother and decide I should sacrifice my life for them?"

He tilts his head to the side, gaze speculative. "I think you'll do it because you know what that man is capable of."

"You do too. Why not take him out yourself? You know where he'll be."

"My priority is to get my daughter out." He shifts his gaze to the dress. "You'll wear that dress. Everything should fit."

"Why?"

"It's what he wants. The car leaves in fifteen minutes."

"Our road trip?"

"I'll be dropping you off on the way. You're going to an opera."

"I don't like the opera."

"That's too bad."

A man knocks on the door then and Jericho turns to him. They talk briefly and he hands Jericho something. Jericho closes the door and we're alone again. He walks toward me and when he shows me what he's holding, I'm surprised.

"An upgrade, as promised," he says.

I look from him to it as he pulls a dagger from its sheath. It's slightly bigger than Matthaeus's switchblade, the handle about three inches long, the fine blade itself sharp. Deadly.

He tucks it back into its holster. "You can wear it on your thigh beneath the dress. He won't search you. He'll assume I've done that." He holds it out to me, but I don't take it.

"Is this a trick?"

"What kind of trick would it be?"

I want to take it. I want to take it very badly, but I don't. "I could stab you."

"You won't." He sets it on the bed on top of the dress and turns to walk toward the door. "I will hand you over to Pérez once he gives me what I need."

"What is it that you need so badly you're willing to do this? Because if I look at you with your daughter or your mother, you don't seem like a bad guy."

He snorts.

I study him now. "What do you need from him?"

"Proof of who ordered the hit that killed Angelique's mother."

"So you can kill him?"

"So I can protect my daughter."

"Why are you giving me a weapon?"

"If there was any other way to do this that didn't involve handing over another innocent to that bastard, I'd do it. But I'm out of options and I will do anything I need to do to keep my daughter safe. That," he says, gesturing to the dagger, "is so you at least have a way to defend yourself if things don't go as I've planned."

"What do you mean?"

"Felix will take you to the opera where the exchange will take place."

"Exchange. Me."

He nods once. "But I've let your lover know where you'll be. Where the transaction will take place."

My lover. Should I correct him? "I'm a person. Not a transaction."

He has the grace to look away. "I know that."

"Dante knows and he allowed it?" My heart twists.

"Not exactly, no in fact, he was adamant you wouldn't be sacrificed."

Relief floods through me but it doesn't last long as I put two and two together. "So, the dagger is in case Dante doesn't make it."

He nods gravely. "Believe it or not, I'm sorry to do this to you," he says, studying me. I wonder if he's waiting for me to tell him it's okay because it's not. When I don't say anything, he checks his watch. "Ten minutes."

With that he leaves, and I turn to pick up the dagger. I take it out of its sheath and press the flat of the blade against my palm. I could kill myself. Here and now. I could put this through my heart and be done with it. But I won't do that, and he knows it, or he wouldn't have left me alone. When I hear Angelique's giggle float up the stairs, I understand why he's doing this. I understand why he will sacrifice me even if Dante won't. I would do the same if I had a child. I have no doubt.

But instead of all that, I think about something else.

I think about what I'll do with this dagger tonight. How I'll bury it in Felix Pérez's stony heart. Because monsters like him don't deserve to live. And if I get the chance, I'll leave one less in this world even if it costs me my life in the process.

47

DANTE

Faust is well attended. When Matthaeus and I walk into the grand lobby of the opera house the fifth act is underway. We made good time. Better than I expected.

Few people are left milling about the lobby, but most attendees are inside. They won't open the doors again until it's over.

"Cameras were already disabled," Matthaeus says.

I look at him.

"Just got the text from Charlie," he says. "Someone beat us to it. Pérez or the buyer, I guess."

Our shoes echo on the marble floors as we make our way to one of the two sweeping carpeted staircases. Two men take the stairs across the large space and a text comes through on my phone confirming that Pérez's men are on site. He could be too for all I know.

Matthaeus reads the text. "The man in Box Four hasn't moved. He's still alone."

"Fuck."

"He'll come."

"Describe him again."

"Nothing has changed, Dante," he says. I know this. We went over this as soon as our men got on sight.

"Humor me."

He sighs. "Late 40's, early 50's. Well dressed. We're too far to hear any identifying accent."

"What about facial recognition?"

"Sent several photos to Charlie but he hasn't been able to get anything yet. Too much shadow or, more likely, he knows how to keep himself in shadow."

"I'm willing to bet the latter. But it doesn't make any sense if St. James was telling the truth. That he paid over a million dollars for her. She's not Elizabeth. Anyone knows that. And after five years with Petrov..." I trail off. I don't want to speak the rest aloud. But this buyer? It doesn't make sense. "We're missing something."

We reach the first-floor landing and rather than proceeding up via the elaborate main staircase, we take a right to where one of my men opens a door to an emergency exit. There's nothing glamorous about this one and our steps echo too loudly on the concrete. We slow as we reach the door and from here, I can faintly hear the sounds of the soprano.

It's a shame Faust will be ruined for me after tonight. I like the story.

Matthaeus sends a text, and we wait for the response. It comes just two minutes later when a door opens, allowing us entry to the third floor and the box entrances. More people mill around the hallways here, men standing at the bars set up at every few intervals drinking. With the private box entrances and the prices associated with them, the rules are different for these people than they are for the general public.

We walk along the rounded corridor toward the box at the far end, where a staircase identical to the one we just climbed, is guarded by two men.

"Perez's men," Matthaeus says, not that I needed him to confirm. We don't slow our steps as we approach Box Three, the one Charlie arranged. The owners of the box had decided to skip this opera which was lucky for us. We show our forged electronic tickets to the man standing outside and he only hesitates for a moment before opening the door to let us in.

Just as the door closes behind us a text comes in. It's Charlie.

Charlie: *Did some digging. Found out who owns the box. I need to call you. Now.*

Me: *Can't talk. We're in the box now. I don't want to take a chance we spook the asshole.*

Charlie: *Shit. Okay. The box is registered to a company by the name of Gray and Associates. As far as I can tell, there's no single Gray. Or not anymore at least. Anderson Gray died about fourteen years ago and since then it's been run by his children. Three brothers. The name changed to Gray and Associates then. Before that, when Anderson Gray was alive, they went by a different name. It's why I didn't make the connection.*

Me: *What connection?*

Charlie: *This group isn't exactly clean, Dante. You want to be careful. They have interests across all continents. Not all are on the up and up.*

Me: *What do they do exactly?*

Charlie: *Imports and exports. It's all very vague. The family is associated with IVI.*

Me: *What the fuck is this Secret Society bullshit? Grown men playing at some game?*

Charlie: *I don't think they're playing games.*

Me: *What else?*

Charlie: *Gray and Associates has ties on all continents, as I said, but the European sector only started to really grow about twenty years ago. And this is where the interesting piece comes in. The connection.*

Me: *Twenty years?*

Charlie: *I could be wrong, but I don't think so. It's the only thing that adds up.*

Me: *What?*

Charlie: *The oldest brother, Drake Gray, was charged with the Europe project. And somehow, he came into contact with David.*

Me: *David?*

Charlie: *Yes. He was in Naples for a meeting with him. I remember this because your father happened in on the meeting and David was beside himself angry. He was trying to make a deal without your father's knowledge.*

Charlie has never stopped referring to the man who raised me as my father. He has not once called David that.

Charlie: *Because David had gone behind your father's back, your father punished him but cutting him out of that particular business altogether.*

Me: *You're losing me. Who cares what happened twenty years ago?*

Charlie: *It's exactly that. The timing. This could be a longshot but the million dollars... Gray, and I'm assuming it's Gray in that box, he put up a million dollars for Mara. Why? It can't be coincidence.*

Me: *What the hell are you talking about?*

But as I ask it, my mind is working, doing the math. As impossible as it is.

Charlie: *Your father had several secret meetings with Gray at the house. I don't know much more because the business never came to fruition. Gray spent some time in Naples vacationing, or so he said, and he was gone.*

Me: *Twenty years ago?*

Charlie: *I'm going to send you a photo of Drake*

Gray from back then. The shots we have of the man in the box next to yours aren't great quality but it's not unreasonable it's the same man and it's the only thing that makes sense. Keep in mind, he'd have been thirty or so then.

A ding signals the photo and I open it. It's a shot at a restaurant and Gray clearly doesn't know it's being taken. He's sitting at a table with a woman. Her back is to the camera and she's a little fuzzy because the photographer had focused on him. She has long dark hair draped over her shoulder. And I only recognize her because the strap of her dress has fallen off her shoulder exposing a familiar birthmark.

I shift my gaze to the man sitting across from the woman. He's a big guy. Blond hair cut short wearing an expensive suit and a Rolex watch, pouring from the bottle of wine into the woman's glass. And he's smiling at her like he's smitten.

I zoom in on his face. The pixels slowly come together. And I see it. The connection.

And all the pieces fall into place.

48

MARA

I ride in one SUV with Jericho while his daughter, mother and a soldier follow in the one behind ours.

The hilt of the blade feels cool and smooth against my thigh, the strap holding it in place tight. The dress itself has a slit up the center which should allow me to reach it easily when it's time.

I think about what I'll do when I see him. When I'll do it. I'll have one chance and as soon as it presents itself, I will take it. If I don't succeed and Jericho is wrong about Dante, I'm dead. But I'd rather be dead than a slave to another Petrov again.

Once we're in the city, traffic grows denser, and I can see Jericho constantly checking on the other SUV in the side mirror.

"Why didn't you ride with them?" I ask.

He shifts his gaze to me. "Everything has to be done in the right order."

About ten minutes later, we slow down in front of a strip club that looks seedy enough to be exactly Felix's style. My heartbeat picks up and a cold sweat covers me. I lay my hand over the dagger and instantly feel Jericho's on top of it.

"Not too fast," he says, holding it in place when I try to pull away. "You have to find the right moment, or you'll lose. You'll get one shot at this. Do you understand?"

I take a deep breath in and nod.

"Good." The SUV carrying his daughter pulls in behind ours but parks at a distance. "Here we go," he says and opens his door to climb out. I count four men in the third SUV who flank him as he comes to my side and opens my door. Again, he lets me climb out on my own rather than manhandling me. The skirt of the dress is loose enough that Felix won't see the outline of the dagger, but I wish I weren't wearing such high heels in case I need to run.

One of Felix's men is standing outside smoking a cigarette. Although I don't recognize him specifically, they have a certain look about them. Like thugs. He looks me over and as soon as he does, instinct has me spinning on my heel. Jericho's hand closes over my arm as Felix's soldier tosses what's left of his cigarette and comes toward us.

"Not yet," Jericho tells him.

The man looks annoyed but accepts this and opens the door.

As soon as we're inside, I see him. Even across a bar full of people and women on a stage dancing, music too loud to be heard over, I see him.

I stop, an old, familiar panic locking my legs.

Jericho turns to me, takes my arm. "Breathe."

I'm scared. Fuck. I'm scared. It's like all those feelings from before, all that terror, it was just waiting, lying dormant and now that he's close again, it's all back and it's paralyzing me.

Jericho leans toward me. "Breathe, Mara."

"I'm scared," I confess, my eyes locked on Felix, his grin making me shudder even as sweat beads on my forehead and pools under my arms.

"Fear is healthy. Look at me." I don't. He takes my jaw and turns my face to his. "Look at me, not him."

I nod.

"Don't think about what he did to you. Only remember your hate for him. Let that be your power. He'll be dead tonight. You'll be alive. Just keep your focus and remember your hate." He subtly touches my thigh where the dagger feels like it's burning into my skin. "You're not a victim anymore."

I nod.

"Good girl." He keeps his hand wrapped around my arm and we cross the room toward Felix Pérez. I somehow manage to do it on my own two feet.

Felix stands when we're a few feet away and looks me over, nods.

"Where is it?" Jericho asks.

Felix seems barely able to drag his gaze from mine as he reaches into his pocket, takes something out and hands it to Jericho.

Jericho takes it and one of his men lifts a laptop out of the case he was carrying. He opens it, sets it on a high-top table and Jericho inserts the drive. He pushes a pair of earbuds into his ears, and I watch him as Felix leers at me. He never looked at me like this before, not when I was a child. I guess I should be thankful for that but he's just a different sort of pervert. I know that.

"You're all grown up," he says to me, but I don't acknowledge him. It turns my stomach to hear his voice. It'll take some doing to look at him.

I can't see the screen over Jericho's shoulders but a few moments later, he pulls the earbuds out, nods and pockets the flash drive. Felix turns his attention to him.

"What you wanted to hear?"

"Not exactly. Our business is finished. Make sure I never see you again," he tells Felix and turns to walk away. I swallow hard when his gaze meets mine briefly but a moment later, he's gone from the club, his men with him and I'm left facing Felix Pérez alone.

The only reason I don't run when he steps

toward me is because my legs won't obey my mind's order. He must see my fear. My panic. Because even as I try to recall Jericho's words, even as I remind myself of the dagger at my fingertips, I'm terrified of this man.

He takes a step toward me, and I feel one of his men at my back. His gaze slides lazily over me and for a moment I wonder if I were to scream, would anyone help me? Would anyone stop him? I don't think so. He'd have chosen a place he feels secure.

He walks a slow circle around me stopping at my back, I close my eyes at the feel of his hot breath at my neck. At the scent of him I'd forgotten. It's a nauseating stench because it carries memory and fear.

"Mara," he says my name, drawing it out. "All grown up. And very, very pretty. I'm tempted to keep you for myself."

I open my eyes, my hands fisting at my side.

"Or perhaps just have a quick taste," he finishes. It's when I feel his tongue slide across the curve of my neck that I steel my spine. I fix my gaze on the dirty mirror in the distance where I can see our reflection. This aging man at my back. This disgusting piece of human filth. And I think of Angelique. Of all the little girls he's hurt. Of all the ones he'll keep hurting.

And it's that that has me standing taller.

Has me focusing my hate. My rage.

I have to keep it together now.

Because Jericho St. James is right. This man will die tonight. And it will be my hands that are soaked in his blood.

49

DANTE

"What is it?" Matthaeus asks. It's been twenty minutes and it's almost midnight. Twenty minutes to make sense of what Charlie is saying. Of who is in that box. Of the one thing that makes sense.

But before I can answer his phone buzzes with a text. "She's here. In the box," he says, and we both get to our feet. If what Charlie thinks is true, it changes things. Changes everything. But I push that all aside. First thing's first. Kill Felix Pérez.

I walk ahead of Matthaeus, stepping into the hallway where I instantly see more men outside Box Four's door. Felix's soldiers. I'd smell them a mile away.

Four men flank us as I take my weapon in my hand. I will shoot up this place if I have to. I will do whatever I need to do to get her back. To kill that mother fucker.

One of the soldiers steps toward us. The way he's grinning makes me think of a hyena. I glance at the bystanders who will witness murder tonight. The hyena draws his weapon.

I wonder if he knows who I am. If he's been warned to look out for me.

I cock the gun. Even silenced it will draw attention and surely when he drops there will be chaos. I prefer to get into the box without commotion, but I'll do what I need to do.

Before I have a chance to fire, another man walks quickly toward the first from behind and at first glance, he looks familiar. I don't know from where, but I've seen him before. He gives me a grin, his face hardening as he focuses on his target. A moment later, he's got his hand on the hyena's shoulder and I see the man grunt, his body jerking.

The face of the one I recognize grows more tense, and I know what he's doing. I did it myself recently. He's twisting the blade he just shoved into the soldier's kidney. I know the moment he draws the knife out because the soldier falls forward. Matthaeus catches him and the man who just stabbed him walks past me, slapping his hand against my chest.

"Even," he says and walks away, disappearing before anyone is the wiser. Then, I realize where I know him from. The night I killed Petrov. The night St. James and one of his men walked me out of Red's. He's that man. A glance down at the bloody card that drops from where he slapped his hand against my chest confirms it.

Jericho St. James sent a man. And he thinks it makes us even.

He's mistaken.

But when the second soldier sees the hyena leaning against Matthaeus, the cocky grin on his face morphs into something else. As he looks up at me, fumbling for his weapon, he's too late to grab it. I push my gun into his stomach and pull the trigger, using him as a shield as I open the door to Box Four. We push our way inside. I see her and for a moment, everything stops because she's here and she's alive and I'll get another chance to save her. To keep my promise to her.

But that moment costs me because I hear the cocking of six different guns over the soprano's aria. Faust comes to an end to a standing ovation. But before it settles, the butt of a pistol slams against my temple dropping me to the floor as Mara, eyes wide with terror, opens her mouth to scream.

50

MARA

"Let's go," the man who Felix called Gray says. "Pick him up. You," he points to Matthaeus. "Lose your weapon."

Gray is casually giving the orders. His soldiers have Matthaeus disarmed in a second.

"My man is dead," Felix says after toeing the one Dante had been using as a shield. "What the fuck?"

"They're both dead," Matthaeus casually adds as he raises his arms in surrender to the one pointing his pistol at him. I can see the faint signs of a smile on his face. He appears so calm. Like he's not fazed at all.

"Let's go. Someone pick Grigori up." A soldier hoists Dante over his shoulder with a grunt.

He knows Dante. What will that mean?

"The rest of your men?" Gray asks Matthaeus. "What about them?"

"Tell them to stand down or I slit this one's throat."

"No!" I yell and Gray turns to me, the expression on his face different than I expect. This situation so reminiscent to the night I met Petrov but so very different.

"They'll stand down," Matthaeus says as we step out of the box. I find the corridor that was only slightly occupied just minutes ago full of men. They're his men. Gray's. And a glance at Felix tells me he wasn't expecting this.

"I delivered," Felix says to Gray, and I see his unease. He's still no match for the people he deals with, and he knows it. "If you'll deposit the second half of the payment I'll be on my way."

Gray gives him a dark look. "We'll take care of it downstairs. You'll come with me. Move."

"Sir," the soldier in charge nods and guides everyone out.

I remain where I am, unsure what to do, very aware of the dagger at my thigh but still powerless with Dante knocked out. Once Gray and I are the only two remaining he turns to me.

"Come," he says, gesturing to the door. He keeps distance from me though.

I study him, trying to figure him out.

"You won't be hurt anymore, Mara."

I'm confused by him and his words. By the tone and his meaning.

He gestures once more to the door. I don't have a choice, so I move through it and follow to where one of the men is holding the door open to the emergency stairwell.

It's loud as we hurry down the concrete stairs, every sound echoing. I hold on to the railing and when we pass the ground floor entrance, we're led through another door, one I hadn't seen before. It's smaller so most of the men have to duck through it. Once we're through, several flashlights light our way. It's dark and dank, smelling like water that's been standing still too long. We keep going and ahead I can see the man carrying Dante, see Matthaeus behind him. Behind me is Gray looking unperturbed in his expensive suit, two more soldiers trail him. Every time I glance at him, I find him watching me.

The crowded corridor opens up a few minutes later, although it's still dark in here, light is coming in from somewhere. A loud sound has me jumping as we get to a cavernous open space.

"Subway train," Gray says.

Subway?

"The tunnels connect," he clarifies as the man carrying Dante sets him down on an ancient looking bench against the wall. Matthaeus goes to him. He's slumped over but moving.

I take a step toward them, but Gray catches my arm and I don't even stop to think. It's pure instinct I act on. I don't think about Jericho's words advising me to choose my moment. I don't think about all the soldiers with their guns around me. I don't care about any of it. I need to get to Dante. That's all.

So I slip my hand through the slit of my dress and take hold of the dagger strapped to my thigh. I pull it out of its holster and brandish it between us.

"Let me go. Now."

I expect every weapon in the place to be cocked and turned on me. I maybe even expect to get shot. But that doesn't happen. In fact, none of the soldiers make a move.

Gray never takes his eyes from me. "You're not a prisoner," he says and does the strangest thing. He lets go of my arm. Surprising, because I expected a fight. I'm sure I'd be easy to disarm. But as soon as I'm free I hurry toward Dante and Matthaeus. I crouch down in front of him keeping hold of the blade as I touch the bloody spot on his temple.

"Dante?"

He groans, and a moment later he's looking into my eyes and I'm so relieved. It's stupid I know because we are not out of this mess or even close to it. But he's alive and he's here and it's all I can think about.

I reach my arms around him, and he wraps one of his around me. Standing, he moves in front of me. He's not quite steady. I can see it. But he's determined.

Matthaeus stands too and I try to move around Dante but he's blocking me with his arm.

"Well, this is very cozy, but I'd just like to get paid and be on my way," Felix says with a forced laugh as he steps toward Gray.

One of Gray's men cocks his gun and points it at Felix's temple. Felix comes to a stop, all the color draining from his face.

I tighten the grip on the dagger, my palm sweaty. Quietly, I slip off my shoes, the ground cold and grimy beneath my bare feet.

Gray studies me, then Dante. Dante is watching him with a curiosity that has me wondering what he knows that I don't.

Felix clears his throat and Gray turns to him. "You want to get paid you little piece of shit?" he asks, stepping toward him.

I follow Felix's nervous gaze and I think we realize at the same time that all of his soldiers are gone.

"What's going on?" he asks.

Gray stops a few steps in front of him and looks him over with contempt.

"Money back?" he asks.

Felix looks confused but I see one of Gray's men punching something into a phone. "Yes, sir," that man answers.

"What the fuck are you talking about?" Felix asks, shifting his gaze to his phone, typing frantically and muttering curses as he does. He then looks up at Gray. "You mother fucker."

Gray barely acknowledges him, and it feels like the longer I study him, the more disgusted he grows, the more contemptuous toward Felix.

"Did he touch you?" he asks, never taking his eyes off Felix.

I know he's talking to me, but I can't answer. I'm too shocked at this strange turn of events.

"Mara?" he asks, shifting his gaze to me.

I shake my head.

"Then I won't cut off his dick and feed it to him before I kill him."

"What the fuck is going on?" Felix asks, taking a step back only to be stopped by one of Gray's men holding the gun to the back of his head.

"Don't shoot him!" I cry out, trying to get out from behind Dante.

Gray turns to me again and Dante shifts his body a little, his gaze still on Gray. I swear I see the infinitesimal nodding of Gray's head. At that strange exchange, Dante shifts his grip to hold my arm with one hand and the wrist of the hand that's gripping the dagger with the other.

"Don't worry, I wasn't going to make it that easy," Gray says as if understanding my meaning. He then looks at Dante. "No one will touch her," he tells him.

"You're not taking her. I don't care who you are," Dante says.

I want to ask who he is because I get the feeling Dante knows.

"Well, I'm not leaving without her, so you and I may have a problem. But we'll discuss that after we take care of this piece of shit." He's eyeing Felix again, his mouth curled with disgust.

"What's going on?" I ask.

Dante glances at me, then at Gray. Gray's eyes lock on me, the look not like any man's I've ever seen. Not hard. Not hateful. And not lecherous.

"Tell me," I say.

Dante turns fully, giving his back to Gray, which surprises me. He shifts his grip, so his hands are gentle on my arms. I shudder as he rubs them. I look up at him, at the bloody spot on his temple, at his scarred face. And all I want to do is press myself into his body, feel his arms around me. Feel him hold me.

"Sweetheart," he whispers, shifting his grip from my wrist to my hand so we're both gripping the dagger. "Are you ready?"

I'm not sure what he means but then, a moment later, I see Felix move behind him. See him reach for a hidden weapon, the glint of metal catching the light of one of the flashlights. But Dante must sense it, so he spins me, one arm wrapping around my middle to hold me tight to his body, still keeping me shielded from Felix. His other hand tight over mine, the one holding the dagger, we lunge together toward Felix. We collide with him as a gun fires and

Felix goes crashing to the ground, us on top of him. Dante's grip shifts to cradle my head as we plunge the dagger into Felix's chest, with our joined hands.

In that moment, something leaves me. Just as a dying man's soul leaves his body, something leaves me. And for the first time in fifteen years, I can breathe.

I look at Dante who's looking down at Felix. He shifts his gaze to me, and we both sit up. I see where Felix's gun is a few feet from him, his hand is bleeding. That was the gunshot. Someone shot the gun out of his hand.

Dante and I don't speak. We just look at each other and it takes me a long minute to drag my gaze away, over to Felix whose eyes are open wide, who is gasping for breath.

"He's yours if you want him," Dante says so low that only I can hear him.

I realize what he did, setting up the kill for me. I nod. Because yes, I want him.

Dante stands and I straddle Felix, my knees bare on the cold, dirty ground as the skirt of my dress settles around me. I close both hands over the bloody handle of the blade and I hold it there, looking at him. I wait until his eyes grow huge with terror. I don't feel a moment of regret at what I'm about to do. I think I know what that says about me. I'm a monster. A monster he had a hand in creating.

And so, with that thought in mind, I drag the

blade down to his stomach, listening to his pain, and then I change direction. I take my time as I draw the dagger out and set the tip over his chest. Slowly, so slowly, I push it through his ribs and pierce his devil's heart.

I can hear sound he makes, the gurgle of his last breaths as I lean over him bringing my face close to his, so he sees me. So he can have no doubt that it's me washing my hands in his blood.

"Go to hell," I tell him and push deeper as blood trickles from the corner of his mouth. I watch life leave him. His dead eyes look back at me, empty, dull, but knowing it was me who did it. Who stole his life like he tried to steal mine.

51

DANTE

Gray watches Mara with intense curiosity. He doesn't flinch at what she's doing. At the blood. At the look on her face as she drenches her hands in Felix Pérez's blood.

"Let's go," I say to her, extending my hand. She doesn't move so I say her name. "Mara."

She drags her gaze from Pérez's dead face to look up at me. I try to dissect what I see in her eyes. It's not triumph. There is no winner in this game. It's not regret either. Maybe it's relief. Maybe it's acceptance and the knowledge that it's over. Or maybe she's still processing. Maybe her brain is still trying to make sense of what she's done. Of the blood on her hands.

"You did good," I tell her.

She shifts her gaze to my hand. Leaving the blade in the dead man, she places her hand in mine and I help her up. I notice she's barefoot, her shoes a few feet away. I get them for her and help her put them on.

She stands tall beside me looking at Gray, her eyes hard. I wonder if she sees the familiarity of his features.

"You're strong," he says with a smile that isn't unkind but doesn't seem quite natural on him either.

Her expression doesn't change. "I'm not going with you."

Gray studies her, then shifts his gaze to me. "You were a boy when I met your father. Your brother, Michael, perhaps would have remembered me, but I doubt you do."

Mara shifts beside me, turns her gaze to mine.

I see the questions in her eyes and pull her closer, wrap an arm around her.

Gray doesn't miss this protective gesture as he turns his gaze back to her. "I only learned about your existence five years ago. If I'd known before, I'd have come for you sooner."

Mara stiffens.

"It was David Grigori who told me, actually," he says to me but only seems able to draw his gaze from Mara momentarily. "I hear he's dead."

He knows exactly how he died. I can see it in his eyes.

I nod.

"Good. Six feet under is where he belongs," he says.

"What's going on?" Mara asks me.

"Let's get out of here. Go home. We can talk then," he says.

"Home?" She asks him shaking her head. "I'm not going anywhere with you. Tell me here. Now."

Gray sighs deeply, smiles again. "I met your mother when she was about your age. She was wild too. A free spirit. I'd never met anyone like her."

Mara stiffens beside me. "I don't know my mother," she says, her words slow because her brain is adding two and two.

He nods sadly. "I tried to contact her but not until years later. Too late I realized."

I tighten my hold on Mara's hand as she seems to grow colder beside me. "What the hell is going on?"

"I'm your father, Mara. And I've been looking for you ever since David Grigori told me you existed at all."

52

MARA

I am reeling. My mind racing. If it weren't for Dante, I'm sure I'd be on the ground right now. But he holds me up and I remember what he'd said a while ago. How he'd never let me fall.

Drake Gray's home is on the outskirts of town weirdly close to Jericho St. James's house. Although he doesn't have the armed guards either Dante or Jericho had, twelve-foot walls surround his property and I get the feeling his security is just a little more discreet.

It looks like no one lives inside the house. He tells us that apart from a live-in maid and handyman, he lives alone. The house is so large most of it is not in use. He's talking about it all as he shows us to an upstairs bedroom where we can get cleaned up. I notice how much of the house is dark, how many of the rooms we pass have furniture covered with dust cloths like no one lives here at all.

This man is my father?

Drake Gray, the buyer Felix Pérez had lined up, is my father?

That's why he'd wanted me back so badly. That's why Felix had sent Samuel with the tracker. Because when the opportunity came, he planned to take me back. To sell me again. Not that he knew who the buyer was. Just a man with money who wanted me, and all Felix needed to hear was the part about the money. By then things were going south with Petrov and now I wonder if it wasn't Felix who'd been the one to let the truth about me come out to Petrov. The fact that I wasn't Elizabeth Grigori but her worthless friend. That's why he'd offered to pay Petrov back. And all the time I'd thought it was me who'd given it away. I'd certainly been the one who was punished.

"Have a hot shower. There are clothes, Mara. Everything is prepared. I'll see if one of my men can find you something to change into," Gray says to Dante.

"I'm fine," Dante says. "I'd like to get Mara cleaned up."

Gray is hesitant but nods. "As long as that's all right with my daughter."

My daughter.

I nod although I'm not sure why. I don't need this

man's, this stranger's, permission. I want to be alone with Dante. I need to figure this out.

"I'll be downstairs. Are you hungry?" he asks me.

"No."

He nods and is hesitant to walk away but he does and closes the door behind him.

Once we're alone, I sit on the edge of the bed and Dante takes my face in his hands, crouching down in front of me.

"Are you okay?"

"I... I don't know. Did you know about this?"

"I found out earlier this evening. Just a little bit before you did. Charlie recognized his name and remembered when he met with David. It must have been when he met your mother."

"It's real?"

"It certainly makes sense. I don't know that your mother ever told anyone about Gray. I think their affair was brief and she was gone so soon after your birth."

"I have a father."

Dante's face darkens with worry, and he pulls me to my feet. "Let's get you cleaned up. Into some warm clothes. Then we can go downstairs and talk to him. Figure out what the hell is going on."

I look up at him. "I... Are you staying?"

He takes my face in his hands, brushes the pad of his thumb across my cheek. "I was wrong, Mara. I thought it was best to walk away. I thought you'd be safer. St. James... What happened to his fiancée, I didn't want that to happen to you."

"Dante—"

"Let me finish."

I wait.

"I never told you how much I love you. It's always been you for me. You were right about destiny. If I'm not too late, that is."

My eyes mist and a bubble of hope inflates inside me. Hope. God. Is this what hope feels like?

"Don't cry. No more of that," he says. "If you need time—"

I shake my head, reach up to touch his face. "That's the thing about destiny. It's always perfectly on time."

He smiles and leans in to kiss me, his lips soft, my kiss cautious. My fingertips come to his chest and the way he looks at me when I draw back shows regret. He cups the back of my head, pulls me close, and I let him. I stand up on tiptoe, weaving my fingers into his hair. I kiss him and this time, it feels different. Not hurried. Not like this may be our last kiss. Because this is our beginning. The start of our destiny.

53

MARA

Drake Gray is waiting downstairs when Dante and I are shown into an informal living room half an hour later. This one is much smaller than the other, with a fire raging in the stone fireplace. He has changed into a beige sweater and dark slacks, crouching before the fire, arranging a new log onto the already large stack.

On our way down I'd peeked inside some of the rooms. It's strange, the house is so impersonal that it's almost like a hotel. Like anyone could move in and call it theirs. It's a little lonely, actually. But this room looks lived in. Personal. I'm glad to see it because when I look at him, he looks as lonely as the house.

He straightens, replaces the brass poker and sips his drink as he turns to us. I'm wearing a pair of jeans and an oversized hoodie with the softest lining I've ever felt, along with a pair of combat boots. The closet and dresser were full of new clothes with their tags still on, all in my size. Did he think I'd just move in? This is all so weird.

Dante changed into a charcoal sweater and slacks the housekeeper sent up. We threw our other things away.

"Better?" Drake Gray asks.

I nod and study him, see the crow's feet crinkle his temples, note the shade of his eyes so much like mine. His hair is a darker shade of graying blond, but I recognize the dimple in his chin. I see it every time I look in the mirror.

"Drink?" he asks.

Dante nods and he turns to me. "You'd better take one too," he says.

I don't argue and a moment later we're settled on the couch in front of the fire. Dante sips his whiskey, while I just hold my glass and study Drake Gray who is seated on the wing chair. He's studying me too.

"I don't understand this," I say. "My mother died when I was very young. I don't have a father. If I did, I'd know about it."

He looks into his glass, nods and sips before he turns to me. I take a sip of mine and have to work through the burn, but it feels good once it's down.

"I didn't know about the pregnancy. We had a brief affair. I was married at the time, Mara."

Ah.

"I am ashamed of how I handled things and I don't want to make excuses, but I was young and ambitious and quite frankly stupid."

"Did she try to contact you?"

He nods gravely. "She did. And I ignored the calls until she stopped calling. But I never stopped thinking of her."

"That didn't do her any good, did it?"

Dante squeezes my hand.

"No, it didn't. And I'm sorry. Very sorry."

"Where's your wife?"

He drinks a big swallow of his drink. "We separated a few years ago."

"Do you have kids?" Do I have brothers or sisters?

"No, we never had children. Her pregnancies were unsuccessful."

"Oh." At that his face darkens and I see a sadness in his eyes. That loneliness in his posture. "I'm sorry."

He nods, drinks, then gets up to refresh his empty glass. My glass is still full, and Dante declines so after refilling his drink he sits back down.

"What's your connection with Jericho St. James?" Dante asks.

Drake Gray looks at him. "Jericho St. James?" He shakes his head. "I know the name but can't say I know the man."

"So David put you in touch with Felix Pérez to find Mara?"

He nods.

"What did he want in return?"

"Connections. I'm part of a powerful organization. A founding family member."

"IVI."

He nods. "David wanted in." His lip curls in disgust. "And he planned to sell me my own daughter to get what he wanted. When I contacted Pérez and learned about the Russian, well, things weren't easy to say the least. The plan was to kidnap you from the Russian, but that's no easy task against a man like Petrov. Then Pérez had an idea to put the truth about who you are out there. I didn't know he'd do that. I wouldn't have agreed to it knowing it would put you at risk, Mara. I hope you weren't hurt because of that."

I don't answer but drink a sip of my whiskey instead, liking the warmth, the lightness of my limbs.

"It's late," Dante says, putting his empty glass down and getting to his feet.

"You can't take her back to the island."

"I don't think you get a say in what Mara wants or needs."

"I'm her father."

"I'd like to see a DNA test before I accept that."

"You can have it." Drake turns to me. "Anything you want or need."

"How about if I get a say in what I want or need," I say, standing.

Both men turn to me.

"I'd like proof," I say to Drake although looking at his face, I know it's true. I see it more and more. And I feel it.

He nods. "Tomorrow. We can get a test."

Dante looks at me. "If it's what you want, I'll take you."

Drake gets up. "Why don't you two spend the night here? Your man too. You can call anyone you need to. We can talk some more in the morning. Go together to the lab."

"I don't think so," Dante says. He takes my hand and walks toward the door.

"Please," Drake says, eyes on me. "I've only just met my daughter."

Dante turns to him and is about to tell him no again, but he continues.

"You're free to go whenever you want," Drake adds. "I would just like a chance to know you after all this time," he says to me.

I see the emotion in his eyes. And in a way, I feel his loneliness. I turn to Dante and nod. "One night," I say quietly. "I'd like to stay. It's late anyway."

Dante isn't convinced but after a long moment,

he nods. I think about how this day started and how it's ended. How destiny has sought us out. All of us. And brought us together. I won't be so quick to trust this stranger yet. Even when it is proven who he is. But I want to. God, how I want to.

EPILOGUE 1

DANTE

One Year and Three Months Later

When I brought Mara back to the island a few weeks later, everything was different. She was different. We were different.

That night in the bowels of the opera house I knew she needed to be the one to drive the dagger into Pérez's heart. She needed his blood on her hands. In a twisted way, it was cleansing.

But you can't come out of a life like she's had and not be twisted in some way.

The DNA results came back to prove what Drake Gray claimed. That he is Mara's biological father.

And he's been good to her. Giving her a lot of space, knowing she needs to go to him in her time. I can see she wants to more and more, although we've only spent a few weeks with him so far. I won't hold her back and I won't leave her to navigate it alone.

As far as Gray, he's lonely. The more I get to know him the more I see it. He's not close with any of his brothers and he no longer speaks with his ex-wife. No children. No cousins. Nothing. In a way I feel sorry for him.

In the year we've lived on the island with my brother and his family, Lenore and Noah and even from time-to-time Matthaeus, Mara has grown lighter. Happier. That glow that I saw on Scarlett and wanted for her, she's getting there.

Scarlett and Cristiano had a little girl, Clementine. And Alessandro, for as little as he wanted a baby sister, is her champion. It's nice to see my brother happy. Nice to be a part of his growing family.

I wanted to go after St. James for delivering Mara to Felix Pérez, but he's once again disappeared. And when I mention him, Mara tells me to leave it alone. Says she understands what he did, why he did it. Says she doesn't fault him. I wonder if he knew who the buyer was all along.

But I don't want to think about any of that today.

Today is Mara's birthday and she hasn't celebrated very many of those. Lenore is preparing a feast. Gray is even flying over for a few days. Mara likes it when he comes for visits.

"Almost ready," Mara says when I enter our bedroom. She's just tying her bikini top.

I look her over. She's stunning. She's put on a little weight finally and looks healthy and on her hip is a tattoo of a single red poppy, the stem long and delicate, the petals of the flower a bright scarlet, symbolizing remembrance and hope. I was surprised at her choice but understand it. She's strong. She doesn't want to forget. Or maybe she's accepted that she never will. And this beautiful, wild flower doesn't so much hide the brand as overwrites it. Gives her back her strength, her power.

She keeps her hair shoulder length but has had bangs cut in. She rarely wears makeup and I love that about her. She's a natural beauty and her most stunning features are her smile and her kind heart.

"Aren't you swimming?" she asks. I'm still dressed in jeans and a T-shirt.

I close the door behind me. "I want to spend some time alone with you first." I walk toward her. "Turn around," I tell her and take the straps of the bikini from her but instead of tying them, I slip it off.

"Hey," she protests, turning in my arms as I let the slip of turquoise drop.

"What?" I ask, wrapping my arms around her and kissing her.

"I promised Alessandro I'd snorkel with him."

"Alessandro can wait." I kiss her again and walk her backward to the bed. Once she's there, I slide my arms down to strip off the bottoms and only when she's naked do I draw back to look at her. "God, you're so fucking gorgeous."

She smiles wide and puts her hands on either side of my face. "It's because I'm happy." She kisses me. "But really, we can't do this now. They're waiting. Lenore has cake and my father will be here—"

"Shh." I kiss her as I push her again to sit on the bed and lean over to kiss her, forcing her to lie down as I pull my shirt over my head. Her greedy hands fumble with my belt as I kiss her neck, her chest, and I take her wrists to draw her hands away. When I bring my mouth to her sex, she opens her legs and arches her back, moaning and weaving her fingers into my hair.

"I love…" she gasps as I tease her sex, licking the length of her before taking her clit into my mouth and sucking. "Oh fuck, I love…" Her breath catches then and within moments, she's coming, her body jerking once as she pulls me closer. I suck harder, drawing every last ounce of pleasure from her. Her taste on my tongue makes me harder, her hands drawing me up to kiss her once her orgasm abates. When I press myself against her she moans with an insatiable need.

"What do you love? You never finished your sentence," I say against her mouth.

"I love your mouth on me," she teases, teeth biting my lip. "And I love my mouth on you." She starts to slide down to her knees, but I stop her.

"You make me crazy."

Her hands are at my belt again, but I pull them away.

"What? You get a taste, and I don't?" she asks.

I smile wide. "I have a gift for you first."

She pauses. She must see something on my face. "A gift? You didn't have to give me a gift." Her eyes get teary. It makes me a little sad to see this still. She's so unused to kindness even after more than a year with me, with her family. But I shove those thoughts aside.

"I wanted to," I tell her, kissing her once more as I reach into my pocket and palm the ring.

"Dante?" her smile wavers and her eyes mist.

"Destiny you said. Do you remember that?"

She nods, a tear dropping down her cheek.

"You believed in us from the start. And while I still believe you can do a lot better than me," I start, taking her left hand as she sniffles and sliding the ring onto her finger. "I'm not letting you go. Ever. You're my destiny, Mara. Will you marry me?"

She smiles through her tears, and I think I can watch her all day. I think I can just watch her face, all her expressions, her emotions. I love her so fucking much I don't know how I existed without her.

She looks up at me and nods, leaning in to hug

me tight. "Destiny," she whispers. "Yes, I'll marry you."

EPILOGUE 2

MARA

Three Months Later

We are to be married on the beach at sunset. Neither of us wanted to wait. What's the point of a long engagement? I don't want to lose any more time.

It's almost time as I look out onto the small gathering. It's just our families, everyone barefoot, the women in pretty dresses, the men in casual suits. Dante is already at the makeshift altar, a beautiful arch he and Cristiano built together. I didn't know he could do that. It's draped with white silks and decorated with hundreds of wildflowers in every color with red poppies being prominent. It's so pretty I can't believe it. The chairs too have bouquets tied to them and white silk ribbon blows in the sea breeze.

The sun will be setting soon. And on cue, there's a knock on my door.

"Come in," I say, turning, picking up my bunch of wildflowers.

My father and Noah enter. My father. It's so strange. So unreal. I have a father. And he's kind and a little bit lonely, I think. Or maybe what I see is the regret at the lost years.

"Wow," Noah says as my father's eyes grow watery.

I catch a glimpse of myself in the mirror. I'm wearing a simple white dress. It's the softest organza silk with spaghetti straps and a small train behind me. My hair is woven with baby's breath as well as one lone sapphire comb. A gift from my grandmother. It's an antique her mother wore at her wedding and Lenore wore at hers. My mother never had a chance to wear it.

"You look beautiful," my father says.

"Thank you."

"We'd better go down," Noah says.

"Just one minute." My father reaches into his pocket to take something out. "I have something for you."

Noah slips out subtly and I look up at my father.

"You made me very happy when you asked me to walk you down the aisle. You didn't have to do that."

"Of course, I did. I wanted you to."

"You didn't but I'm happy you did. And I'm just happy to have found you and I want you to know however much time you need, I won't rush you."

"I'm glad I found you too."

He holds his palm up and inside it is a key. "This is for you and your husband. You're always welcome. My home is yours whenever you're ready."

I smile, look up at him and I hug him. I'm happy to see each time we go to stay at his house that more and more of it is opened, windows no longer shuttered, life slowly returning. "Thank you. Thank you so much. I'm so glad you're here."

A knock comes on the door again and we straighten, both of us wiping our eyes. Noah peers in. "Sunset…" he says.

My dad sets the key on the nightstand and extends his arm. I tuck mine inside his and we walk out of the room and out of the house. Noah comes to my other side, and I take his arm too as we walk onto the beach where the harpist begins to play.

I curl my toes in the sand as everyone turns to us and I think how magical this is. Us on the beach like this. Waves rolling softly in. The delicate sounds of the harp. My family all around me. More family than I ever thought I'd have. And at the end of the aisle, my heart.

When Noah and my father hand me over to Dante and he takes my hands, I feel my eyes mist with happy tears. He wraps his arms around me, hugging me close to him, his forehead to mine, nose touching nose.

"Destiny," he whispers.

"Destiny."

We kiss.

WHAT TO READ NEXT
SAMPLE FROM TAKEN

Helena

I'm the oldest of the Willow quadruplets. Four girls. Always girls. Every single quadruplet birth, generation after generation, it's always girls.

This generation's crop yielded the usual, but instead of four perfect, beautiful dolls, there were three.

And me.

And today, our twenty-first birthday, is the day of harvesting.

That's the Scafoni family's choice of words, not ours. At least not mine. My parents seem much more comfortable with it than my sisters and I do, though.

Harvesting is always on the twenty-first birthday of the quads. I don't know if it's written in stone somewhere or what, but it's what I know and what has been on the back of my mind since I learned our history five years ago.

There's an expression: *those who cannot remember the past are condemned to repeat it*. Well, that's bullshit, because we Willows know well our past and look at us now.

The same blocks that have been used for centuries standing in the old library, their surfaces softened by the feet of every other Willow Girl who stood on the same stumps of wood, and all I can think when I see them, the four lined up like they are, is how archaic this is, how fucking unreal. How they can't do this to us.

Yet, here we are.

And they are doing this to us.

But it's not *us*, really.

My shift is marked.

I'm *unclean*.

So it's really my sisters.

Sometimes I'm not sure who I hate more, my own family for allowing this insanity generation after generation, or the Scafoni monsters for demanding the sacrifice.

"It's time," my father says. His voice is grave.

He's aged these last few months. I wonder if that's remorse because it certainly isn't backbone.

I heard he and my mother argue once, exactly once, and then it was over.

He simply accepted it.

Accepted that tonight, his daughters will be made to stand on those horrible blocks while a Scafoni bastard looks us over, prods and pokes us, maybe checks our teeth like you would a horse, before making his choice. Before taking one of my sisters as his for the next three years of her life.

I'm not naive enough to be unsure what that will mean exactly. Maybe my sisters are, but not me.

"Up on the block. Now, Helena."

I look at my sisters who already stand so meekly on their appointed stumps. They're all paler than usual tonight and I swear I can hear their hearts pounding in fear of what's to come.

When I don't move right away, my father painfully takes my arm and lifts me up onto my block and all I can think, the one thing that gives me the slightest hope, is that if Sebastian Scafoni chooses me, I will find some way to end this. I won't condemn my daughters to this fate. My nieces. My granddaughters.

But he won't choose me, and I think that's why my parents are angrier than usual with me.

See, I'm the ugly duckling. At least I'd be considered ugly standing next to my sisters.

And the fact that I'm unclean—not a virgin—means I won't be taken.

The Scafoni bastard will choose one of their precious golden daughters instead.

Golden, to my dark. Golden—quite literally. Sparkling almost, my sisters.

I glance at them as my father attaches the iron shackle to my ankle. He doesn't do this to any of them. They'll do as they're told, even as their gazes bounce from the closed twelve-foot doors to me and back again and again and again.

But I have no protection to offer. Not tonight. Not on this one.

The backs of my eyes burn with tears I refuse to shed.

"How can you do this? How can you allow it?" I ask for the hundredth time. I'm talking to my mother while my father clasps the restraints on my wrists, making sure I won't attack the monsters.

"Better gag her, too."

It's my mother's response to my question and, a moment later, my father does as he's told and ensures my silence.

I hate my mother more, I think. She's a Willow quadruplet. She witnessed a harvesting herself. Witnessed the result of this cruel tradition.

Tradition.

A tradition of kidnapping.

Of breaking.

Of destroying.

I look to my sisters again. Three almost carbon

copies of each other, with long blonde hair curling around their shoulders, flowing down their backs, their blue eyes wide with fear.

Well, except in Julia's case.

She's different than the others. She's more... eager. But I don't think she has a clue what they'll do to her.

Me, no one would guess I came from the same batch.

Opposite their gold, my hair is so dark a black, it appears almost blue, with one single, wide streak of silver to relieve the stark shade, a flaw I was born with. And contrasting their cornflower-blue eyes, mine are a midnight sky; there too, the only relief the silver specks that dot them.

They look like my mother. Like perfect dolls.

I look like my great-aunt, also named Helena, down to the silver streak I refuse to dye. She's in her nineties now. I wonder if they had to lock her in her room and steal her wheelchair, so she wouldn't interfere in the ceremony.

Aunt Helena was the chosen girl of her generation. She knows what's in store for us better than anyone.

"They're coming," my mother says.

She has super hearing, I swear, but then, a moment later, I hear them too.

A door slams beyond the library, and the draft

blows out a dozen of the thousand candles that light the huge room.

A maid rushes to relight them. No electricity. Tradition, I guess.

If I were Sebastian Scafoni, I'd want to get a good look at the prize I'd be fucking for the next year. And I have no doubt there will be fucking, because what else can break a girl so completely but taking that of all things?

And it's not just the one year. No. We're given for three years. One year for each brother. Oldest to youngest. It used to be four, but now, it's three.

I would pinch my arm to be sure I'm really standing here, that I'm not dreaming, but my hands are bound behind my back, and I can't.

This can't be fucking real. It can't be legal.

And yet here we are, the four of us, naked beneath our translucent, rotting sheaths—I swear I smell the decay on them—standing on our designated blocks, teetering on them. I guess the Willows of the past had smaller feet. And I admit, as I hear their heavy, confident footfalls approaching the ancient wooden doors of the library, I am afraid.

I'm fucking terrified.

One-click Taken here!

ALSO BY NATASHA KNIGHT

To Have and To Hold

With This Ring

I Thee Take

Stolen: Dante's Vow

The Society Trilogy

Requiem of the Soul

Reparation of Sin

Resurrection of the Heart

Dark Legacy Trilogy

Taken (Dark Legacy, Book 1)

Torn (Dark Legacy, Book 2)

Twisted (Dark Legacy, Book 3)

Unholy Union Duet

Unholy Union

Unholy Intent

Collateral Damage Duet

Collateral: an Arranged Marriage Mafia Romance

Damage: an Arranged Marriage Mafia Romance

Ties that Bind Duet

Mine

His

MacLeod Brothers

Devil's Bargain

Benedetti Mafia World

Salvatore: a Dark Mafia Romance

Dominic: a Dark Mafia Romance

Sergio: a Dark Mafia Romance

The Benedetti Brothers Box Set (Contains Salvatore, Dominic and Sergio)

Killian: a Dark Mafia Romance

Giovanni: a Dark Mafia Romance

The Amado Brothers

Dishonorable

Disgraced

Unhinged

Standalone Dark Romance

Descent

Deviant

Beautiful Liar

Retribution

Theirs To Take

Captive, Mine

Alpha

Given to the Savage

Taken by the Beast

Claimed by the Beast

Captive's Desire

Protective Custody

Amy's Strict Doctor

Taming Emma

Taming Megan

Taming Naia

Reclaiming Sophie

The Firefighter's Girl

Dangerous Defiance

Her Rogue Knight

Taught To Kneel

Tamed: the Roark Brothers Trilogy

THANK YOU!

Thanks for reading *Stolen: Dante's Vow*. I hope you enjoyed it. Reviews help new readers find books and would make me ever grateful. Please consider leaving a review at the store where you purchased the book.

Click here to sign up for my newsletter to receive new release news and updates!

Like my FB Author Page to keep updated on news and giveaways!

Join my Facebook Group, The Knight Spot, by clicking here!

ABOUT THE AUTHOR

Natasha Knight is the *USA Today* Bestselling author of Romantic Suspense and Dark Romance Novels. She has sold over half a million books and is translated into six languages. She currently lives in The Netherlands with her husband and two daughters and when she's not writing, she's walking in the woods listening to a book, sitting in a corner reading or off exploring the world as often as she can get away.

Write Natasha here: natasha@natasha-knight.com

Click here to sign up for my newsletter to receive new release news and updates!

www.natasha-knight.com
natasha-knight@outlook.com

Printed in Great Britain
by Amazon